LOVE AT PEAK BLISS

MR. STARK
- Small Town Billionaires -

ALICIA NICHOLS

MORE BY ALICIA

Doctor's Heat (Dr. Wright, Book 1)
Get it for FREE Here:
https://getbook.at/doctorsheat

Wedding Night Stranger (Complete Series)
Read It Here:
https://mybook.to/WeddingNightStranger

Reality Love (Complete Series)
Read It Here:
https://mybook.to/RealityLove

Daddy's Off Limits (Complete Series)
Read It Here:
https://mybook.to/DaddysOffLimits

Darwin Brothers (Complete Series)
Read It Here:
https://mybook.to/DarwinBrothersBoxset

Dr. Park (Complete Series)
Read It Here:
https://getbook.at/DrParkBoxset

Dr. Stone (Complete Series)
Read It Here:
https://getbook.at/DrStoneBoxset

Dr. Wright (Complete Series – Vol. 1)
Read It Here:
https://getbook.at/DrWrightBoxset

Dr. Walker (Complete Series)
Read It Here:
https://getbook.at/DrWalkerBoxset

Dr. MacLean (Complete Series)

Read It Here:
https://mybook.to/DrMacleanBoxset

Dr. Pierce (Complete Series)
Read It Here:
https://mybook.to/DrPierceBoxset

Dr. Blackmore (Complete Series)
Read It Here:
https://mybook.to/DrBlackmoreBoxset

Dr. Grant (Complete Series)
Read It Here:
https://mybook.to/DrGrantBoxset

Dr. Hayes (Complete Series)
Read It Here:
https://mybook.to/DrHayesBoxset

Dr. Campbell (Complete Series)
Read It Here:
https://mybook.to/DrCampbellBoxset

Dr. Hale (Complete Series)
Read It Here:
https://mybook.to/DrHaleBoxset

Dr. Costa (Complete Series)
Read It Here:
https://mybook.to/DrCostaBoxset

Dr. Duncan (Complete Series)
Read It Here:
https://mybook.to/DrDuncanBoxset

CONTENTS

FREE GIFT

Hi my lovely!

Thank you for reading my book!

Stay up to date with everything going on in my world. Exclusive books, giveaways, tons of new reads, chapter reveals, and so much more.

Plus, I'll send you my exclusive ebook "Coveted (Dr. Stone, Book1)" that is available nowhere else, absolutely FREE, of course!

Just sign up and enjoy the love and steam:

https://dl.bookfunnel.com/46pg16ndzd

Much love 🖤

Alicia Nichols

To love.

CHAPTER 1

- JENNA -

Mark Harris.

Nine months. Nine fucking months of dating him and he'd been a total gentleman. Hell, he'd set off endless fantasies of happily ever in my mind, and I didn't even want that. Well, that wasn't completely true. I wanted happily ever after. I wanted to have a home to settle in and a man to love with children I could raise — a fucking big happy family. And while I'd not been head over heels in love with Mark, I'd thought I could maybe find some of that with him.

And then it all went to shit.

I poured a shot of whiskey into a glass and emptied it straight down my throat, feeling the heat burn a path down to my stomach. It was crazy that once, when I'd thought of that name, it was with love and affection because now all I wanted to do with my ex-boyfriend was to forget him.

I picked up the bottle and glass and walked out of the kitchen, my feet making squishy sounds across the padded carpets. It had been a crazy past two months, from losing my job to Mark brutally breaking up with me. I'd really thought he was the one, the man for me, but I quickly realized that I'd been expecting too much from the man. My eyes went to the huge picture hanging on the wall in the living room — that was the last thing of his I still kept in the house. At times when the pain became unbearable, I'd hurl things at the picture hanging over the fireplace.

I walked up to it now, studying the picture. Mark Harris knew how to make an appearance. I guess that was easy when he was a couple of inches taller than the average man. His light blonde hair was framed by dark streaks coming in at the temples and the roots. He'd told me that he'd dyed it blonde after an important incident that changed him forever. He'd never told me what that was though. Mark was always that way, dark and broody. I stared into those warm brown eyes with the slightest hint of crow's feet that formed with the smile in the picture. He wasn't smiling that night. In fact, if I'd interpreted the look he had on correctly, it was pain. Pure, unadulterated pain. All the times I knew him, he'd always been suave, with an air of confidence–cocky, some might say–and rightfully so because he was one of the hottest men in Taos. I shouldn't have been too surprised he found someone to cheat with easily.

The crazy thing was, I'd always known Mark was a ladies' man. Growing up in Taos, unlike my own quiet family, the Harris family had been on the receiving end of speculation and gossip. Mark's parents divorced pretty bitterly, and his mother left town with a junior brother who only visited during the summer. Ladies have always flocked around Mark. He had a lot of the bad boy reputation going for him, but he'd always been that forbidden fruit most young wanted.

Now that I think about it, I should've run the other way when he bumped into me at that festival last year. But I'd been drawn in by those brown eyes, wanted to really flirt with danger, and this is where that had led me.

Now was the time to let it all go. I'd decided to forget him totally and move on with my life. I have a job interview tomorrow at the mountain resort, and I didn't want to carry any of this bad energy with me. I slowly removed his picture from the wall and tossed it into the fireplace. The lights flicker as it licks at the wood and the scent of burning wood filled the air.

"Fuck you, Mark," I giggled.

The whiskey made my mind blur, and I felt the alcohol's warmth in my cheeks. My gaze drifted to the firelight and an idea slipped into my mind. I rubbed my thighs together, feeling a brazen desire start to climb through my body. I should fuck him, one last time as a right of passage.

No. I shook my head trying to shake out the naughty thoughts from my mind, but it didn't work. I was already hot and horny, and I needed relief. I had to do something about it. Now.

I stood and reached underneath my dress, slipping a finger past my panties and swiping tentatively through my folds, slick with want. *This would be part of the process of purging my mind.* I was already so wet; my core was molten with need. I rushed my bedroom, grabbed my vibrator, and then headed back to the living room.

I looked into the fire, my lips opened slightly, as I draw in a huge breath. And then I slipped into the old leather chair across from the fireplace. The framed picture was still burning as I used the tip of the vibrator to lift the hem of my skirt across my thigh. I imagined him watching me, his eyes moving up my body, darkening as they traveled, pleading to let him touch me. Of course, I wouldn't, he'd lost his chance.

My heart began to pound with anger and desire. Memories of when I'd walked in on him flashed through my mind. He'd been tied to the chair with his tie, the wench grinding on his lap.

"No, no. Not now," I whispered. I turned on the vibrator and heat bloomed between my legs as I reached for the hem of my skirt, sliding the fabric up my thighs, exposing my skin to the warmth from the fire across from me.

My fingertips trailed along my skin to the satin of my underwear. I felt so daring in the moment. Nothing—and no one— had ever made me feel as sexy. And it's about time after months of bottling it all up. It was as if Mark took all my thoughts. My job, my life, and my goals, but all that was over now, and I was free.

I closed my eyes, letting a devilish half smile spread across my face as I chewed my lower lip. My left hand traveled higher, cupping my breast and squeezing. With my other hand, I pushed the center of my panties aside and turned on the vibrator. I gasped, fingers leaving my breast to clench the chair arm tightly. I began moving my toy, slipped it against my pussy and let out a little moan. Holding the tool to my clit, the vibrations sent me rocking against the chair, whining now, desperate for release.

I moved it faster, my eyes falling close as my head dropped back against the chair. I tried to be quiet, biting down on my lip when a tiny moan escaped. My body shook taut with the desire, muscles tensing beneath my skin as I kept moving the tool inside me.

I closed my eyes and imagined a man touching me. My dream man here with me in the living room – strong body pressed up against mine, big hands grabbing my hips and waist and thighs as he drove into me and his thick cock buried deep inside me – and then I was coming, clenching and fluttering to the thought, whimpering several obscenities. My climax was near the edge, an overwhelming wave building around me.

Suddenly the doorbell pinged, and I froze. The moans on my lips turned into a startled gasp. Before I could stand up from the chair, another buzz sounded on the door, followed by a loud knock.

Who would come to visit me? I'd barely had any visitors in the past couple of weeks. I rose from the chair and headed to the door, I stumbled on a chair's leg and almost fell. "I'm coming, please. Hold your horses."

When I pulled open the door, I stopped short, my eyes raking along the stranger standing. It was the delivery guy. The baseball hat on his head read Peak's Bliss. I remembered that I had ordered some food earlier this afternoon.

"643, Downtown Taos. Am I at the right place?"

His face...he was gorgeous. Wide, strong jaw, steely green eyes, and lips that cried out for a kiss. My delivery man's shaggy dark hair peaked out from beneath his cap, his sculpted features dusted with stubble.

"Yes," I managed to whisper. "That's me."

He nodded and stretched the package forward. "Your package ma'am."

I stretched out my right hand to collect it, forgetting that I was still holding the vibrator. His eyes locked with mine right as I yanked my fingers out from under his eyes.

4

Oh no.

I shuffled backwards and the force of my body knocked the door open behind me. I stumbled into the house, slamming and contemplating on locking it up from the push-button on the inside handle. I'd been so struck by his looks that I'd completely forgotten about the vibrator. I was mortified. I wanted to crawl into a hole and disappear.

"Should I leave this outside, ma'am? We can put this on your tab."

"No, please." I reopened the door. "Please step in while I get the money for you."

My head was hot as I watched him gingerly step into the house. This man was hot beyond compare, and that didn't help me think. He was tall and strapping, easily around 6'4, with a body built as solid and strong. It was obvious he took his workouts seriously, those broad shoulders and huge biceps revealed by the sleeves of his shirt rolled up along taut forearms. He had on rugged jeans, a big belt buckle, and a pair of boots to complete the picture.

Only the baseball hat showed that he was really from Peak Bliss.

"Sorry for the embarrassment."

"Hey, there's nothing to be sorry about, ma'am. We all have needs." His eyes darted down my body.

"I–oh. Thank you," I said, flustered. "What's up with Jude? He's the regular guy for my deliveries."

"Oh. He's okay, just unavailable this afternoon, personal business. He mentioned that you are one of our frequent customers. I hope you find my services satisfactory."

Oh, I could imagine how satisfactory your services would be.

I smiled. I didn't have a response. My brain was stuck on the fact that this man was a hunk that just gave off strong sexual vibes — without even trying.

"Uhh, I'll just quickly get the money, and drop this off as well." I sheepishly smiled while raising the vibrator.

"Ah." He smiled too, his jaw twitching with his green eyes fixed on my face. "I hope you're not doing that on account of me?"

I shrugged, feeling less and less embarrassed with the cool way he'd reacted.

"Maybe a little on account of you, who needs toys when you have studs standing in touching distance, eh?"

"Oh, really?" He laughed.

Oh, God. Being alone with this man in a room should be illegal. Standing only a few short inches away from him, I could feel the heat coming off his torso and enveloping me in his musky, manly scent.

Any questions or hesitations I had were drowned out by an instinctive, visceral need deep inside me. On impulse, I leaned in and tilted my head up to his.

"Yes, really. Wanna go for it?"

He blinked rapidly, clearly shaken by my words. His eyes roved over my face. "That's hard to say no to."

He looked in control but then I noticed his trousers. Tented, with a bulge that suggested he was not only hard, but huge. When I looked back up, I licked my lips, watching his chest heaving as his eyes raked up and down my body, landing on my hand clutching the wet, glistening vibrator. His pupils were blown out to a dark shade of green and was wide with desire. He wanted me. Why else would he have that deep longing look in his eyes?

His eyes flicked to the couch and back to my face. I knew he was considering how much time he had for a quick one. The idea that he was now considering that made me blush furiously, my cheeks hot and my hands suddenly sweaty. It was crazy to see him desire me that much, and I felt like I would melt this instant under the heat of his gaze.

I had to get out of there. It was too weird, too much. A man I didn't even know had this profound physical effect on me, that threatened my composure which was slipping from my control the longer I stood near him.

"If you'll excuse me," I said, managing a smile. "I'll get the cash while you think about your answer."

He responded with something incoherent as I walked away. His eyes were on my back. I could feel his burning gaze as I turned down the hall, trying not to seem like I was in too big a hurry, yet desperate to get out from under his fiery attention just to be able to breathe. I slipped inside the room and rested my back on the wall, trying to breathe. After a few moments, I walked back outside to find out he was gone. He'd left a note with the packaged food:

Have this on me. If we somehow meet again, maybe we'll definitely go for it.

I sighed, half relieved, and half frustrated that I didn't get to at least kiss my delivery man. Christ. I am so fucking screwed.

I'd been staring at the man like I wanted to devour him. I sank into the couch. At the moment, my brain was a hot mess and my body was still feeling little tremors of excitement. I scowled at the flames still flickering in the fireplace. Mark's framed picture had entirely disappeared now. I thought briefly about picking up my toy to finish what I started, but I discarded the thought. It didn't matter how many times I came off with the vibrator, this feeling would never go away.

And even though it shouldn't be possible, I felt like I'd just made things a hundred times worse by flirting with the delivery guy. Because this time, I had a feeling I now knew what I was missing, what my body wanted. And I had gotten so close to enjoying it. But here I was, still stuck in my house, horny, not only because I hadn't come in weeks but because a man had now walked in to make the situation worse.

I looked at the clock, it had only been a few minutes since he left and it felt like hours already. I decided that I needed a cold shower and I headed to the bathroom immediately, scrubbing myself roughly as if to remove any trace of him.

This was going to stop, this had to stop. I shouldn't be acting like some horny teenager, and I certainly did not fuck around with strangers and delivery men. The last thing I needed was another man coming in and ruining everything. I couldn't allow a random man I'd never met before to have this sort of control over me. Everything was so much better when I was ready to satisfy myself with a toy, but now I knew what I really wanted.

As awful as I felt previously, giving in to this was million times worse.

After my bath I headed to my bedroom and flipped open my laptop to prepare for my interview on Monday. An intermediary had linked me up with the boss of Peak Bliss Resort — the biggest resort and business conglomerate in Taos. I'd heard that the owner was a billionaire who liked to keep a low profile and he had only relocated here five years ago and started a business to manage tourists. I'd gotten an email from him last week to come in for an interview. I glared at the mail blinking from my computer screen. For some reason, I felt a sort of panic and I didn't know why. Likely this was just a formal meeting where we discuss if I was fit for the job.

Well, fuck. I took a deep breath through my nose and closed the laptop, leaning forward and crossing my fingers as I stood up and walked toward the window to stare out at the mountains in the distance. Getting a job at Peak Bliss would be a dream come true — a fresh start to wipe the slate clean of these horrible past few weeks.

That was what I should focus on — not some sexy mysterious delivery man.

CHAPTER 2

- TYLER -

I stood looking out the upstairs window, craning my neck to see my daughter playing in the field downstairs, my face close to the glass. She looked really happy, skipping through the field and waving her hands as she chased her dog. My lips twitched in a little smile. Her blonde hair was in a ponytail, and she wore a loose t-shirt and cut-offs, a pair of flip-flops on her feet. She paused for a moment and looked around the resort like she was taking it all in.

The resort was a sprawling compound that spread hectares over the mountainside of Taos. The front porch where she played was a patchwork of reclaimed wood I had used to shore it up, and it carried a fresh coat of paint. The yard was tidy, mostly because my housekeeper treated it like an extension of her gardens. Flowers bloomed in window boxes, and we had workers take care of mowing the lawn around the guest houses that lined this side of the resort.

Emma looked up at the window and caught sight of me. She waved energetically at me and I waved back. Five years now since I learned I was going to have a daughter, and it still only felt like the gift of having her had only been delivered yesterday. The whole situation around her birth was entirely crazy, and it was one that now — after years of reflection, I was not proud of. I'd gotten into a whirlwind relationship with my brother's girlfriend to get back at him and then one day Ellie had walked in to tell me she was pregnant with my baby.

It was at that time that I realized I could no longer keep on living life the way I always had. I needed to be there for my daughter, especially since her mother had become a drunkard and was in no way fit to take care of a kid. I'd taken away Emma from her and settled in Taos to give my daughter the best life; Ellie hadn't taken the news well and of course, didn't agree that Emma living on the resort with me would be the best. I couldn't blame her – what mother would be okay with having her baby yanked out of her grasp —but in five years, I think our shared parenting had been good so far.

I returned to my seat in the office, trying to get the next week's activities organized at the resort. My main job managing the resort was to ensure the tourists who stayed on the property never had a shortage of things to do, from hikes to fishing trips to horseback rides and hiking and skating. I loved the work and loved helping the city folk get a taste of rural life in Taos. This kept me good and busy, and I liked it.

Juggling the work with caring for my daughter was hard work, but I couldn't complain about it. She was my little girl, and I loved her to pieces since the first time I held her. But the workload was getting increasingly high, and it was why I was looking to hire an assistant.

As much as I tried to focus on work, however, the fight we'd had earlier in the day was still fresh in my mind.

My phone buzzed on my desk, and I snatched it up. It was Edwin, my friend, and the man in charge of foreman duties at the resort.

"Edwin?"

"What's up, man?"

I tilted the chair backwards and propped my feet up on the table in front of me. "I hear you have quite a lot on your plate. You holding up alright?"

"What, you talking about that little hiking crowd coming in this afternoon? Not bothered in the slightest."

I chuckled. "I guess you can handle them."

"I was born to do this man, it's why you hired me."

He was right. Edwin Goldricks was born in Taos and he'd spent all his days in this town. That was why I hired him to help me manage the resort.

"Thank you for working with me, Edwin. I'm not convinced I'd have been able to do this without you, especially with a kid who needs me. Maybe I should pay you more."

"I sure as hell am holding you to that," he chuckled. "You're doing fine, man. What's Emma up to right now?"

I left the chair to stare out the window again. "She's playing with Randell, doin' a little throw and fetch in the yard. Seems she can handle being on her own sometimes."

Edwin chuckled again. "Now you know how kids can be. Or at least you're learnin' real quick."

He'd been married for six years and has three kids already. Edwin had always told me that family was the best gift a man could have and that I would look good with a woman at my side. The mental picture brought a smile to my face; unfortunately I had no woman in my life, none since the Ellie debacle with my brother and I couldn't imagine I'd be getting married, ever.

I sighed. "Hell, Edwin, is this how they always are? Massive bundles of energy that I'm not even sure I can keep up with?"

"Nah, don't you worry about that. The girl of yours is one of the best-behaved kids I've met. It might look bad now but sorry to say, you'll have to hunker down when it gets worse."

"It's gonna get worse?" I scoffed.

He chuckled. "Picture yourself walking into a room to find her necking with a totally random playboy from the next town."

Fucking shit. I could imagine myself ripping the boy's head off.

"Thanks for nothing," I grumbled. "Hoping that never has to happen."

11

"It'll be sooner than you think. So I'll advise you just keep being a kick-ass daddy and enjoy her needing you while it lasts. You'll kill it."

I chuckled. I was a kick-ass man, a kick-ass businessperson, and a kick-ass boss. But a "kick-ass daddy" is something I still needed to work on — a lot.

"Well, thanks for the vote of confidence, bro."

"Anytime. But that's not the reason I called."

"Oh?"

"Yeah. You got someone here at the house."

"Really?" I asked, wracking my brain. I didn't have an appointment that I could remember.

"Yeah. She said she was here for an interview about an executive assistant role."

"Ah, hell – that's right. Slipped my mind."

It was a busy season with tourists and I was trying to find an assistant to help take some workload off me. The lady coming in today was well-recommended by people around town.

"Oh," Edwin started, "It's not like you to get your schedule all scattered at all, man. Hell, you probably really need this assistant badly. Half of your job's making schedules."

"I know right. Just hope to get my head back in the game a bit now."

"I get it – kids have a way of putting a wrench into plans. A good kinda wrench, but a wrench all the same. You want me to tell her to come back later?"

"Nah. If she came out all the way here, the least I can do is meet with her."

"Alright, I'll drive her over to your place."

"Sounds good. Thanks, Edwin."

I ended the call, took my feet off the desk, and climbed out of my leather chair. Once up, I started some coffee in the French press. About the time the water reached a boil, I heard the grumble of Edwin's truck as it pulled up in front of the cabin, followed by a car door opening and closing, then the sounds of soft footfalls on the gravel of the cabin's driveway. I poured myself a cup of coffee as a soft knock sounded at the door.

"I'm coming," I said as I set down the steaming mug on my desk and hurried over.

I threw the door open, and it was a damn good thing I wasn't taking a sip of coffee because I would've spat it out. A shock went through me as if someone had just tasered me.

I stared into the blue eyes that I'd not been able to forget since I saw them last Friday. The last person I expected on my doorstep was the woman I'd delivered food to on the absence of one of my staff.

I saw the moment she recognized me. Her blue eyes flashed and her face immediately flushed pink. Damn, she was beautiful. As beautiful as she was when she opened the door clutching that vibrator last weekend. She was petite, with curves in all the right places. Her dark hair was long and straight, framing that heart-shaped face to perfection. Her features were delicate, pert nose over full lips that screamed for a kiss. Her blouse clung to her body, accentuating her full breasts. And it looked like she'd been poured into jeans she wore.

I was stunned. I had spent the better part of the weekend regretting that I'd not taken up the offer to fuck this woman and now I'd be interviewing her for a role as my assistant.

"Hi!" she said, her voice nervous as she extended her hand. "I'm Jenna Roberts — here about the assistant position."

I cleared my throat, trying my best to snap myself out of the daze she'd put me in. "Tyler Stark," I said, shaking her hand. "Pleasure to meet you, even though I believe we've met before."

The moment our hands touched, a wave of electricity danced through my body. It was so intense, and exciting that I felt like I was on the verge of jumping out of my own skin.

13

"Come on in," I said.

She nodded, giving me another nervous smile as she stepped into the cabin. She had a folder tucked under her arm, and she set it down on the table before slipping off her purse and then turning to take a seat. I swallowed hard. I couldn't help but appreciate her backside in her tight jeans. Her ass was so perfect that an image of her bent over in front of me flashed through my mind.

Fucking hell, Tyler. This was not getting an already strained working relationship off to a professional start. I cleared my throat again, trying to push the arousal running through me out of my mind.

She looked around the small cabin room I used for my office. "This so cute," she admired with another smile.

I laughed. "Cute ain't really what I'm goin' for. But I'm glad you like it. Coffee?"

"I'd love some."

"Coming right up."

I stepped over to the kitchen and poured her a mug. When it was ready, I handed it to her as I sat down in the chair across from the couch.

"So," I began. "I gotta admit you're not who I was expecting."

"I'm sorry about the other day," she groaned. "I was quite deep in the bottle."

I nodded. "I understand." I scratched the back of my head as I sank into my chair and crossed my legs. It was clear that the whole thing made her feel ill at ease. I wasn't supposed to have seen what I did. She probably now thought it was some stupid mistake to flirt with me. "Well, when I heard your recommendations, I gotta say I was picturing someone a little more...I dunno – matronly?"

14

"Yeah, I guess no one pictures their assistant holding a dildo, really." She gave a twittering laugh and I couldn't help but chuckle.

I took another sip of my coffee. "Yeah, you're right. I don't think I'd have it any other way though. That's quite memorable."

The image of that day flashed in my mind again. Thinking about her like that was probably a huge mistake. But damn, I couldn't help it. A woman as beautiful as her, standing with a vibrator clutched in one hand and flirting with me. How could I not think about it? And if there had been any doubts the first time we met that she was a breathtakingly gorgeous woman, the glimpse of her perfect, body right in front of me now was more than enough to put that question to rest.

She was like a damn dream – curvy hips, round breasts, and an ass like I'd never seen.

Her eyebrows rose. "Is that your way of saying our first meeting is going to be taken into consideration in the decision you make, because if that's the case, I might as well leave now?"

I was already impressed by Jenna – she had poise and confidence and looked like the kind who could speak her mind without nervousness around her boss.

"I can assure you it won't make a difference at all."

She nodded and blew out a soft breath. "Thank you, so now I hope we can put it behind us."

"Don't mean to offend, but that'll be a bit hard."

Her eyes flashed as she focused on me, clear confusion written on her expression. I wondered if truly she'd just been tipsy the other day. That would be a huge reason to get myself in check.

"Well, I just wanted to be truthful with you. I still have shivers when I remember that day."

The confusion slipped off her face and her eyes darken as she bit down on her bottom lip. "Ah—"

15

I chuckled. "Nah, as long you can do the job, I don't care about anything else." My eyes flicked to the folder on the table. I picked it up and opened it, seeing that it was all her documentation and work history.

"My background's majorly been around town," she muttered.

"I can see that. So you're no stranger to managing events?"

"Not at all. I worked in management at the high school and we organized quite a number of trips for our students. I'd reckon that would be much harder than tourists."

"So, why did you stop working in the school?"

For the first time since she'd come in, a brief expression of worry flashed on her face. "Um, it's a long story. I'd lived in Taos for years and decided I needed a place where I can impact the community more and that's with tourists."

I nodded. There wasn't a doubt in my mind she was hiding something. But from what I could tell, her record was clean, and my contacts did a deep background check. If she wanted to keep her secrets, I wasn't about to pry unless she gave me reason to believe it would impact my business.

"This ain't a school, you know. Working on a resort like this is gonna be at a scale of nothing you've ever done before."

Her confidence returned as she smiled sweetly. I ignored the twist in my gut and focused on her words.

"And that's why I'm so eager for the chance. Working one-on-one with tourists in a place like this...it seems almost too good to be true."

"Well, I'm happy you're excited about it. But what have you heard about the resort?"

"Peak's Bliss is quite a legend around Taos to be honest. The resort is on everyone's lips. But personally, you're quite a mystery. When I asked about you, the only thing I'd heard is that you were born in Taos, but you didn't live here until recently."

16

I laughed. "I generate quite some interest in town it seems."

"When you run the biggest resort in the area, it kind of comes with the territory."

"Exactly. Doesn't help that the gossip-mongers around town can't get enough of talking about my business, either."

"A handsome man who has some past history with the town?" she asked, one perfect eyebrow lifted. "Sounds like a subject made for gossip." As soon as she spoke the words, a tinge of red broke out across her stunning features.

"So," I went on, pretending not to notice her embarrassment over calling her prospective boss handsome. "Seems you know about the place. Want to know why I'm hiring you?"

"I know it's a busy time of year with tourists. You need extra hands to manage it all."

"You're not entirely wrong," I said. "But I'm hiring you because I need time to focus on my daughter."

"You're married?" A look of shock crossed her face as her eyes raked across my fingers for a sign of engagement ring.

"No, I'm not. I dated her mom for a time, but it didn't work out."

Her look was sympathetic. "Oh, I'm sorry. But I don't know how that affects me?"

I smiled. "I need to make more room for Emma to have time with her father."

She glanced away, and I could tell the gears of her mind were turning. After a brief silence, she met my eyes again. "I'm a quick study. I should be able to alleviate most of the workload after shadowing you for a few days."

I nodded. "Sounds good so far."

She flashed her gorgeous smile. "I think so. I don't have any doubt you're a great dad and are doing your best for her. I'm the partner you need."

The word partner rang hard in my ears, but I ignored it, smiling gently instead. "Sure as hell feels that way."

"And if I were to be your assistant, we'd be on the same team — might even give you some tips on how to handle things and keep her happy. I love kids — I worked in a school after all, so we can help each other out."

A grin spread across my lips. "Now, that's a damn good point."

Hell, I was impressed. Jenna sounded like an expert with a sky-high IQ, but I could also read a slight sense of desperation in her voice.

"Hm," I said, sitting back. "Now, this all sounds good. But the real question is how you're going' to react to things around the resort."

Jenna smiled. "I'd love the chance to find out."

Right after she spoke the words, I rose to my feet and grinned. "Well," I announced. "Hope you are ready for this because now's your chance."

She grinned right back. "I can't wait."

And neither could I. For some reason, I felt like this was meant to be. I was supposed to meet this woman and she was supposed to be my assistant. I wondered how I was going to handle the desire burning through me at just the sight of her.

CHAPTER 3

- JENNA -

When we stepped out of the cabin, I felt my phone buzz and I checked my phone and saw Mark's name flashing on the screen. My heart started to beat furiously. *Why the hell was he calling me now?* I silenced the call and dropped my phone back in my pocket.

"Do you have a call?" Tyler asked. "I can wait for you to take it."

I shook my head. "It's nothing important, just a notification."

I wasn't about to ruin this opportunity with Mark's call. I was certain Tyler had been impressed by how I'd handled myself during the interview. I was glad because it had been so hard to focus with those steely green eyes staring at me. And whenever he talked, the first thought that ran through my mind was that his lips were calling out for a kiss.

I knew most of the men in Taos; they were hard-edged and serious, while most of the touring men that came here could be described as softer. And neither hard nor soft were words I'd use to describe Tyler at all. The man was a different breed; he combined the best of both worlds with grace and poise as if he'd been precisely made to combine the best features. Most women would kill just to have him flash that wide-toothed grin at them.

Focus, focus. The real interview's about to start. I pushed how insanely hot Tyler was out of my mind as he opened the door and led us out into the sprawling estate of the resort. He led me from place to place, and I was in total awe. When we turned toward the residence, my eyes widened as I stepped into the entry hall, The place was as impressive as anything I'd ever seen.

"Damn," I murmured. "This is some place. And it doesn't look like what I'd imagine from the outside."

"That's because it's not," he announced excitedly. "My mom has always been interested in decor and how things look, so when I had this place built, I had her in mind. We decorated the inside according to an unpublished interior decor manuscript she wrote."

"It's amazing." I stepped to the grand spiral staircase that led to the other two floors, running the tips of my fingers over the intricate designs of the hand-carved rail.

"All built from trees around the area. It's Taos and New Mexico all in one building. Love to call it home," he said with pride ringing in his voice. "Come on – I'll show you to the rooms."

We climbed the stairs to the third floor. A few guests were wandering about, and I said my hellos as we passed them in the carpeted hallway. The walls were decorated with landscape paintings of Texas, a few specifically painted at Peak Bliss resort. Each door was closed and fitted with locks for privacy, though we had keys to every room just in case.

"So, you live here with the guests?"

"Kinda," he said, wiggling his hand back and forth. "Most of the staff — especially those who live far away — all have rooms in the house that are their own where they can stay if they need to. I've got a room here too, but Emma and I mostly stay at the cabin at the edge of the property, where we met earlier today." He smiled at me and my heart melted. "We meet here for meals daily though."

We walked past several doors as we moved back down the stairs and a number of people who looked like staff greeted us. He gestured as we stepped out the door. "This is where I'll be needing your help the most. I will be working very closely with you until you get settled. So if you need anything, don't be bashful about hollering."

I thought about how there was a whole other way I wanted to holler – one that involved him over me in a bed. I shook my head quickly. I needed to get things like that out of my mind.

He is your employer now, dumbhead. I felt a pang of disappointment that I might not get to experience the feeling of his hands wrapped around me and his cock buried deep in me.

"I won't," I responded with a smile.

"Alright. Today's for getting rested and acclimated, you hear?"

I smiled and nodded. "I hear. It's been a beautiful place so far." I followed him across the resort, heading through the grassy knolls and on the trip down, I spotted a little girl out in front of the house.

"Daddy?" came a sweet voice and then little feet carried her across the lawn. "You're back here?"

He grinned. "Well," he announced. "I guess I am."

I looked up to see Emma stepping out of the lawn, looking so tiny and precious. She looked so much like her dad — the same steely green eyes, the same full lips, the same dark hair she'd pulled back into a long ponytail. She was dressed like her dad too, in a green-and-black checkered shirt and faded jeans, and a pair of adorable boots on her little feet.

She clapped her eyes on me, her mouth opening slightly in surprise. "Who's that?" she asked, raising a tiny finger in my direction.

"Come on and meet her, kiddo."

Emma took a few hesitant steps and stopped a few feet away from me, her expression uncertain.

I leaned in and stuck out my hand. "Hi, Emma!" I exclaimed. "My name's Jenna."

"Who are you?" she asked, her voice soft.

"Well, your daddy's thinking of hiring me to help out around here."

She blinked and frowned at me. "But we have lots of people working here already. Do we need more?"

I smiled, squatting and putting my hands on my knees. "I would be helping your dad with his work," I dropped my voice into a whisper. "So he'd be able to hang out with you much more. You think you'd like that?"

Emma turned to her dad, her eyes bright. "Is that true?"

"She'd be my assistant," he clarified. "And I'd be able to take you to school more, play with you in the park – all kinds of fun stuff."

"That's so cool." She punched her fist in the air and turned to me. "Thank you for coming to work with my dad."

I smiled at her and nodded to Tyler. "I think we should thank your dad."

"I'm going to see Gray, dad," she said, "Wanna come see my horse with me?" Her eyes were bright, the smile bright on her face.

I glanced at her dad, asking without words if it was alright with him. "Sure," he said. "We can all go see her. But not for long, yeah?"

The smile faded from her face. "Because I stayed too long yesterday."

"That's right," Tyler said, smiling at her and chucking her chin a little. "And we can't because I've still got some things to discuss with Miss Jenna."

She nodded and glanced at me and when I stuck my hand out to her, she took it, her tiny palm disappearing in mine. "Let's go."

Emma led me out of the resort, her hand still in mine. I felt relief as soon as we started walking down the path. My phone started buzzing again, and when I fished it out of my pocket to see it was Mark's call again. I slammed on the red button again and turned towards the girl.

"You know, Emma," I began. "You're a really lucky girl."

We walked along the trodden path away from the cabin, the worn grass winding through the emerald green around us.

"I am?"

"Look at this place." I swept my hand toward the vast expanse of the resort. "You have this beautiful place all around you, and you get to live here. Plenty of grownups pay a lot of money just to stay here for a little while. But it's all yours."

"I guess," she said. "I like staying here too. Is that why you've come to work with Dad? Because you like here?"

"Yeah. That's part of it. I used to work at the high school in the valley, but working on a resort like this is even cooler."

"I'm glad that you came to work here." She smiled again, and I couldn't resist grinning in return.

Emma seemed like a great kid, and it was clear that was down to her having a great dad. Hiring me to be able to spend time with her was enough proof of that. I looked back at Tyler who had given us space and was casually strolling behind us. The sight of him made my heart skip a beat. I never thought I'd be so into someone so quickly. He looked sleek, tough and rugged at the same time, exuding such a manly aura that turned me on in ways I could hardly wrap my head around.

Behave yourself, Jenna. The man's kid is here.

"Here's where she lives." Emma's voice pulled back my attention and I followed her through the side door to the barn. Sunlight flooded the space, and the scent of hay and horse filled my nostrils. The sides of the barn were lined with horse stalls, the magnificent animals snorting and eating their food, their deep eyes locking onto us as we walked through. They were all incredible. I wasn't surprised to see the graceful beasts because I'd heard that one of the programs that Peak Bliss offers tourists is a wilderness survival class and other basic skills like horse riding.

"Okay," Emma said as she led me through the barn. "There's Artax, and that's Bailey, and that's Trigger." She pointed out the horses as we passed. "And that's Dusty. Dad told me she's Gray's mama."

"Hi, Dusty!" I greeted, peeking at the big, gray-and-black speckled mare in front of me. The horse snickered slightly and turned its attention back to nosing the hay around it.

"And here's Gray!"

We stopped in front of one of the stalls. Gray had seemingly been named after her color. She was a gorgeous yearling, sleek and trim, clearly smaller than the rest of the horses on account of her age. Emma opened the stall and stepped in, and I followed her. Her lack of fear fascinated me.

"Good girl," Emma said, patting Gray on her long muzzle. "You're so pretty. Isn't she pretty?'

"Very pretty," I agreed.

"You should pet her – she likes that." Emma took my hand and slowly moved it toward the horse's muzzle. Her fur was bristly but soft, a light snort sounding from her nose as I petted her.

"She likes you," Emma nodded confidently. "I can tell."

"I like her, too. I bet it'd be fun to ride her."

"Yeah!" Emma whooped. "I want Daddy to teach me how."

I looked back at Tyler where he hung back staring at us with a smile on his lips. "Maybe he can teach both of us. I'd really like to ride."

It was until he cleared his throat that I realized the double entendre of my words. I flushed badly as he sauntered over to us.

"We'll see, Jenna." He said the name like he was savoring it. I loved hearing it come out of his mouth, hearing him say my name with that sexy tone. His eyes flashed at me before he turned to his daughter "Anyway, you oughta get back to the house now, sweetie. You should tell Isabella to start setting up the table for dinner."

"Yes!" Emma celebrated. "I'm starving." Then she turned to me. "Are you going to eat with us?"

I glanced at Tyler, unsure of how to answer.

"I think that'd be alright," he said. "But I'm gonna need to talk to her for a bit before we do that, alright?"

"Okay," Emma agreed. She hurried out of the barn quickly to deliver her dad's errand.

"If you are willing to dine with us tonight, I'll walk you down to the house later. Isabella likes having new people taste her food."

I nodded, unable to speak. With Emma gone, I was very aware that we were alone in the barn. Tyler placed his hand on the small of my back to guide me out of the stall, and the sensation of his touch on my body sent a thrill through me. Even though it was simply a polite gesture, it felt electrical. I involuntarily wondered what it'd be like for him to put his hands on other private places in my body.

Stop it right now, I ordered myself. *You have just been hired, and you're already fantasizing about fucking the boss. How are you going to handle working day to day with him when you start the job? Gonna go and have some kind of stupid schoolgirl crush on him?*

Get real.

"I think you would be a natural fit here. Would you be staying the night? I can have a room prepared for you, and we can work on some things through the night."

"Huh?"

"I promise I'm not a slavedriver," Tyler grinned, a sexy, wolfish smile on his lips. "I just need to get you settled as quickly as possible. It's the rush hour over here."

25

I kept my mouth shut. I wanted badly to stay the night, but mostly for work that would involve him thrusting his cock into me, deep and hard until hot spurts of his seed shoot into my body. I closed my eyes briefly as I feel warmth pool towards my lower belly. I could feel the wetness in my panties already.

Fuck! No man had ever aroused me like this before. Not one had even come close.

"What's wrong?" He pulled me closer to himself and I almost exploded in orgasm right there.

Can't he feel this? Can't he feel the desire blasting through my body. I clenched my teeth, trying to stamp down on the raging need for pleasure and focusing on the worry instead, letting that rush through me to drown out the lust.

When I opened my eyes, his expression was sympathetic. "What's wrong? Tell me."

I didn't know what to say or how to say it. I slipped out of his hands and away through the barn, walking through the hay. I staggered out of the closed space filled with the smell of horse and an irresistible man, rushing out as quickly as possible.

"Jenna," he called out after me. "Talk to me."

I opened the door to the barn, letting the sunlight stream in. It covered him in a golden glow that made him look surreal. I shook my head. "I...I can't do this."

"What?" he asked, with confusion in his voice and on his face.

"It's...I can't control myself around you. And I can't risk this. I just...I need some time to think."

I slipped out of the barn, ignoring the millions of shivers around my body, striding away from the barn. Tyler called out, but I kept on walking through the grass and to the deck. Luckily, no one was there to see us. I didn't stop until I was a few yards away from the cabin. I waited, panting, my heart still racing.

I knew he was coming. No way he'd let the matter drop like that. But I couldn't think of what else to do other than give myself some space. I gazed off to the west and heard rustling grasses behind me, I didn't bother to turn back to confirm who it was.

"Jenna," he said, his voice low so as not to attract attention. "Come on."

He wasn't going to take no for an answer. After letting a full breath move through my lungs, I turned to him. Tyler had a genuine look of worry on his face and even at that, he looked sexy as hell.

"I know you're not gonna make me just stand out here like this." The side of his mouth curled up in a cute, sexy smile. "I thought we were cool."

"Okay," I nodded and stepped over toward him. "We can talk about it. This thing between us…" I gestured with my hand. "It's making me worried."

"So," he said. "You're worried about your job?"

"Not just the job," I said. "Everything about it. I shouldn't want to fuck my boss so much."

"We shouldn't."

My eyebrows rose and he glanced aside and nodded. "That's right…yeah. I want this so much too."

"It is one thing that you walked in on me using sex toys and we flirted and we laughed about it the next time we met. But I think I should be dead-set on not making that mistake again."

"But you can't resist me."

I grinned, in spite of how I felt. "Someone's cocky."

He grinned too. "Nothing cocky about it – it's a statement of fact. You can't resist me, and I can't resist you. So we gotta figure out what we're gonna do here."

"I know. Sounds like we both tried resisting today, but all it takes is for us to be alone and…"

"And we want to get our hands all over each other."

"Right."

Silence. My heart was pounding hard and fast. This man was totally irresistible. I licked my lips nervously and opened my mouth to speak, and then my phone started buzzing again. I didn't bother digging it out of my pocket this time, I already knew who it was.

Tyler's eyes narrowed. "Are you involved with someone?"

"No," I cleared my throat and spoke quickly.

"Okay then," he nodded. "What if we just...let it happen?"

I gasped slightly. "Let it happen?"

He smiled softly at me. "Nothing serious or certain or carved into stone. We just go with it. See what happens."

I looked into those steely green eyes that were focused on my face. "That's what you want? Does that mean that if it doesn't work, we can just stop?"

"I don't think it would be that easy," he countered.

"Affect our working relationship?"

He sighed. "I didn't mean it like that. Of course, it would be hard if it didn't work. But we're adults, right? We could figure out a way to go on."

"But there's still the matter of Emma and other people working here. News spread fast in Taos, you know?"

He nodded. "You're right. We have to keep this under the cover for the time being."

"Yeah. Don't want anyone to get too confused about anything going on between you and me." I sighed.

The conversation was setting a low fire in my belly. I was anxious and excited at the same time. Tyler apparently felt the same way. He stretched, his powerful body curving back, his muscles popping and tautening. "We let things work out naturally," he said.

"Yeah, naturally."

He turned to me in the silence that fell between us. Neither of us seemed to know what to say.

"They will be expecting us for dinner already." His eyes settled on my lips. The look lingered, and the longer it went on, the more I wanted to grab his neck pull his mouth down to mine.

But I didn't.

"I'll be staying the night, Tyler."

"I'm glad," he chuckled, giving me a sexy smile before pulling me along with him. I fell into step with him, a big smile on my face. A feeling of excitement danced through me as we headed toward the residence area.

CHAPTER 4

- TYLER -

I could barely take my eyes off Jenna for the rest of the evening. She was cool during dinner, spoke to the other staff she met, and chatted a bit with Emma. Every move she made set me on fire — every soft laughter, every word she spoke, every time she slipped the spoon between her lips. Just the sight of her across the table made my dick twitch. I stared down at where I tented my trousers. I'd worked hard to get the stupid appendage under control so it didn't get me into mess to begin with, and that had worked for me most time. *Not now though*.

Since the moment she'd walked in for that interview I'd been thinking about several ways to keep my distance, and I'd actually thought I'd be able to do it, and then one moment of standing in that quiet meadow, with her smell all around me and her eyes flashing with desire, those curvy hips, round breasts and perfect ass in display and I just lost it.

I looked across the table and our eyes met. She tucked her hair behind her hair and flashed a smile. *Fucking hell*. I rubbed my hands across my face and sat up. Why couldn't I just keep it in my pants around this woman?

"Ready for bed, Emma?"

My daughter nodded and started to climb out of her chair. "Goodnight, Jenna. Goodnight everyone."

A chorus of goodnight went around the table as I grabbed Emma and hurled her across my shoulder and ambled down the hallway to her room. I gently helped her into her PJs and then tucked her in before placing her favorite sleep partner — a stuffed bear under her arm.

I read out a short passage from her favorite collection of stories to her and when I closed the book I pressed a kiss to her forehead.

"Good night, baby. Have sweet dreams. You mean the world to me, and I want you to know that."

"I love you, Daddy," she muttered, well on her way to the dreamland. I smiled and ruffled her hair before getting up and heading to the door, flicking off the light and shutting the door behind myself. I immediately turned and walked back to library.

I was focused on trying to get the schedule for the next few days finished when the door opened, and Jenna walked in and plopped on the couch.

"You said you'd be getting me up to date, so when do we start?"

"Alright," I answered and packed up the sheaf of papers to go drop them on the table in front of her. "Think you're ready for a nightcap with this stuff?"

"Hmm," she nodded. "A drink should help me get through the worst of it."

I found myself smirking as I poured both of us a small glass of whiskey and then the two of us settled down on the comfy couch. I watched her go through the papers, the only sound was the papers rustling as she started to speak. "These are your plans for the next few days."

"Yes," I took a sip of my drink. "You have any input?"

She stood up suddenly, my eyes following her as the index of her right hand absently traced the edge of her glass and her face frowned in though as she paced the room. There seemed to be a crazy sway to her hips and when she finally stopped at the desk and leaned over, jutting out her round ass, I sucked in a breath. It felt like she was taunting me.

She turned back to face me and I saw a hint of a smirk before she resumed pacing and she "accidentally" brushed her hand across my shoulder. Twice.

For the next half an hour, she started explaining how she thinks things could go, but I barely heard anything. Every time I looked at her she was doing something that sent arousal through me: sly glances, biting her bottom lip, sitting for a bit to cross and uncross her legs, or absentmindedly twirling a tendril of hair around her finger. At one point, she dropped a set of papers and casually placed her hand on my thigh as she bent down to retrieve it from under the table. The torment both excited and frustrated me and I nodded and spoke at appropriate times, but I was never fully thinking about the schedule anymore.

"Tyler?" Her voice called out sultrily. "Did you hear the last thing I said?"

"Sorry," I said. "I get like that sometimes – wrapped up in my own head."

"Oh, really?" She flashed another smile, settling next to me on the couch. "You must be a thinker then."

I chuckled. "Don't know if I'm a thinker, per se. More that I find an escape from the moment sometimes. I kind of create more engaging scenes in my mind."

"Oh." Her expression dropped. "Then I've been boring you."

"Not at all," I quickly assured her. "Quite the opposite, in fact."

"Oh really?"

"Sure is, ma'am."

A sly smile spread across her lips, exposing a sliver of white teeth peeking through her full, red lips as she wrapped around her glass, lifted it to her lips, and took a long, slow sip, smacking her lips. "Now, that hits the spot like nothing else."

I'd never been more jealous of a thing as I was of that lifeless cup at that moment. I immediately stood up and went over to the big, grand table. Once there, I tried to distract myself by picking a few books like the ledger and other notes I'd made. I could feel her eyes on me. There was another fire deep in my belly and the only reason I was not jumping Jenna right now was because I was worried if I should go ahead with this. It was simpler talking about our feelings, but acting it out was a different thing entirely and there would be no going back once we crossed that line. And at the same time, I wasn't ready to let her go quite yet.

When I was done going, I dusted my palms on my jeans and turned around, winking at her. "Think I've got just a bit more for you to look through?"

"That's why you need me here, ain't it?"

No way! I needed more than that, but I said nothing. I returned and sat in the chair next to her as I handed her the books. We were so close that her hand was only a hair's breadth away from my own, but I focused on sipping my drink while she read. She flipped through the pages, at one time, she tongued her finger to be able to flip the page. I felt a light, pleasant buzz dancing with a wave of heat between my legs and traveled to the rest of my body. I rubbed my thighs together, hoping that'd take my mind off what I wanted.

"You are very detailed," she commented. "These are going to make things easy for me."

I nodded. "It helps that I got a great assistant too. Seems we'll develop chemistry."

"Thanks." She smiled, setting her drink down between us and turning to narrow her eyes at me. "I think we've got the chemistry already. Or else I'm mistaken."

"Ah, I think that—" I tried turning to face her and my hand collided with glass, tipping it over, and splashing the drink over the front of her blouse. She let out a sharp gasp as the liquid landed on her clothes.

"Aw, hell," I groaned, I couldn't believe what I'd just done. Just a line of flirtation and I became a lummox. "You alright?" I got up immediately, hurrying to one of the closets.

"I'm fine," she assured me, finally opening her eyes. "It's not that bad actually."

I opened the closet and took out a small towel. "Just stay right there," I instructed as I approached her. "I'll handle it."

Before I thought about it, I squatted down in front of her, placing the towel on her blouse and firmly pressing it against her chest to soak up the drink. A bit had seeped into the fabric, but fortunately, there wasn't a lot of whiskey left in the glass.

"I assure you, I'm not that much of a blunderer, just so you know?" I joked.

I looked up to see those deep blue eyes staring down at me, a hint of a smile on her lips. It was that moment I realized I'd been pressing the rag on her boobs.

"Fuck," I gasped and retreated.

The smile on her face widened and she threw her head back in a laugh. "It's nothing really. You owe it to me to finish what you started."

"Really?" I grinned at her, continuing to clean up, pressing my other hand on her lap to keep myself steady. "Is there a reason why you don't want me to stop?"

"Well, you seem to know what you're doing. I should just follow your expertise and get this dry quickly."

I chuckled. "And what if my expert advice is that you take these off," I tugged at the blouse. "Hang it up to dry."

The wet silk of her blouse clung to her, accentuating every curve. I traced the fabric along her breasts, feeling her tight nipples underneath. She moaned and brought her hand to rest on mine, guiding my movements.

"I guess I should really hang it up to dry." Her voice was rough with need as she pushed me back and stood up from the couch to stand near the desk, looking at me calmly. With shaky hands, she unbuttoned the blouse, fumbling some buttons in her haste before sliding the wet fabric from her shoulders and tossing it away.

I stopped dead in my tracks at the sight of what lay underneath. Damn me to hell. She was a goddess. I slowly

35

climbed to my feet, one hand leaning against the couch for support. She stood still before me in a white strapless bra that tied on the front with a little bow. I closed the distance between us, wrapping my hand around the back of her neck. Her nipples were hard and visible beneath the bra, and I couldn't stop myself from reaching out to touch them.

"Fuck, you are so beautiful," I said, running my fingertips along her taut breasts. She shivered as my hand traveled upward, across her collarbone, along her neck, and finally to her jaw.

I wanted her more than anything. I pulled her to me, meeting her gaze as I drew her mouth to mine. There was an unspoken challenge there. Both of us knew that this—whatever it was—was beyond our control, but we didn't care at that moment. The moment our lips touched, I was overtaken by a familiar buzz coursing through my body. I fisted my hands deeply into her hair, forcing her head back, to take everything I poured into her through the kiss.

Pressing my body to hers, I groaned at how perfectly each of her curves seemed to fit against me. I wanted this need to go away, to be satisfied and move on; but the fiery need that burned now was too vast, too crazy and I could feel the buzz of electricity at every point where our bodies touched.

I wanted to satisfy this mad need, but I also wanted to make her feel every piece of it. I wanted her to go wild with desire, to push her off the edge.

Falling to my knees, I grasped her hips and pulled her closer, my lips moving across the waist of her pants. I lapped at each inch of visible skin, biting softly and then licking it, enjoying feeling her muscles tense as I explored. I looked up at her, smiling as I hooked my fingers into the waistband of her jeans. Her eyes closed immediately, and she bit her lower lip. I felt my cock harden in anticipation of what I was about to do and with a groan, I unbuttoned her jeans and pulled it down her thighs, watching goose bumps break out over her skin as my fingers trailed down her legs. Her hands settled on my head, clutching my hair and pulling roughly. I groaned and looked back up at her. Her eyes were wide and dark, her face pink with blush. I traced the edge of the delicate satin of her matching panties, stopping at the thin straps on her hips.

36

"I'm sorry," I said, wrapping one strap around each hand. "But you won't be leaving here with your underwear."

I yanked it off, hearing the rip as I pulled the white material away and stuffed it into my pocket. A sense of urgency took over me then, and I quickly freed one of her legs from the jeans, placing it over my shoulder and kissing along the soft skin of her inner thigh.

"Oh, shit," she gasped, exhaling hard as her hands ran in my hair. "Oh, shit, please." I smiled against her skin, gently nuzzling her between the thighs and then slowly licking along her clit.

"Fuck it!" She gripped my hair tightly, her hips undulating against my mouth. Other words fell from her lips in groans and hoarse whispers, most of them unintelligible. I took pleasure in seeing her come undone so completely. She was completely helpless and out of her mind, and in the next moment, she might hook her leg around my neck and strangle me.

I loved seeing her out of control, knowing that this was, in many ways, so much more intimate than simple fucking. I was on my knees, and she was vulnerable and bare. I lapped her, again and again, enjoying the fact that she was also warm and wet and tasted just as fucking sweet as she looked. "It feels fucking consuming yeah?" I whispered, pulling back enough to glance up at her expression.

"Yeah," she gasped, "yeah!"

Kissing her hip, I murmured, "I want to find a bed where I can spread you out. Should we head to a room, perhaps."

She tugged on my hair, pulling me back to her with a sneer. "Not yet. Don't you dare stop."

I didn't, I couldn't. And I immediately buried my face in her lap again. I grazed my teeth against her as she shivered against my mouth, memorizing every curse and plea that escaped her mouth and knowing that I was the reason for it. I moaned against her, causing her to cry out as she twisted her body closer.

I slid two fingers inside her, pulling on her hip with the other hand, urging her to find her rhythm with me. She began rolling her hips, slowly at first, pressing into me, and then faster. I could feel her tense gradually: first her legs, then her abdomen, and then her hands in my hair.

"So close," she panted, "I'm so fucking close."

Her movements started to falter, the orgasm too close for her to follow any rhythm as her hips jerked in wild motions. I felt a little wild myself and I let loose on her, biting and sucking, and pumping my fingers inside her wetness to completely unravel her. Her breaths turned into little pants and every word was a plea not to stop. When I twisted my wrist and pushed in deeper, she cried out, legs shaking as her climax overtook her.

Before she could collapse in my arms, I grabbed her, her breasts pressed against my chest as the waves of orgasm passed over her. She went still for a moment, and then I felt her hand on my cock over the fabric of my trousers. Just her touch was enough to drive me wild. She smiled up at me, lifting to her tiptoes and planting a long lingering kiss on my lips. Her taste filled my mouth, driving me wild and I let our tongues tease for a moment or two before I backed up.

"You liked that?" I couldn't wipe the grin off my lips.

"Yes, and now it's your turn..." Jenna flashed me a sly smirk before dropping to her knees. Flicking her eyes up at me, she stroked my cock through my trousers before reaching below the waistband and pulling it out, her eyes flashing with surprise for a moment.

"Damn," she groaned. "I had a feeling you'd be big, but..." She shook her head as if trying to wrap her mind around it then she glanced up, her eyes on mine, those gorgeous grey-blue eyes narrowed hungrily, with a sensual promise.

Jenna curled her fingers around my cock, stroking it slowly as she planted her lips on the tip. She licked my head once, then twice, before opening her mouth and taking the end of my cock into it. I trembled as her warm, wet mouth closed all around my cock, her tongue flicking out and teasing the end, the sight of her, kneeling down there with her mouth full of me was crazy. She slid her mouth down my length, taking as much of it as she could into her before dragging those plush lips back up and going again, pushing me deep in her throat.

Pleasure tingled from my cock, spreading through my body. Before too long, she was sucking me at a quick, steady pace, her hand following her mouth as she pulled me in and out of her mouth. It was overwhelming and I could feel the first waves of an orgasm building inside. But I didn't want that yet.

"Get on up here, gorgeous," I said, reaching down to pull her face off me.

Sam did as I asked, letting my cock drop out of her mouth before rising to her feet. "Now what?"

I made a spin around motion with my finger. "As great as you swallowing every last drop of me would feel, I'm not gonna be satisfied with just that."

She chuckled as her hands clutched me and stroked slowly. "You really think everything's yours for the taking, huh?"

"Only what I truly want."

"Oh yeah? And what do you truly want?"

I reached around and smacked her perfect, round ass. "I think you know.

She pressed her hips against mine. "Then take it."

I didn't need to hear another word. My hands on her hips, I turned Jenna around and carried her to the couch. The sight of her bent over in front of me, her pussy glistening and waiting to be fucked was the most perfect thing I'd ever seen. She wiggled her backside a little, inviting me with her body. I slipped out of my trousers, grabbed my cock in my hand and dragged the head against her lips, enjoying the sigh of pleasure pouring from her mouth.

"Please," she moaned. "I need you inside me."

I could no longer resist as well and I pushed into her slowly. A low hiss escaped my mouth as I felt her wet heat encircle me. Raw, primal need flushed through every part of me and I leaned over her. Jenna groaned, shaking as I thrust every inch of my hard cock into her. I waited until I was buried to the hilt, and then I pulled back and then drove into her again, watching her hands grip the couch arm hard. Her whole body seemed to shake and I held her in place, thrusting into her again and again, as she threw her head back, her eyes clamped shut in pleasure and then she dropped it again.

"Fuck. You...you feel so fucking good inside me," she moaned, her face partially muffled by the couch. "Like nothing I've ever felt."

"You feel incredible too."

And though it was just the first time, I somehow knew without a doubt that no woman would ever feel the way she did. I knew she was special, that Jenna was somehow different. It was crazy, but I knew, and I couldn't shake the knowledge.

"Yes Tyler," she gasped again, wiggling hard against me, pushing her hips back to meet every thrust. The image of her ass bouncing on my cock pushed me over the edge and in mere moments I was draining myself deep into her, her ass squirming against me as the orgasm flowed through my body.

CHAPTER 5

- JENNA -

The shrill ringing of a phone pierced through my sleep-filled mind. I wanted to ignore it, trying to force the sound away because I didn't want to wake up. I was too warm and comfortable to wake up now because this was the best sleep I'd had in years. I snuggled into the warm, sweet-smelling pillow near me and it snuggled back. It was when the warm, hard body pressed against me snuggled closer that I realized this was no pillow. My eyes popped open in shock to see the face of a man covered with messy hair inches from my face.

Tyler!

A hundred images of the previous night flashed through my mind in that second as reality came crashing down on my muddled brain. *Holy shit. It was real.* I'd truly ended an interview with my prospective boss giving me mindblowing orgasms all through the night. My heart rate quickened and I turned around quickly to grab my phone, quickly hitting the button to end the call as soon as I saw Mark's name on the screen.

I turned back toward Tyler to see he was still sleeping, and I heaved a sigh of relief. His head lay on the bed, his perfect mouth slightly open as he released puffs of warm air across my bare breasts. His long body was tangled with mine, our legs over each other and his right arm wrapped tightly around me.

After we left the library, he'd carried me into his room and we'd fucked all through the night until we both collapsed with exhaustion.

Now that the night was over, what was to become of us? The realization of our situation hit me with a crushing force that actually took my breath away. I might not know what he wanted, but I wished I could spend every other night in his arms. I was employed by him, and that made this inappropriate, but my body didn't care about that.

I struggled to find my breath and not panic. I could feel the powerful thump of his heartbeat against my chest. His semi hard cock was pressed against my thigh, still huge even in his sleep. My fingers itched to touch him to kiss him and run my hands across his body. He'd given me the best night ever.

I heard the buzz start with my phone again and I shut it down before it could wake him. *Why the hell was Mark calling me now?*

For the first time in more than a month, I'd been able to sleep well without needing the help of alcohol. Being with Tyler had made me forget my pain of losing Mark quickly, and I selfishly didn't want to lose that for any reason. *Mark had no reason to call me. He'd been clear enough when he told me it was over between us.*

I decided I would only give him a call only when I was ready and away from Tyler. He didn't know who was harassing me yet, and I intended to keep it that way. I managed to roll off him gently, freezing when he began to stir. I reached out to hold him close, silently willing him to go back to sleep and when he mumbled some words and his breathing evened out again, I slipped out from underneath him.

I stared at him for a moment. He looked so peaceful in slumber. I gently brushed back a thick curl that had fallen down across his forehead, and my fingers itched to touch him more. He was just too good-looking — long lashes, perfect cheekbones, full pouty lips, and a stubble-covered jaw. He was extremely gorgeous and fucking skilled. He'd shown just how great he was in every move, every touch, every word, and every kiss.

It was like we had been together a million times before. Nobody had ever made me feel that way, as if my body were made to fit his. I'd been with other men, but with him, it felt as if a whirlwind of pleasure was carrying me away and there was completely nothing I could do to change the course. I closed my eyes, trying to quell the sense of panic that was building. I didn't regret what happened. It was—as always—intense and easily the best sex I'd ever had. I just needed a few minutes alone before I could face him.

I started to make my way to the bathroom when I caught my reflection in the mirror over the bedroom vanity. I stopped in front of it, staring at my rosy face and bright eyes. Sated. That was definitely the one word that described my look this morning.

I leaned over to examine the small red scrapes that were scattered along my skin to prove what I'd spent the night doing. There was a small bite mark on the underside of my left breast, a scratch on my shoulder and little tingling feelings down between my legs. I ran my fingers along the red marks on my inner thigh, nipples hardening as I recalled the feeling of his unshaven face brushing along my skin as he buried his face down there. His hands had made my hair a tangle of wild mess, and an image of his hands twisting in it as he slammed his hips against my backside.

"Thinking about sneaking out?"

Turning, I caught a glimpse of his naked body as he twisted in the sheets before he sat up and pulled them over his hips but leaving his torso bare. I smiled brightly at him. I didn't think I would ever get tired of looking at his broad, muscular chest, pressing my hands against those lean washboard abs, and running it down the tantalizing happy trail that led to the cock that had blown me through multiple glorious orgasms just last night. When my eyes—finally—reached his face, I saw him scowling at my lopsided grin.

"Caught you sneaking out did I," he murmured, rubbing a hand over his jaw.

"No, I was not."

Seeing him rumpled and vulnerable in his half-awake state was disorienting. We never bothered about consequences last now, but right now with the daylight spreading across the sky, I was starting to realize that I'd never see this gorgeous man as just my boss. As his eyes raked over me, I remembered that I was completely naked too and his intense dark stare started another flame of desire in my belly.

43

"If you're not sneaking out, then why are you there?" His tongue darted out to wet his lips. "Come here," he growled.

I obeyed him, moving to the bed to sit beside him, but he pulled me across his thighs, and said, "Tell me what you're thinking."

How can I condense a million thoughts into a single sentence? I opened my mouth and let the first thought out: "I was wondering how I'll ever be able to see the man who gave me so many orgasms last night as my boss." I stared at his collarbone so I wouldn't have to look him in the eye.

"Is that all?"

Finally, I looked up. He nodded in encouragement and slipped his fingers beneath mine to link our fears together.

"I'm also scared that the deeper this goes, the worse things will become." I confessed. "I'm worried that I might be doing all this as a rebound because I got dumped two months ago, I've been lonely, and you're the most attractive man I've met in that time."

He closed his eyes for a moment and shook his head. "I understand what you mean."

I wasn't sure how to interpret that. Did he mean he agreed that it was dangerous but was still open to it? Or he meant that we should actually end things. Tyler said nothing else, he just kissed along my shoulder, to my collarbone and up my neck. I reached around him, grabbing the complimentary bottle of water on the nightstand and taking a sip when I saw him stare at the water, I handed it to him. He finished it in a quick long swallows.

"You're thirsty?"

"I was. Feeling a little hungry now."

"Not surprising, considering how much energy we expended—" I stopped as he wiggled his eyebrows and grinned. I rolled my eyes, but they fell closed as he leaned forward and kissed me once, sweetly, on the lips.

"What is the expectation here?" I asked.

"After what happened last night, I think you should be the one to tell me."

I didn't know how to answer that. I wasn't even sure I could be with him like this. The idea of how that would work made my head spin. How would we actually act at work . . . friendly? Loving? Would he even feel safe criticizing my work?

"Give me time to think about it?"

He nodded and spread his fingers over my lower back, pressing me into his side and pulling me out of my rambling thoughts. "Can I keep doing this while you make up your mind?" he whispered.

"Okay." I didn't know how to resist this man. I leaned back to give his mouth better access to my throat. He kissed me quickly, and his fingertips found my breast, slipping back and forth over the soft underside.

"What time is it?" I asked, trying to see behind him to the clock but in the process of leaning away from him, I'd exposed the skin just above my hip, his eyes fixed on that.

"Don't give a shit."

"That means you're ready for me walking out into an already busy resort wearing last night's rumpled clothes that tells a thousand stories. I might as well wear this bedsheet and nothing else down to the breakfast this morning."

His laugh was low and playful. "Like hell you will."

I was finally able to get a glimpse of the clock. "It's almost seven, Tyler!"

He let out a disappointed breath and moved away from me. "Alright go bathe. I'll drive you to your place to go your clothes and we head back here."

"Thank you," I gave him a quick kiss on his forehead and dashed into the bathroom.

I showered quickly and wrapped a thick towel around myself, wishing that there was one of the residence bathrobes in

45

here with me or I'd had the sense to bring my clothes with me. With a deep breath I opened the door and stepped out. He was still sitting on the bed, and his eyes rose to meet mine as I entered the room.

"I just need . . ." I trailed off, motioning to my clothes.

He nodded but made no move to speak. I was usually never self-conscious about my body. But standing here in nothing but a towel, knowing that he was watching me, I felt uncharacteristically shy. I grabbed my clothes and rushed past him, not stopping until I was once again safely behind the bathroom door. I dressed faster than I thought possible, deciding I would pull my hair back and finish the rest later.

When I returned to the bedroom. He hadn't moved. Sitting on the edge of the bed with his elbows resting on his thighs, he appeared lost in thought. What was he thinking? All morning I'd been a nervous wreck, my emotions shifting wildly from one extreme to the other, but he seemed so calm. So sure. But what was he sure of? He might have left the decision to me but I wanted to know what he really thought about this.

We hurried out and climbed into his car and he drove me straight to the door. When I stepped out in front of my apartment, I leaned over to ask him. "Do you have a uniform you want me to adhere to?"

He lifted his head, he looked slightly surprised, as if the thought hadn't occurred to him. "Um . . . we just have a few meetings this afternoon, right?"

I nodded.

"Whatever you pick will be fine. I'll drive down to Reeds to get their early bagels though. We might not be able to catch breakfast this morning, we have quite a lot to do."

I nodded and waved him off as he drove to the east toward the rising sun. After I walked into the house, I couldn't stop myself from imagining Tyler in here, on my bed after another long night of romping. I paused briefly, realizing imagining how it had felt waking up in his arms this morning, his scent, his body, his arms all around me. A heavy pang of desire washed through me

46

and I quickly opened my eyes. Not again! I was looking to stop this, not compound it.

I began looking through the neatly packed items for clothes to wear for a few days. In just a night, I'd noticed everything about Tyler was so tidy and organized, and I was the complete opposite of that.

Were we even compatible in any way? How far can we go before all of this comes crashing? Was I even ready for the risk? I paused as I realized that I wanted to risk it. But wouldn't I end up regretting it?

It struck me that I was stalling and I continued searching through the clothes before finally settling on a charcoal dress, and flat official shoes. Putting everything back where it belonged, I gathered up the clothing and changed into them quickly. Regardless of my nerves, it was clear that the man excited me. I was unable to stifle a chuckle as I walked into the living room, shaking my head over the sheer absurdity of the situation. I made it two steps into the living room before I froze. A man stood in front of the fireplace, staring up awash at the now empty wall where a picture used to hang.

Mark was here.

When he turned, he shook his head, staring at me intently. "I see you discarded me already."

I swallowed. "You need to leave here Mark."

"We need to talk, Jenna." His words were spoken so simply in a way that I'd never seen him speak before.

"You've said all you wanted to say. I was no longer needed, and I heard you loud and clear. You don't need me in your life any longer and you only dated me this long because you didn't know how to tell me."

"I was wrong, Jenna," he muttered and reached out to hug me. "Please listen to me, you're about to make a mistake."

Red hot rage surged through my veins, giving strength to my straining muscles. My hands landed on his chest and I pushed. "Get the fuck off me."

47

He staggered back a step, his eyebrows lifting in surprise and he put his hands up. "I heard you're thinking about working at Peak Bliss, hey! Don't make that mistake, Jenna."

"What the hell? You don't just walk in here and tell me what to do," I screamed at him. "You haven't got that right."

"Jenna," his eyes swept up and down my face. "Damn, girl. You need to listen, please. Tyler—"

I couldn't tell if he was truly worried, or just that much of an asshole that he was worried I'd moved on from him. Maybe both.

"Get the hell out, Mark."

I stomped toward the door and pulled it open. He followed me outside the house and his hand clamped around my wrist. I twisted, shouting for him to let go, and an instant later an arm hooked around my waist and pulled me away from Mark's grip.

"She asked you let her go, Mark." It was Tyler. I was so shocked that he knew my ex that my mouth dropped open.

"How did you know him?"

"Don't tell me he's fucking got to you already!" Mark screamed. When I looked up at him, he had a look of rage that I'd never seen on him before.

"She told you to leave, man," Tyler responded, looking as cool as cucumber as he faced Mark with a stance that scared me that they might go for each other's throats soon.

"Fuck you!" Mark screamed and made a threatening move and I quickly stepped around Tyler to raise my hands up.

"Mark, don't," I shouted, "Please don't."

He stopped suddenly and stared at me, and then scoffed and pointed to Tyler. "Do you even know who he fucking is? You're about to make the biggest regret of your life getting associated with this guy!"

What the fuck was he talking about? I turned to Tyler to see his cold emotionless stare in his green eyes. *What the hell was going on here? Did the fight even have anything to do with me?* At least they were not at each other's throats yet. I took a step toward Tyler and raised my eyebrow.

"He's your ex?" he asked flippantly.

I nodded and saw his face fall and he closed his eyes as if I'd just sent a lancing pain through his heart. "How do you know Mark?"

Tyler opened his eyes and shook his head. "We've got an history that goes way back. He's my brother."

"What?" I staggered back, I felt like a strong hand hit me across the face, making me so dizzy that I certainly couldn't see anything. My stomach knotted and I staggered back, and Tyler caught me, keeping his iron grip around me.

"Leave her the fuck alone!" Mark shouted.

"You broke up with her brother," Tyler bit out, his voice cold as ice. "You don't have any rights over her. She chooses who she wants with her."

"Tyler," Mark's tone was threatening. "You don't get to taint this one. You find a way to leave her alone or I swear to God I'm gonna reveal your secret. You'll be hearing from me soon."

I took ragged breaths and the red tinge that hazed my vision started to recede. When I opened my eyes, I saw Mark leaving. I tried to lunge at him again but Tyler's thick arms wrapped around my chest, pinning my arms down.

When I looked up at him he shook his head. "Let him go."

My gaze swung from him to Mark's retreating back. My mouth opened, but I closed it again, not knowing what to say. I followed Tyler to the car and he climbed behind the wheel, still saying nothing.

"What does that mean?" I finally asked.

"Nothing," he answered, driving out toward the main road.

49

"Are you serious?" I asked. "That was nothing?"

"He's my brother. We've got history and we're not in each other's good books. I'm not letting that crap affect anything."

Fuck. I didn't even know what to think. My morning had just gone from indecision to the most confusion I'd ever felt in my life. My eyes flicked from him to the road. Tyler was obviously not ready to explain anything to me, and I couldn't help the sense of foreboding that settled over me as we drove through the gates of the resort.

CHAPTER 6

- TYLER -

Jenna was avoiding me.

I stared at her through the window while she waved at co-workers and walked toward the main resort building. If there was one thing I'd learned about her in the past week, it was that I'd made the right decision to hire her. The whole staff at the resort had warmed up to her, and it was already like she'd been a part of the team for months. She wore a knee-length trench coat that shielded her clothes but showed off her amazing legs. Oh shit . . . For the love of God, soon I would have no willpower to resist walking up and grabbing her.

My recurring fantasies for the past few days have been stripping her naked and grabbing a handful of hair as I fucked her. I couldn't do that, though. It was clear that Jenna's mind was still boiling over what happened in front of her house on Tuesday. After we left the scene, she'd asked me what the secret was, and even though I had said it was nothing, it was clear she was still shocked that Mark was my brother and angry for something I couldn't put my finger on.

God, it pissed me off.

She barely acknowledged me these days, just polite greetings and business talk. I shook my head and sank into my seat, flipping open my laptop to start work for the day. An image of Jenna smiling brightly filled my mind. Everything she did was cute as hell. Not to mention sexy. I'd hoped that avoiding each other would put the desire I had for her on ice, easing the sexual tension a bit. But it had the opposite effect. I was glad plenty of other people were often around us because if it were just her and I in private, I had no idea if I'd be able to control myself.

I was still totally focused on work hours later when the door opened and Emma flew into the living room, plopping on the couch.

"Hey, dad?"

I cocked my head to the side in mild confusion. "Hey, baby? How's your day been?"

Emma was being homeschooled and her teacher had come around earlier in the day. She was always kept pretty busy until around this hour.

"It was exciting," she said with a bright smile. "We played Scrabble and did maths practice."

I grinned at her and raised my eyebrows. "Since when have you been anxious to start studying?"

"I don't know," she said with a dramatic shrug. "Jenna makes things interesting."

"Really?"

She nodded and I reached forward to ruffle her hair. "That's good to hear, baby." Since Jenna came around, Emma had shown enthusiasm I'd never seen before. I loved it but I also didn't want to start doubling her workload with my daughter. "But you must also remember that Jenna has other duties on the resort, so you shouldn't disturb her." She pursed her lips. "Can't Jenna teach every time?" she asked.

Her question struck me. I hadn't even expected her to think like that. "You have a teacher already, Emma. Jenna is my assistant and she has a lot to do as my assistant. Do you understand?"

Emma sighed and nodded. "Jenna told me to come to find you for the hike. She's waiting for you on the deck."

"Oh, I lost track of time." I checked my watch; it was way past noon, and I'd missed lunch.

"Are the tourists set?" I asked.

"Yeah. They're ready to go."

"That's great." I rose and cracked my back, the hours at the desk had taken their toll. We had a family hike planned for that afternoon with some of the tourists, and I was eager as hell to get outside and take in some fresh air and sunshine.

"Let's go hike!" Emma squealed, bouncing out of her seat. "Are we gonna drive?"

I looked out the window and back at my girl's excited face. "No, let's walk to the cabin – it's nice and sunny outside."

"Okay!"

Emma bounded out the door, and I had to hurry to catch up. I fired off a quick text to Edwin to tell him we were heading out to hike. My daughter's enthusiasm seems to have doubled and that made me happy as anything could. She's always been quite a bright girl, but the presence of a woman seems to have made her freer, more playful. Maybe that was exactly what she needed.

We headed toward the main cabin, the huge building growing in the distance with each passing step. As we walked, Emma chattered about whatever was on her mind, mostly about how her morning lessons had gone. It was the most excitement I'd heard from her since she'd moved in with me. And damn, was it nice. It fills me with relief and confidence that maybe I could truly figure out how to make my little girl happy. That was all that mattered to me, and seeing this smile on her face brightened my day.

Before long, we reached the main cabin. I opened the door, and the smells I'd been looking forward to greeted me. It smelled like steak and deep fried potatoes. A group of people were already standing and set to go in the lounge, Jenna was with them and speaking to a woman. She looked stylish as always, but completely casual and sexy in her dark fitted jeans and a red tank top. Her hair was in a sexy ponytail, and she didn't look much older than twenty without makeup or the glasses she sometimes wore around the office.

My heart started to pound hard. Hooking up with Jenna should've been the last thing on my mind. I had a resort to manage, not to mention a kid to watch out for. But damn, I couldn't stop thinking about her. It was a bad situation, no doubt about it. Jenna was my employee, and aside from that, there was the issue with Mark.

History was repeating itself in a cruel way. There was no way Mark would believe that I didn't hook up with her intentionally. I wouldn't put anything past Mark when angry, he'd never forgiven me for taking Ellie from him and I wondered what he would do now.

Jenna smiled brightly at me, surprising me. She reached over and touched my shoulder, giving it a light squeeze. I smiled back at her, wanting to grab her close to me. But I couldn't do that here in the open with dozens of eyes watching.

"You're late," she mouthed silently.

"I know right," I whispered back. "I'm sorry."

She nodded towards the waiting guests, signaling they were the ones I needed to address. I nodded and broke away from her side and made my way to the front of the group. I called out to them, letting them know we were about to set out to hike the mountains and they should stay together as a group.

I walked back to Jenna. "Coming with us?"

She shook her head and I felt disappointment ripple through me. "I've got to get their meals and their rooms cleaned and readied for when they return, you know?"

I sighed dramatically. "I can get someone else—"

She put a hand on my arm and shook her head again. "This is what you hired me for."

There was no argument I could come up with against that so I grabbed my whistle and called the hikers together. We walked through the lush peaks and valleys for about two hours before we eventually turned back toward the resort grounds and arrived in front of the main cabin. I was eager to return to the cabin to see Jenna and when we arrived, the kitchen and the dining hall was set as she had promised and she was waiting at our own corner.

54

I announced to the tourists to enjoy some dessert and coffee and beer inside the dining hall, and the majority headed inside to take me up on the offer. By the time dinner was over, the sun had set, and the cool night ushered in thousands of stars twinkling above. I walked to the front door and stared out.

"Wow," Emma ran to me and tugged on my arm. "There are so many more stars out here. It's so pretty!"

"It's beautiful," Jenna agreed, walking up beside my daughter.

Emma let out a big yawn, stretching her arms.

I grinned. It was clear that my baby girl was dead-on-her-feet. "Alright, kid – let's get you inside and ready for bed."

"But I'm not tired yet."

Jenna and I both laughed at the same time.

"Sure, sure," I said. "How about you get washed and get in your PJs, and if you're not ready for bed after that, you can stay up for a bit. That fair enough?"

"Alright," she nodded and then she turned to Jenna. "Wanna come with us?"

"Ah—" she stuttered.

"You can stay in the main house tonight until I sleep. Please?"

Emma didn't wait for her answer before pulling her hand and hurrying to the front door. She threw it open and rushed into the cabin and up the stairs.

I grinned. "I wonder where she gets the energy sometimes."

"Yeah," I could hear Jenna's slight chuckle. "She's feeling quite excited."

"And you?" I turned toward her. "How're you feeling Jenna?" I asked "Good. I'm a bit tired myself."

"Not surprising. It's been a long day. But a good one – I'm thinking I made the right call in bringing you on board."

She smiled slightly. "I'm happy to hear that." Her eyes went up the flight of stairs. "Do you want to check on Emma? I can wait for you in the library."

"Sounds good." I didn't know what to make of her words, and her tone had given nothing away. My mind started to ponder about what she might want to talk about. Work? Mark and our relationship? I wanted to rush up the stairs and down here immediately, a strong tension boiling in my bowels.

We shared a little smile before she headed down the hall to the library I watched her for a couple of seconds before I turned and I went up the stairs to Emma's room just in time to see her pulling on her pajamas.

"Feeling well, kiddo?" I asked, taking a seat on her little bed.

She blinked. "I'm pretty sleepy…" she admitted, her little voice trailing off in another yawn.

I chuckled. "It's alright. You had a long day. But I tell you what – if you get to bed early, then tomorrow you get to start another good day early enough and spend some more time having fun. How's that sound?"

"Good." She nodded, then climbed onto the bed and slipped under the covers. There was something on her mind. Her brow was furrowed, and she'd pulled her lower lip between her teeth in that characteristic way she did when something was bothering her. I was still wondering if I should ask her when she broke the silence.

"Daddy?"

"What's up?"

"Mommy's going to come around soon to visit me, right?"

"That's right, baby girl."

56

"I—" she heaved a breath. "Would Mommy be mad if she saw that you and I really like Jenna?"

Holy hell. That was the last thing I expected to be bothering her. Emma had always been smart and quite attuned to people's emotions, but I wouldn't have thought she could understand her mother's current fragile ego.

I cleared my throat and leaned closer to brush her hair off her forehead. "Don't worry baby. I don't think she can be mad that you made a good friend."

That was hopeful, I knew. But what else was I supposed to say? Thankfully, she could barely keep her eyes open.

"Good night, kid," I said, kissing her on the forehead.

"Good night."

I smiled down at her before turning off the lights and closing the door. It had never been easy nurturing a child on my own, but it had been worth it. I'd looked back on every moment grateful that the adorable little bundle was mine.

As soon as I stepped out of Emma's room, all I wanted was to see Jenna as quickly as I could. What the hell was wrong with me? How the hell had I only known this woman for a short time, and she was already having an effect as this? My heart pounded as I hurried across the house toward the library.

When I stepped into the library, Jenna was waiting for me. Her back was turned toward me as she leaned over the coffee. The moment my eyes caught her body, a wave of something amazing ran through my body. Seeing her perfect shape right there in the dim-lit room. The air suddenly was so intense, such a turn-on, that I felt like I was on the verge of jumping out of my own skin. It quickly crossed my mind that this was the first place we did it.

The image flashed in my mind. *Frenzied movements as we twisted and turned our naked bodies around each other, her hands gripping my hair tight as I pressed my own hand against her mouth, stifling her scream as she came apart around me. I'd muffled my own moans against her shoulder and with a few more thrusts before I exploded deep inside her.*

"Is she asleep?"

I realized she was speaking to me and when I looked at her. She turned toward me and I expected a look of indifference, but there was something vulnerable in her eyes before they snapped shut and she looked away.

"Yeah, she is. Thank you for today, organizing everything and all—"

Jenna shook her head. "No, don't you worry about that. That's part of my job, remember?" She looked back at me and finished her words with a smile.

"I know. But I still feel like I'm slacking if I'm not taking care of those things."

"Well, I'm here to help and make your life a little easier in the process. So you just let me know what you need."

I need you naked and writhing under me for the night. The words popped right into my head, totally out of my control. But they remained in my head.

"Care for a drink?"

She smiled again. "That sounds nice, but I'm going to have to take a rain check on that."

I regarded her for a long moment, and I could tell there was something more on her mind she wanted to say but I didn't want to pry.

"You know you can talk to me right?"

She nodded. "I know. I know business and personal life shouldn't be mixed but I think we crossed that line from the first time I stepped in here, Tyler."

I stared into her wide eyes. I truly understand that she was probably feeling disoriented by what happened between Mark and me. I smiled reassuringly at her. "I don't regret any of that, Jenna."

"You serious?" Her eyes flashed.

"Yeah."

She nodded at me and then sighed. "I'm glad to hear that because Mark has left me voicemails that has made me question things."

"And what'd he say?"

"He said a lot, Tyler. But I want the assurance from you."

"I told you before, Jen. He's my brother. We've got a history and we're not in each other's good books and I'm not letting that crap affect anything." As I spoke the words, I realized they were vaguer than I realized at first. I could see in Jenna's eyes that she would have liked a bit more information.

If I told her how much of an asshole I'd been, would she even look at me the same? A cold spike of fear jabbed into my stomach and spread out through my limbs.

"Nothing more?"

"None that is important. I need you to trust me here, Jenna. I'll tell you everything in good time."

Yeah, after you know me for who I truly am, not the asshole I once was years ago. I didn't know why what this woman thought of me mattered so much, but it did.

She smiled, putting her hand on my shoulder. Immediately, her touch started a buzz deep in my belly.

"Alright, I won't say I'm not a little confused, but I'll give you the benefit of the doubt."

Relief washed over me, a small smile forming at her words. "Thank you," I said. "I really appreciate it."

"It's only right. You've been a good guy and I guess I can cut you some slack." She flashed me a grin, and a little chuckle left my mouth.

"Alright," I said nodding. "Makes me feel a hell of a lot better. I'll be more of a good guy from now on."

A frown crossed her brow and then she leaned toward me and whispered. "A little bit of badness now and then wouldn't be bad for balance now would it?"

I threw my head back and laughed. "I have to ask you if you don't wanna take that drink."

She stared at me and her eyes darkened. She bit her lower lip as her eyes danced across my face and then she closed her eyes and shook her head. "I'm really sorry but I can't tonight."

I nodded. "I understand. I should let you get to bed," I announced. "Got a full day tomorrow."

Jenna nodded. "Exactly. I want to start bright and early with the event we have for the weekend."

"Good idea with that. I'll help you get it going in the morning."

"Thank you," she said, rising. "I should get going now."

"I'll walk you up there."

Another smile and we left the library. I tried to stamp out the disappointment brewing inside me as we continued the rest of the walk in comfortable silence. My thoughts returned to Mark. I had no idea what he was planning. An angry Mark was capable of anything. I only hoped I hadn't just put Jenna in the middle of my personal shit show. We made our way to her car without saying a word. Jenna turned to me.

"I'll see you in the morning."

"Bright and early."

She nodded. "Bright and early."

That was the moment when, if we'd been on a date, I'd have dragged her close and kissed her. But I did nothing. She offered one last half-smile before opening her door and stepping inside. I watched as she got in and drove off.

And as soon as I was alone, all I wanted was to see her again. What the hell was wrong with me? How the hell had I only known this woman for a short time, and she was already having this effect? I should've gone to sleep, but I knew I'd be tossing and turning as soon as I was under the covers. A drink sounded about right, something to at least put my mind at ease before turning in. I headed down to the lounge and found a handful of tourists in the huge room. I said my hellos as I passed them in the carpeted hallway. The walls were decorated with landscape paintings with little mahogany stools. Little neon lights scattered bright colored lights across the room, making it quite cozy for staff and tourists alike to hang out before retiring for the night.

Edwin was at the bar, and he caught my attention as soon as I stepped in.

"Hey," he called out and I walked towards him. "You look like a man who needs a drink." He stepped around the bar and grabbed a bottle of whiskey off the shelf.

"That obvious?"

"Man, I can read that look from a mile away." He grinned as he poured the drink.

I watched the brown liquid fill the glass. "Make that a double?"

He chuckled. "Coming right up."

He added extra booze and pushed the glass over to me before making one for himself. When that was done, he took a seat at the bar next to me. We watched the tourists milling about and chatting for a few moments before he tapped my shoulder.

"Alright," he said. "So what's going on?"

I sipped my drink, completely at odds. I couldn't tell him what was going on. Sure, we were close, and we were usually open with one another. But I needed to keep what had happened with Jenna and me had private for now. I needed some time to process it before I talked the matter over since anything said out loud could affect both of us, not just me. But I had to say something. Edwin, the foreman, wasn't the type of guy to let things go, and if I said nothing, I'd just be boosting his interest.

"You ever…want somethin', but you know you can't have it?"

He laughed. "You kidding? My wife's family were in a life-long dispute with mine. Of course I know a thing or two about wanting what I can't have."

"But that worked out for you."

"Well, I guess it did," he agreed with a shrug. "But it took more than a little while for our families to wrap their heads around our relationship – not to mention sell them family on the idea of the feud ending. But we're happy together now…at least I'd like to think we are.

"How did you do that?"

He grinned. "Truth is none of that would've happened if we'd worried about what other people might think, or any of that shit."

I gulped some more of my drink. He was right. The situation with him and Regina was strange, but it worked. These feelings between Jenna and I was strange too. Her being my employee was enough problem and now the issue with Mark. He looked at me as I remained silent. "Why?" he asked. "You thinking about something you want but can't have?"

I took another gulp. I had to play it carefully. Letting him know that less than an hour ago, I'd been thinking about having sex with Jenna wasn't right. But neither was lying.

"Just thinking about…I don't know – it might sound kinda stupid. But I'm wondering what line I should and shouldn't cross when it comes to things I want…" I trailed off, not sure how to finish.

Edwin let out a laugh. "You've never let that stop you before, bro."

"What's that?"

He clapped his hand hard down on my shoulder. "You've always gone for things you wanted and faced the consequences regardless of what it was. That was one thing that used to scare and excite me about you." He grinned broadly, showing off two rows of white teeth.

"And see where that led me— an estranged brother who hates my guts and a baby girl with no mother."

He paused and sighed. "Let me ask you this – does this indecision of yours have to do with a woman?"

My eyebrows raised in mild surprise at his question.

"Now, now," he said, raising his hand. "You don't need to get explicit about it. I've gotten my answer, so how about this — how long since you've even been on a date?"

I thought about it, trying to remember the last time. "Hell, a date? Like going out to dinner and drinks and all that? Must be years."

"Now that is quite long ago, don't you think?"

"Yeah," I nodded. "Too long."

He laughed. "Now why the hell do you think you let that happen?"

"Too busy with work, I guess. No time to fit in a girlfriend or anything like that. And one-night stands aren't really my thing anymore. Last few times I've gone into town to have a drink I've had a few women make it clear they'd be down for some fun. But...I don't know...the idea just..."

"Bored you?"

I raised my eyebrows, surprised that Edwin found the word I'd been searching for. "Yeah. I had my wild years back in my twenties, but now that I'm a grown man and I have a kid, you know, you can only hook up with so many women before it loses its luster."

Edwin laughed again.

"Now, what's so damn funny?"

"You've been uninterested in women so far and suddenly your interest spikes again. She's a special one, man."

"What're you saying?"

"I don't want to ruin the surprise for you. But what I can say is this – go with your gut. And don't be afraid of wanting what you want." He threw back his drink, swallowing nearly all the whiskey.

As he set his glass down, his eyes widened, and he took his phone out of his pocket. "Shit," he said. "Regina wants a little help with the baby. Gotta scoot." He pushed aside the rest of his drink. "Responsibility and whiskey don't mix all that well, you know?'

"Oh, I know."

He rose from his chair and gave me another smack on the shoulder. "Whatever it is, you'll figure it out. Have a good night, kid."

"Night, Ed."

With that, he walked out, and I was alone. I kept on sipping my whiskey, the conversation with Edwin playing in my mind. He was probably surprised I'd said what I did – everyone had always known me to be the wild kind of guy who played by his own rules. That was why I'd dated Ellie even though I knew my brother was in love with her.

I was not that guy anymore. Fatherhood had taught me to put other people's wellbeing before mine. Since Emma came into my life, I'd barely ever made a decision that satisfied my needs first — until Jenna. But it was what he'd reminded me of during the conversation that really stuck. I hadn't been with anyone in a long while, and that was my own doing. Like I'd told him, plenty of gals had thrown themselves at me over the last few months. I hadn't found the idea of taking them for a spin appealing in the slightest, though. With all of them, I'd always been in control.

With Jenna, on the other hand, it'd been the opposite. I'd lost control, given in to what I couldn't resist. And that scared me.

What would happen the next time we were alone? Would Jenna and I give in again? It couldn't happen – one of us needed to be able to resist. I'd let my guard down once and once was enough.

I knew what was happening between us wasn't ideal and I should be glad Mark had walked in on us and caused her to step back, but I wasn't. I'd almost kissed her twice tonight and I was pretty much sure if I'd done it, I'd be in bed with her right now instead of sipping whiskey.

A little screw-up every now and then was human, but there were a thousand and one things that could go wrong with this situation.

Mark's threat still hung over my head, and even though I didn't care much about his threat, deep down I wanted reconciliation with my brother. There was also the question of how Emma would react to me dating another woman, and also the crux of her being my employee. I don't want Emma to feel like I was trying to replace her mother and even though she liked Jenna, I couldn't risk getting her too excited about a relationship that might not work out for various reasons.

I shook my head and finished my drink, finally feeling ready for bed. As I headed to my room, I tried to shut out the image of Jenna licking her lips before she climbed into the car. It had almost seemed like she wanted the kiss as well.

I sighed deeply. It was going to be another long night.

ALICIA NICHOLS

CHAPTER 7

- JENNA -

It was party day at Peak Bliss. I'd learned quickly that it was a fundraising event to finance some amenities for the town like new pieces of equipment for the science department of the local high school. It was a pretty well-acknowledged in town and both locals and tourists liked to take part in this. I poured orange juice and rum into the punch bowl that sat atop a buffet table. We had hung up festive red carnival lights as decorations like it was the holidays, and Bob Marley was playing in the background while I helped Isabella set out some appetizers. She was still working on the dessert to be served at the party. A makeshift bar was stationed in the corner, with the foreman, Edwin, serving as both the bartender and DJ.

Avoiding Tyler for the last couple of days had been really difficult, but I felt like I needed to step back for my own good. The truth was, I couldn't trust myself around him. Any little bit of contact would have probably ended up with me riding his cock all night. It was bad enough that I thought about him all day and dreamed of orgasms with him at night, every day I came into work, I made sure my legs were shaved and that I was wearing the laciest lingerie I had. I also made sure my birth control was up to date.

Butterflies swarmed in my stomach at the thought of Tyler. I was still wary of him because of my discovery that Mark was his brother. It was clear enough that there was something wrong between them, but Tyler was obviously not ready to talk about it.

I wanted him badly, but I didn't understand the situation and what it meant for me. For all I knew, I could be a pawn in a twisted situation between two brothers and I didn't want that to happen. It was hard suppressing my desire for him though, I loved the excitement of being around him, wondering what he'd say or do, wondering what would happen next. Giving in and having a fling with him was a risk I wasn't sure I wanted to take, nevertheless, I was prepared for whenever we might tumble into bed again because I didn't really trust myself not to happen again even though I vowed not to have sex with him for now.

Checking my phone incessantly, I noticed that Tyler was about five minutes late. People were starting to arrive, but he was all I could think about. I hurried toward the buffet table, deciding to distract myself by stuffing myself with some candy. That was when I heard Mark's voice.

"I have been trying to reach you, Jenna. Why have you been ignoring my calls?"

My heart started beating out of control at the sight of Mark standing in the doorway, his arms crossed over his chest. *Oh. My. God.* He had a desperate look I'd never seen on him before and a dangerous light in his eyes.

The last thing I needed this morning was Mark in an ill mood. Too bad it looked exactly like what I was getting.

I gave him a casual nod. "Good morning to you too, Mark. I have been quite busy, and maybe we can meet after the party. I'm working." I smiled at him, hoping he would give me a nod, and then this conversation would end.

I tried to slip past him, but he stepped in front of me.

"Really? 'Good Morning,' Jenna? Why in the world can't you understand that you shouldn't be working with Tyler?"

I lifted my neck to meet his anger in his eyes. Mark had an aura about him that made me uncomfortable most of the time, even when we were dating. I'd put it down to his dominating size, but funnily enough, I didn't feel that same aura with Tyler — who was equally as impressive as his brother. It felt perfect with Tyler. His look, demeanor and carriage felt like a fitting pair to mine, whereas Mark's was a problem.

"Jenna?"

I blinked and my eyes focused on his face. "What makes you think you have a say on where I work or who I work with, Mark? The last time I checked, we're no longer together." My voice came out steady, but ice-cold and I could see his eyes flashing.

With that, I managed to slip past him, put my purse on the wide table and focused on setting the table, trying to act like he wasn't standing right there, watching every move I made.

"I'm doing this for you, Jenna," he bit out, and then looked around before his voice dropped into a whisper. "Fraternizing with Tyler is only going to get you hurt...bad. Do you even know him? Did he even tell you about Ellie? I'll bet he's never mentioned her."

Ellie. My heart dropped. Swallowing my jealousy, I specifically chose not to ask the question I was dying to. *Who the hell is Ellie?* It felt like my ears were burning. The only thing worse than worrying about Tyler not opening up to me was the possibility that there was someone out there who had actually meant something to him—meant enough for him to hide her from me.

Mark looked at me, sensing my discomfort. I glanced up at him, striking an antagonizing pose, glaring, arms crossed over my chest. "And what has that got to do with anything?"

"Fuck!" He groaned. "Maybe I need to bring you to mee—
"

"Hello, Mark."

Tyler's smooth baritone greeted in a crisp curt tone. He was standing directly behind me, and I felt his body stiffen. "Jenna."

Oh, fuck. How did he get here so fast? He grabbed my hand and wrapped my fingers in his.

"Brother," Mark greeted with a snide smile. "I take it you're here to know why I'm speaking to her."

Tyler drew me even closer to his side. "Actually, no. I could not care less about the seeds of discord you're trying to plant, I just need her attention. Excuse us."

69

I heard Mark suck in a breath as Tyler abruptly steered me away from the table and him. I was relieved to get away from him myself, but curious about what had made the relationship of both brothers so sour. Tyler dragged me across the large, mostly empty dance floor on one side of the room. On our way, we made a stop at the bar and Tyler picked up drinks for both of us.

I could barely take my eyes off him. He was wearing a black polo shirt that fit his chest like a glove, displaying his pectoral muscles. He was also wearing dark jeans and his hair was slicked back to the side, making him appear younger. God, this sexy casual look was really working on me — maybe a little too much. My body reacted more with every step he took beside me, my nose dragging whiffs of his signature scent and nearly passing out from it. While I had been trying to restrain myself, Tyler pulled me into a corner and leaned across me.

"You okay, Jenna?" The strained sound of his baritone was enough to do me in. The night hadn't even started, and my panties were already wet. I was ready to pull him into one of the supply closets and hump him until I exploded into stars.

Jesus. Grab a hold of yourself.

Tyler's eyes were searing into mine. I felt those eyes burn a path across my chest as they trailed down to my cleavage and back up again. I was wearing a simple red dress and red heels, but the look in his eyes made me feel like I was wearing the sexiest thing ever.

He took a fistful of strands and gently tugged, whispering seductively in my ear, "Surprised to see him, huh?"

I cleared my throat. "Yes."

"I'm sorry. I should have told you these events are open doors to the whole town."

"So I should expect more surprises, right?"

"A few maybe." He smirked.

"I see. Is there anyone, in particular, I should keep an eye out for?" I narrowed my eyes.

70

"Not any that can make as sparkling an impression as you make in that red dress."

We stood there gazing into each other's eyes for nearly a full minute before he leaned over, his lips nearly on my cheek. He ran his hand down my back, causing a shiver to run through me. This was going to be a long night.

"So, does it all match?"

I leaned back and stared into his face. "What?"

"The colors. Red dress, red heels. Looks like you chose a pretty bold color, I can't help but wonder if it spreads to places my eyes can't see right now."

I lifted the hem of my dress. "Are you talking about my setup down there?"

"Hmm," he cleared his throat. "So are you set up in red down there?"

I stood on my tiptoes, my lips a hair's breadth apart from his, and spoke against them. "You're dying to know, right?"

He grinned. "Absolutely."

"What are you ready to give me for that info?"

Tyler cocked his head to the side, studying me. He suddenly brought up his mug to drink, but instead of the mug going to his mouth, his hand shivered slightly, and a drop of red liquid dripped down my cleavage. Before I could wipe it off, I felt Tyler's long finger run a line up the middle of my chest to mop it up.

"Anything," he muttered as he licked the punch off of his index finger.

That one single swipe practically did me in. I was so incredibly attracted to him but never had I wanted him as badly as tonight. The light mixed with the hungry look in his eyes flashing like that...it was all too much. But more than anything, the lingering jealousy over this mysterious "Ellie" was driving me nuts the most. A foreign and uncontrollable sense of possessiveness came over me.

"Are you in love with Ellie?"

Tyler looked at me when he answered, "No, Jen. She's an ex-girlfriend."

His expression right then lacked the aura of easy humor he always carried, and it made me even more curious about what might have happened between him and this woman.

"So…I take it you two have a history?"

"We do. But it's not what you think."

"Meaning what? That you wish you could still fuck her?"

He pulled his head back and his brow arched. "Jealous?"

I looked away. The thought of him being with anyone else stirred something irrational inside of me.

Tyler leaned in and his breath fanned my face as he chuckled. "I like that you're jealous. It means that you're possessive of me. I feel the exact same way about you." I lifted my eyes to meet his. Our gazes held for a long time before he spoke again. "No. I don't wish I could fuck Ellie."

"Oh."

"So now you get to tell me if it's red. Not knowing is killing me."

I grinned and put a hand on his chest. "There's no red, Tyler. I'm completely bare down there."

His eyes widened. I laughed at him until he grabbed me close, his hand on my lower back. He pressed me firmly against him. I could feel his erection poking into my hip as he leaned in closer, gravelly speaking in my ear. "Now speaking of fucking. I'll have a hard on all day now that you've told me you are bare."

I looked into his eyes and swallowed, my mouth suddenly dry. The man was attacking all of my senses at once—the raspy sound of his needy voice, his masculine smell overwhelming my senses, the touch of his hands on my bare arms—God, I wanted to taste him. It didn't help that the way his body controlled mine as he held me tightly, reminding me of how dominating he'd been in bed. Nothing else existed for me at that moment, and my head was trying to figure out if there was an unlocked closet around somewhere nearby. It would be so easy to give in to him right now.

But instead, I forced a snide tone through the haze of lust that threatened to swallow me. "How am I sure that erection has anything to do with me?"

"Because," he muttered, "when I'm around you, Jenna, I feel like the hardest thing to do is to resist you. There is nothing more that I want to do than come inside of you."

"Hmm, you sound eager, you know?" I was joking, but Tyler pulled back and chuckled.

"Of course, I'm serious. I've waited days now, spent time reflecting on what I wanted, and I've decided that no chance in hell was I going to miss an opportunity with you again, everything else be damned. I want you that much."

His admission was bizarrely endearing. And it sent a happy buzz across my body. I wanted him too, I wanted him so much that I was ready to risk anything.

I leaned my head on his chest and sighed. "I want you too, to be honest."

He nuzzled against me. "So what do you say to a rendezvous tonight?"

I swallowed again. My guard was slipping for this man, and there was nothing I could do about it. "Okay," I managed a whisper.

"Good." He nodded. "Now let's get to the party."

He winked and dropped my arms as he headed over to where guests were now milling about, greeting them heartily. I watched him go, my eyes glued to his ass — it looked amazing in those jeans, and my hands longed to grab and squeeze it as he slammed his cock deep and hard into me. I wondered if that was how it'd happen tonight. A slight thought of Ellie crosses my mind but I brushed it off. I wanted to believe Tyler, so far he'd been more open to me than Mark had been. Mark was probably just trying to get under my skin and there was no need to let him do that.

Another thought crossed my mind that I was only going that way because I wanted Tyler, but I ignored it.

The party went on quite well, but Tyler was busy for most of the rest of it. I took my seat at a large round table set up to accommodate at least a dozen other guests. I'd picked the table because apart from a few couples on either side, most of the chairs were still empty, and I could observe the party from there. I regretted that decision when Mark's huge body slipped into the chair next to me.

"So what lies did he tell you, Jenna?" he asked, nodding at Tyler who was standing at the podium talking about the business of tourism and appreciating the tourists on the other side of the room.

"How many times do I need to tell you I don't owe you any explanations for anything, Mark?"

"So he's gotten into your head. How wonderful." I ignored him, but he placed a hand on my arm and whispered, "Look there."

I followed his direction, eyeing one woman who was blatantly staring at Tyler as he talked. She was wearing a unique green dress, and her head moved to follow his every step.

"Who do you think that is?"

I shrugged. "Why should I care?"

"Because he'll want to keep you away from that one."

That comment made me stare longer at her. She looked like a perfectly normal guest to me. "Why?"

"Because she is the one who can taint your view of him much more than I can accomplish on my own."

74

I shook my head. "I'm not looking for a tainted view of him."

"Don't you want to know who Ellie really is?" Mark raised his eyebrows. "Knowing you, you inquired as to her identity, and knowing him, he most likely lied or avoided the question."

"I don't care. I'm not interested."

I decided to ignore the woman and avoid her, but that was easier said than done. As the event went on, I felt her glare at me, and I caught her a few times blatantly staring. And even when I wasn't sneaking peeks, for some reason, the woman enjoyed making me feel uncomfortable. She made no effort to speak to anyone else at her table.

After dinner, I excused myself to go to the ladies' room. I closed myself in a stall and attempted to figure out the best way to go to the bathroom without dipping my dress in toilet water, touching the seat, or dropping my purse. I caught sight of myself in the mirror and chuckled at my desperation. I barely found a way without falling forward on my stilettos. The restroom had been empty when I walked in but a few seconds after I stepped in, I heard the door open, then close, and then the clickety-clack of heels stop somewhere in the vicinity of my stall.

Hackles rose on the back of my neck and I could immediately guess who was on the other side. Taking a deep breath, I stepped out. Ellie was lining her lips in the mirror, but her gaze was set on me as I walked out.

"If it isn't Tyler's latest plaything."

I smiled at her. "Is this how you get your kicks? Following women into the restroom to speak ill about their bosses?"

"Boss, indeed." She snorted and then rubbed her lips together to even out her fiery red lipstick, blotted on a tissue, and then capped her lipstick. "I'm doing you a service you don't seem to deserve by warning you about that man."

"What's the matter? You don't like the way he broke up with you, so you need to warn me off?"

75

Her mouth spread into a malicious smile. "Is that what he told you? That I simply don't like the way he broke up with me?"

"He's said nothing other than you're his ex." I hated the smug look on her face. "I don't think he considers you important enough to tell me your whole history."

"Oh, that's exactly him. He knows how to discard quite well."

The flash in her eyes was mocking, like she knew something I didn't about Tyler. I pushed away the urge to ask her. Instead, I washed my hands and took my own lipstick out. When I was all done, she was still standing there with that look, and it was hitting me so hard that I could no longer ignore it.

I folded my arms over my chest. "Well get on with it. Tell me what you are dying to enlighten me with."

She took a few steps, stopping behind me to study my reflection in the mirror. Then she spoke directly into my eyes. "On second thought, I think you're not worth my time. And I should leave you to figure it out on your own, eventually. Or maybe you can ask Tyler why he is set on destroying the relationship between his daughter and her mother by keeping them apart."

I took a minute to compose myself after Ellie walked out. I sighed, my head whirling. She appeared to be every bit a bitch, and her eyes had become glazed over as she said those final words. I wouldn't be surprised if she was in cohorts with Mark against me and Tyler, but this was personal for her in some way. There was something about those eyes; somewhere I'd seen that look recently, but I couldn't put my finger on it and that didn't sit right with me.

Tyler was waiting outside the bathroom when I walked out. There was a frown on his face. His jaw twitched with irritation his eyes flashed with an angry light as he reached for me.

"Everything okay? I saw Ellie follow you in. I wanted to storm in."

"Why?" I forced a smile. "You didn't want her to meet me."

"Jenna–"

"I only need you to answer one question, Tyler."

He nodded. "Of course."

"Is Ellie something other than your ex-girlfriend?"

"Yes," Tyler raked a hand through his slicked-back hair. "She is Emma's mom."

It felt like a bomb went off in my ear and I staggered back in shock. Tyler grabbed my arm but I regained my balance and shrugged him off.

"Let's not create a scene, Jenna." He pleaded. "I can explain."

I looked around at the crowd and nodded. "Not tonight, Tyler. I doubt I can hear or understand anything you have to say tonight."

"Jenna–"

"Let me go, Tyler. Please."

He released my hand, and I walked away from him, my heart pounding hard and fast as I managed to put one leg in front of the other, until the sound of the party faded in the distance.

CHAPTER 8

- JENNA -

Tyler walked in, stalking me as I backed into the bedroom. I staggered over the edge of the bed and fell on the mattress. He climbed over me until his face was only a couple of inches from mine, his breath coming out in sharp bursts against my cheek.

"Jenna?"

The heat from his eyes burned into my skin. Every muscle in my body tensed, and it felt like my insides were melting. He lifted his hand carefully and caressed my face.

What the hell was he doing? A voice screamed in my head, telling me to push him away, to run out of the room as fast as my legs could carry me, but a louder voice drowned that out. The new voice told me I wanted this and no matter what I did I should know I had no control over how he made my body feel.

I stared at him, my heart pounding in my chest. At least half a minute passed with neither of us saying anything. His hand traveled down, across my face and neck, softly grazing my breasts and down my belly until his hand moved down, caressing my thigh. I couldn't move, couldn't speak. The only sound in the quiet bedroom was our heavy breathing.

"Why didn't you wait for me, Jen?" His quiet voice broke the silence, and I straightened my back, eyes staring into his.

"I can't wait for you, Tyler. I don't even know who you are anymore. I don't think this can ever work."

"You don't want this?" He exhaled, bending over my neck.

"No…Yes, I do." I pulled back as much as I could, gaping at him. *"I want this. I want you. I want you so much I'm scared of how much power you have over me."*

"I have power over you?"

"Yes. Here you are in my dreams."

He shook his head. *"You're the one who wants this dream."* His hand slipped between my legs to gentle rub my wet panties.

I gasped, desperate. *"See what you're doing to me."*

He shook his head again, his lips curled in a little smile. *"You're the one doing this to me, Jenna. I'm the powerless one."*

He was right. This dream was my doing. *"I don't want this, Tyler."*

"Then say the word, Jenna. Tell me to leave."

I opened my mouth, but no words came out. The silence around us was heavy and poignant as we stared at each other. A low hum started in my navel and moved lower, between my legs, the ache for touch intensified, and my pussy throbbed against his hand. He waited for a while and when I said nothing, he bent over, kissing my jaw, then kissing my lips. I wrapped my arms around him, and his hard cock pressed against my stomach.

"Fuck," I groaned.

My body reacted on its own, controlled by wild lust. A shiver ran through me. I reacted quickly, wrapped both legs around Tyler's waist, pressing my wet pussy as close as possible to his arousal.

He pulled back his fingers, teasing the edge of my waist, his eyes flickering with need.

"Say the word, Jenna," he whispered.

Placing his hands on my shoulders, he looked into my eyes and slid my clothes to the floor. Goosebumps spread along my skin as he took my hands, turned me around, and held my palms in one hand against the pillows. The other hand reached up and removed the comb in my hair, letting it fall down my naked back. He grabbed my hair and jerked it to the side, his lips spreading hot kisses down my neck and shoulders.

"Say it, Jenna." He whispered as his teeth grazed my spine.

I opened my mouth, but the only words I could utter were soft groans. Every inch of skin he touched was tinged with electricity. He leaned back on his knees behind me, grabbing my ass and pressing his teeth into the flesh, spurring a sharp gasp from me before he leaned over me again.

Holy hell, how does he know to do these things to me?

"Don't you want me to leave anymore?" His fingers circled around my breasts, pressing and pulling. "Changing your mind?"

"Maybe," I yelled out in surprise as I felt his hand smack hard where his teeth had just been, and my only response was a moan of pleasure.

"I need you to be sure about what you want." I breathed in another sharp gasp as his hands clasped the delicate ribbons of my underwear and ripped them off. "Leave or stay?"

My voice was muffled and incoherent as I screeched into the pillow. He chuckled darkly and pressed up against me again, his hard cock pushing against my backside and his weight pressing my breasts into the pillows. Shivers danced through my body, and I felt every bit of his touch that set me on fire.

"You have to tell me." His hand slid around my waist and down my abdomen, slipping lower until his finger rested on my clit. "You know, I think you don't want me to leave at all. That's just a lie you tell yourself."

Was he right? Was I hypocritical, thinking I wanted him to leave? The pressure from his touch caused me to ache, his

81

fingers pressed and released, leaving me wanting. Moving lower, he stopped right at my entrance.

"You're so wet, Jenna. You wanted this all day and now you're dreaming about it. You don't want me leaving anymore do you?"

"Damn it," I groaned, gasping as his finger finally pushed inside, pressing my back against his fingers.

"Say the word, Jen. You know you want this."

He slipped another finger into me. My teeth clenched as I bit back a low groan as the finger circled the slippery wetness. I shook my head, bit my lip, clenched my thighs, doing everything and anything as I tried to find a way to regain control.

"Tell me now, please, Jen."

There it was — that needy sound in his voice that I couldn't guard against. I felt wave after wave of hit scatter all around my body from the spot his finger stimulated. Every new wave scattered whatever control I'd managed to gather. The feel of those graceful fingers slipping in and out sent my mind spinning. He pressed his thumb hard on my wet clit.

"Oh, fuck." I moaned.

He leaned over my back. "Say it," he whispered as his thumb rotated. "You know what you want." I was so close. And then he added another finger. "Say it now."

"Don't leave!" I gave in, my voice coming out in a hoarse whisper. "I want you. I need you inside me."

"Yes!" He groaned and started pumping his hand fast and hard. I could feel the tip of his erection rubbing against me, and I pushed my hips back, wanting more.

"Oh, God," I groaned. All of my senses were focused on the pleasure that he was building. Only one thing mattered — the climax his fingers were pushing me toward. I groaned and moaned and twisted the sheets in my hands as I felt the first wave of orgasm hit, then a shrill noise broke out around us, and Tyler disappeared.

When I opened my eyes, the buzzer was still ringing, I rolled around quickly and stared at the bedside clock: 7:30. *Fuck!* I'd spent the whole night fantasizing about Tyler again.

"Who's there?" I grabbed the intercom and muttered into it, ignoring the head-splitting headache that pounded in my head. That was probably as a result of my dreams breaking up before the orgasm.

"You've got a delivery, ma'am."

"Hold on a sec."

I rushed toward the bathroom and threw some water on my face before pressing the button to unbolt the main door downstairs. I was awestruck when the two men walked down the hallway from the elevator to my apartment, carrying flowers of different kinds.

"What's this?"

"Ms. Robinson, Mr. Stark requested that these be delivered to you. Along with this." He handed me two sealed manila envelopes.

"What is it?"

"I don't know, ma'am. I was instructed to deliver it, so here I am." He gave a polite nod. "You have a good afternoon."

As I watched them walk away, my heart began to race a little faster. Why had Tyler sent me these? I'd stopped going to work since that night three days ago, and I was contemplating sending in my resignation letter once I'd learned about Emma's mother. Tyler had tried calling me, but I'd ignored his calls, needing my head clear to think about the situation. I'd barely had a clear head, with most of my time spent fantasizing about him.

I should send these back.

I sighed and then stared at the envelope and then back at the flowers. For three long minutes, I stood there staring at the flowers: orchids, tulips, roses, and lilies. I closed my eyes and took a deep breath, wishing I wasn't such a wuss for caring about what he'd put in the envelope.

I hurried toward my couch and sat down before ripping open the sealed envelope. Lacy lingerie was hidden inside. I lifted it up, staring at the vivid red color when the card fell out.

Can I see you? Of course, I'm aware that I've passed up the opportunity to meet you bare, which is why I'm sending these.

Please say yes. Just once, hear me out.

I shook my head slowly.. I left the flowers and note and headed to the room, trying to think about the message, and by the time the sun was setting, I knew we needed to have some sort of discussion.

I couldn't keep missing work, and I was becoming increasingly concerned about... everything. Why would he stop Ellie from meeting Emma? What did he want to tell me?

I also went because I wanted to be with him more than anything else, and not just to be naked and wild; I just wanted to be near him, and while my need for self-preservation had plagued me all week, I was in desperate need of it now. I couldn't understand my desire for him because it was the first time in my life that I was unable to push something out of my head and focus. Even with Mark, I'd mourned our breakup, but the feeling paled in contrast to this excruciating need to be with Tyler.

I needed to know. I needed to understand the relationship between him and Ellie, and how Mark fit into that picture. Maybe clarity would help dull the constant—and painful—thorn in my heart. My head knew I was right to put distance between us. This pull we felt when we were together was entirely unhealthy and nothing good could come from it, but my heart wanted something more. So I headed to Peak Bliss mountain in the evening.

When I got to the resort, I stopped at the kitchen and was told Tyler was away for the evening and wouldn't be back for hours. I decided to spend the time waiting for him to see Emma. I'd missed the little girl too. I was walking down the hall of the main building when I stopped at a picture of Tyler hanging on the wall, and I looked into his eyes in the photo. I missed those eyes flashing at me.

"Boy, I can't wait to see you," I whispered to him under my breath.

"Jenna?" Emma's voice excitedly called from behind me.

I turned around and sucked in a breath. If I thought I was having a bad day before, it became abundantly clear that the worst was yet to come when I saw who was holding the little girl's hand at the bottom of the stairs. Emma dashed at me, wrapping her arms around my legs before I leaned over to hug her too.

"Where've you been all these days? I've missed you."

"I missed you too, sweetheart." I grinned and patted her cheek before I raised my head and nodded to her mother. "Ellie."

"A word, please, will you, Jenna?" Without giving me a chance to respond, she motioned for me to follow her and began to walk toward a set of French doors. "Emma, go to Isabella in the kitchen."

The little girl looked at me for a second before nodding and heading off. "See you later, Jenna."

I waved after her. Ellie was the last person I wanted to speak to at the moment, and yet I followed along. She entered an antechamber and closed the doors behind us.

"Have a seat." She gestured to a brown leather couch. Unlike the rest of the resort which was bright and airy, this room was dark. Built-in bookcases lined the walls, and a massive cherrywood desk was positioned on one side.

"Where is this?"

She chuckled. "Do you think you're the only one who gets to have a room on the resort? After all, I'm the mother of his child."

"I thought you said he doesn't allow you to see her?"

"And that's the truth. He calls the shots." Ellie shrugged, walked behind the desk, and opened a cabinet. She pulled out an ornate crystal liquor bottle and two glasses, pouring amber liquid into both before offering one to me.

"No, thank you."

"Take it. You may need it." Her tight smile was laced with more spite than charm.

Screw it. This whole situation was a shitshow. I took the glass and sucked half of it back in one gulp, feeling it burn a path from my throat to my stomach.

The snide smile was still on Ellie's lips. "I thought it was time the two of us had a little woman-to-woman talk."

"Another one, you mean. And since you've cornered me in a dark room, I assume whatever it is you want to talk about isn't something you want either Tyler or Emma to hear."

"That's right. Some things are just better off between women."

"Well, go ahead, Ellie." I settled back on the couch. "Get whatever you want off of your chest so we can all move on."

"Alright. I won't beat around the bush then." She sipped her drink. "I want you to stop fucking my daughter's father."

"Excuse me?"

"What part didn't you understand?"

"You have no right to tell me what to do."

She scoffed. "That's where you're wrong. Your actions have a direct impact on my daughter and she deserves to have her family."

"What?" I leaned forward, shocked. "Tyler being involved with me has nothing to do with Emma."

"Of course it does. You're being selfish."

"I'm being selfish? You are no longer Tyler's lover, yet here you are laying a claim to him. And I'm the selfish one."

She raised an eyebrow. "We're not talking about me."

"Like hell we're not. The only reason you want me away from Tyler is so you can attempt to dig your claws back into him. This has nothing to do with the welfare of your daughter.

She let out an excessive sigh. "You wouldn't understand, Jenna. He's not even told you anything yet, has he? I doubt he even likes you that much."

I felt it at that moment. A gurgling of emotions began to bubble up within me. The bathroom and now her not-too-subtle talk. *What the hell was she talking about?*

"What do you think I need to understand, Ellie?"

"That's not my business to tell you. But you should see that this is a chance for Ellie to have her family. Also, Tyler and I have a lot in common. We have a child together."

"But he doesn't love you."

Ellie laughed. "You can't really be that naive, can you? Believing some ideologic notion that love will conquer all."

"No, but..."

"I'm the mother of his child. If you were out of the picture and I wanted to, I'd be back sleeping in his bed after a few weeks and he would forget you even existed."

I flinched. Being in a highly emotional state, the image of her in Tyler's bed was as if I was struck with a physical blow.

A wolfish smile crossed her lips and then she went on me. "We've fucked right there on that couch you're sitting on. There's nothing he could have with you that I've not had with him." She shrugged and finished the remnants of the drink in her glass. "If you think that Tyler has anything special with you, then I'm sorry. You never really knew him very well."

"Tell me, Jenna. Why do you think Mark is hell-bent on separating you from him?"

I stayed silent, watching her smile satisfactorily as she twisted razor-sharp words in my guts. She took a deep breath and continued.

"Because you're a pawn in their game of vendetta. The only reason you matter to Tyler is because he wants to get one over his brother and hurt him."

No! No that, surely that can't be true. This couldn't all be a game to Tyler. But as I stared at Ellie, I could see a mixture of pity and derision on her face. My heart pounded hard against my ribs as I watched her stand up and open the door. "He'll get over you as soon as he conquers you. You're way in over your head."

The thoughts racing in my head made me so dizzy I couldn't speak as I staggered to my feet and out of the door. What was I to do with all of these? There were no answers. The only sound I could hear was the blood pounding in my ears as I hurried off.

I didn't understand this and I didn't know what to do, the only thing I understood was that I was in a huge mess.

LOVE AT PEAK BLISS (MR. STARK)

CHAPTER 9

- JENNA -

I rushed out of the resort. The urge to hit something filled my gut and made my chest tight. I was so fucking angry, and I had nowhere to put all this rage. Because I was angry at myself. Furious that I'd been foolish enough to fall for a man that was unavailable, that could have been playing a game all along. I was so fucking broken, didn't know how to handle the emotions boiling in me. I didn't know how long I wandered. Hours, maybe, walking in circles around the streets of her neighborhood. The stars had begun to shine in the darkness of nightfall before the chaos in my brain eased. My heart rate finally slowed and my breath wasn't so ragged. Clarity, and at least a bit of rationality, started to return.

She could be lying. I needed to confirm her words from someone else, and I also needed to understand why things had led to this, and the only man who could answer my question is Mark. I pulled out my phone and dialed him.

"Hello, Jenna."

Panic seized me in a cold grip as I heard his voice. I changed my stance and cleared my throat. "Where are you?" I asked frantically. "I need you to answer some questions."

"Finally," he grunted. "I've been waiting for this." His voice was cool and calm. No doubt he was anxious, but he was the kind of person who didn't let the situation get the best of him.

"You're free? At home?"

"No, I'm not, Jenna. I'm at the fair," he murmured. "How about this – you come over here and we find a suitable place to talk." He cleared his throat. "It should be easy enough to find me.

Just go west of the fair grounds and make a big half-circle to loop back around the Ferris wheel. One of us is bound to spot the other."

His voice was calm and even, with no emotion on display. I did a few deep breaths, sucked in, and released, steadying myself. "Alright," I said, my tone more even. "Meet back there in fifteen?"

"Sounds like a plan."

As soon as he ended the call, I rubbed my hands across my face before I nodded to myself, trying to convince myself that talking to Mark was the best course of action, despite the risks. Taking a few more breaths, I nodded and headed off, following the descriptions he gave.

Mark was easy to spot in the crowd on the fair ground, his massive height towering over just about everyone else there. I waved at him through the crowd, my heart racing as I drew closer and closer to the entrance.

"There you are!" Mark exclaimed, a mixture of excitement and interest in his tone. I nodded at him and both of us fell into step beside each other. The first several minutes were spent in total silence. I silently wondered about how he'd react when he found out I was here to drop a bomb on him that he might not be prepared to deal with. But those worries were inconsequential when compared to the fears that I needed to allay.

He reached over and put his hand on my arm; his eyes fixed on the milling crowd in front of us. "I know this isn't what you expected," he broke the silence. "None of this is your fault and even though it looks like it's a situation full of shit, I promise I'd help you understand it the best way I can. I'm sorry for being pushy and insensitive earlier, okay?"

I frowned. Those were the exact words I wanted to hear. I thought he'd actually freak out and tell me to never talk to him again. Months ago, I'd have argued he was not that kind of man. Not anymore. It was becoming clear that I didn't know him like I thought I did. Hell, I dated him for so long and I didn't even know he had a brother in town or that his brother was Tyler Stark. I sighed, the uncertainty between us meant more uncertainty about this new situation.

"It'll be fine. Things work out the exact way they're supposed to. I just need you to answer my questions." I was looking at his eyes calmly. He nodded and we kept on walking through the crowd.

"Where are we going?"

"Small town," he said. "People talk. And I don't want unwanted attention before we've both had a little time to process things on our own, one way or another."

I nodded. Made sense. We walked through the center of the fair ground, continuing until we eventually reached the west end,

"We'll go to my stall at the other end," he announced. "You might need to sit to process some of the things I need to tell you."

"Thanks."

My heart raced as we walked back to the stall. Soon I'd know the answers to my questions and understand why I felt on the edge as if I was so close to my life potentially changing forever…I had no idea how to feel. I had to at least try to play it cool. At the west end gate, I watched Mark open the padlock and pulled the metal gates open smoothly. A few minutes later, we were settled on the stools in the workshop with different woodwork surrounding us. I breathed slowly, my hands wringing each other feverishly as my heart slammed hard against my ribs.

"I met Ellie at the resort when I visited earlier today."

"I know."

"She told you?" I asked, shocked as I looked at his face.

He offered me a small, half-smile. "There is more to all of these than you understand, Jenna. So much more."

"Then can you help me understand?"

He bobbed his head up and down. "I said I would explain, didn't I?"

I crossed my arms. "Then let's get to it."

"Give me a second, please."

I took one more deep breath as I watched him walk around a huge table, heading to a side of the stall used as some sort of minikitchen on the left side of the workshop. I'd been in this workshop a couple of times. It held memories of my time with Mark, and pain for how it had ended. I sighed as I looked around, I could recognize some of the little figurines hanging on the wall. I recall times when he explained what each of them meant to him. Once this business was taken care of, I needed to get the hell out of this house. When Mark returned to the living room, I was still sitting on the couch. He raised the two mugs in his hands and then set them on the coffee table.

"Made a little tea," he said. "It's that special blend you used to like. How did you say it– supposed to calm the nerves, huh? I figured coffee would get us both more keyed up than we need to be right about now so I made this. Put a little honey in there too."

"You're stalling."

He sighed. "I am."

"Why?" I walked up to him at the huge work table, my eyes locking onto the dark contents of the big, ceramic mug. Mark put his hand on my upper back to soothe me, but I shrugged out of his arms and picked up the cup of tea. The touch was too intimate.

"I need you to stay calm," he muttered. "I want to show you something, and it's all for you to understand."

I frowned. "What?"

"I'm sorry," he spread his hands in a helpless gesture. "You've got to see it for yourself."

"I hate moments like this," I confessed with a snide chuckle. "I like to know things, one way or another, good or bad. But when all you can do is wait...it drives me crazy."

"I know what you mean," he said. "There's nothing worse than waiting. But it's only a couple of minutes."

"Was that why you started stalking me? Because you couldn't wait any longer?"

"I couldn't afford to watch you make mistakes." He stood and brushed his hands together. "Figured I'd help you clear things up."

"Why?"

"Because I put you in that position by breaking up with you. It was my duty to look out for you."

"Oh really?" I turned away from him. "I assume you think I should have been grateful for that? Well, I'm sorry I am not in the mood for gratitude, and I didn't need your help."

"I'm sorry, Jenna. But I'm going to help anyway. It's the least I can do."

I clenched my teeth. God, he was so stubborn. "What is this, a way to ease your guilt? You're convinced this is somehow your fault, so if you help clean up, that'll make you feel better for ending things the way you did?"

He didn't answer. Just looked at me. Which only made me angrier.

"I don't need your help. What I need are answers. You don't matter to me beyond that."

He flinched as I'd slapped him. "Jenna—"

"No. I don't need you to butt your ass into every situation playing your knight in shining armor on the pretense of protecting me from myself, when you really have your own motivations at play."

94

"That's not what I'm doing." The pain in his eyes reflected mine.

This was killing us both and it made me furious. And I snapped. "Yeah, we dated for nine fucking months, and I didn't know important things about you." I knew it had nothing to do with what he'd just said, but the words tumbled out just the same. "And now I'm realizing how crazy or stupid I looked because it had never been real from the start. I should have listened to my gut, but did I listen? Nope. I dug my heels in and convinced myself this was just a bump in the road until another and another and you finally had the chance to tell me what had never really started was over."

I paused to swallow and wipe my cheeks. It was hard to speak clearly but I couldn't stop this avalanche of emotion.

"I'm sorry."

"Yeah, you are," I scoffed. "For days after the breakup, I'd stare out the window and picture you coming back to me, standing in my yard to tell me it was all a mistake and I'd run right into your open arms and you'd hold me and it would mean we'd never have to be apart like that again. But that was just a stupid fantasy. The truth was that was never going to happen because we were done in your mind a long time before you had the balls to say it."

"You're right," he muttered, dropping his cup. "I tried, Jenna. I wanted to make this work for you, but I couldn't. I couldn't hold on to you when I couldn't give you what you deserve."

"Typical," I shot back. "Hiding behind the moral high ground."

"What did you expect me to do?"

"Would it have killed you to just talk to me? Help me understand what you were feeling and why?" I clenched my teeth, getting angrier by the second.

He crossed his arms and his jaw hitched. "How would that have helped?"

"It would have helped me find closure. Not almost go crazy wondering what had gone wrong. Did you forget that I loved

95

you? But of course, you can show up now that you want to get one over your archenemy, not when it actually would have helped me."

"What is that supposed to mean?"

"Would you even have approached me if I'd been involved with another man other than your brother?"

"For fuck's sake!" He groaned. "It's not that big of a deal. I'm not here just to sabotage your relationship."

"Maybe not, but don't talk like you care about what I do when you can't even acknowledge that your problem is Tyler."

"Fuck!" He grabbed my arm. "I need to show you now."

We walked out of the shop, and he led me to the center of the fair. Right at that moment I feared the worst. Whatever mark had to show me could never be pleasant and I felt like a lead had settled in the bottom of my belly. He pointed in the distance and I spotted Emma. She was carrying a stuffed bear and the thing was so big I could hardly see the kid behind it. But there she was, talking to someone just out of sight behind a tall set of stands. I rushed forward, wanting to grab her and see the stranger she was talking to, but Mark pulled me back.

Seconds later, the person stepped out. The figure was tall and reedy, with a familiar toned physique. Tyler. He wore a pair of black jeans and a black sleeveless shirt, his long sandy blond hair falling across his shoulders. His features were sharp, and he carried himself with swaggering confidence as he grinned at his daughter. Pain washed over me when I spotted Ellie's unmistakable slim figure as all three walked away from the fair stall, her hand casually on Tyler's arm. He wore a big, friendly smile on his face, talking to Ellie like intimate lovers. He squatted down to get to Emma's level and whispered something that made Ellie throw back her head and laugh. He reached for the bear and gave its arm a squeeze, causing Emma to laugh too as she turned around to face her mother.

Waves of pain hit me. Hard, grueling, grabbing at my throat and choking the breath from my body. I stared at them, unable to speak and barely breathing. Even though my body trembled slightly, I felt so numb, like something had short-circuited my mind.

"Can you see why you can't keep up this idea of Tyler? It's a mirage."

Mark's voice rang in my head and I froze, having no idea what to say or do. I had to say something. I couldn't believe Tyler and the rest of his family were there. Then why had he sent that message? I wanted to move my legs and go on to ask him but I couldn't because fear held me in its grip.

"It's fine. You're not the only one hurt seeing them together. That has been my life for the past five years."

"What?" My eyes widened, and heart was racing with shock.

Mark smirked. "I tell myself daily that I don't care anymore, that Ellie doesn't want to be in my life anyway, so it doesn't matter. But that's not true. She was my greatest joy, my greatest pride. I used to be happy just because I knew she was in the same room with me, and how did that end, huh?"

"Mark, I—"

"No. I'm not done. If you go on with Tyler, it would just be history repeating itself, and trust me it would not end well."

The reality was hitting me square in the face. This was really it. I shook my head. "No, it's not the same."

"Isn't it?" His dark brow furrowed, and his hands clenched into fists. "Don't make the same mistake Jenna. That's all I have to say. Everyone else gets hurt, me, Ellie and even Emma in some ways. We're all carrying some sort of pain, but you know the only person who is invincible to all of this? He who loses nothing?"

I let out another long breath and I took another look at the trio. I was too angry to cry so I left the fair ground, my heart pounding, my soul feeling hollow like I had a gaping hole in my chest. Which I did. It was where my heart used to be. Pain and grief were exhausting, so I clung to anger.

My mind was far away from the scene before me, and someone barreled into me so hard that I lost my breath and nearly staggered into another person.

"Watch where you're going, lady," I mumbled an apology and kept on walking, shallow breaths gasping out of my mouth.

I was angry at Tyler, at Mark, and at myself for stupidly falling for Tyler. I needed to forget him, to forget it all and get back to work like nothing had happened. The thought of walking up to him crossed my mind, and then the fear stormed in. It didn't creep into my mind in a simple way, it hit me hard and fast. I paused at the corner of a stall and closed my eyes, trying to regain my breath. Gritting my teeth, I called a cab that drove me home.

When I got home, I stepped out and slammed the car door shut. I marched inside, which still smelled of those dozens of flowers —it should be such a beautiful memory, but now it felt traumatizing. I took a deep breath, swallowed hard, and started to pick up the flowers. My hands shook as grabbed them all in my arms, stormed out the door and I shoved them into the huge trash can outside the house.

I went back inside, holding back the sobs. My heart beat too fast and my hands wouldn't stop trembling. I walked to the kitchen and reached into the high shelves to pull out a bottle of vodka. I picked out three glasses and filled the whole three. I knew I shouldn't, but it didn't matter right now, nothing mattered. I was vulnerable. Alone. I had to get the pain and anger out of my head. I had to get away from consciousness—had to bury this feeling under liquor's intoxication. My hands shook violently as I grabbed the first glass and downed it in one go. I felt the hot liquid sear down my throat as tears streaked down my face.

An image flashed in my mind of Tyler bending over me, cradling my face in his hands as he leaned over to kiss me.

Fuck! What was wrong with me? I should never think about that night. Not that part, at least. But I knew I'd never forget. *Oh my god.* I'd get rid of anything. It would all still be there, deep inside me. The realization hit me as hard as the fear, like a storm breaking in my chest.

I wished I could go to him now. I craved the solace of his arms around me with a desperation that I could hardly bear. But I couldn't do that to myself. Even if he comforted me tonight, tomorrow he'd break my heart again, because the one person that mattered to him most was Emma, and that brought Ellie into the picture. And now that Mark had revealed the secret to me, it all seemed even crazier. Much more than I could handle. There was no hope, and there were only so many times I could put myself through pain. Only so many times I could live through the wound in my soul being ripped open before I broke apart completely. If it hurt this much now, then that only meant it would hurt more if I didn't end it now.

I picked up the second glass and downed it, and then the third before going to the room and collapsing on the bed.

CHAPTER 10

- TYLER -

I missed Jenna…

The last week had been so busy that I hadn't given myself a break or any time alone. That didn't mean I hadn't been thinking about Jenna like crazy. Whenever my mind would drift, I'd imagine the two of us back in my room, Jenna's shapely legs wrapped around my body, my cock buried deep in her, and her face twisting into beautiful torment as I brought her to orgasm.

I wanted her again so badly it almost hurt. But then I'd think about our conversation the other night, how it had ended without her needing time before she heard my side of the story, but she hadn't asked again. I was hoping and praying she'd come around soon enough. Every now and then I'd imagine her around the property, and just the memory of her was enough to get me thinking about how much I wanted her, how desperately I needed to have her naked and underneath me, pounding her hard, watching her tits bouncing, and her full, curvy body squirming as I made her come. I needed to feel my soul connect with hers in a way that had become so familiar whenever I touched her or kissed her. I craved that buzz that filled my heart and the contentment I had that one time in her arms. It felt like things were perfect whenever I was with her and I needed that then.

I shifted where I sat, trying to put all that out of my head. But damn, was it tough.

The last few days had flown by. Since Jenna had walked out on me, she'd not been back to work, so I'd allowed Ellie to come in to take care of Emma while I focused on business. Work was the only thing that could distract me from thinking about her and I'd focused solely on that, allowing Emma and Ellie to develop a nice little babysitting routine, with the two of them spending most of the day together. Ellie helped her with schoolwork also and most time they finished up around the time for dinner. After that, I would have my own time to spend with my daughter before I tucked her into bed.

The week was busy as hell. A holiday weekend was coming up, meaning tourists from the city were looking to spend a few days out in the country. I took groups out on hikes and trips around town, not to mention horseback rides and other activities. By the time the next weekend hit, I was exhausted. Most of the groups had gone back to the city, with only a few tourists left at the resort.

That day would be my first evening free in over a week. I was in my office, sipping on some coffee and going over some odds at ends at my desk when Emma and Ellie showed up.

"Hey, Dad!" Emma shouted as she ran into the house, her little feet pattering on the hardwood floor as she ran to the fridge and opened it.

"Hey, kid," I said.

"Now baby," Ellie said as she entered behind her, shutting the door. "You know we're eating dinner in a little bit, right?"

"I know, I know," Emma said, her face still buried in the fridge. "But I'm starving. Can I have a snack or something?"

"You can have whatever you want." Ellie smiled at her.

"I can have that slice of pecan pie Jenna used to give me?"

Ellie's flashed. "No, you can't have that."

"Why mom? It's delicious, she made it herself."

"It's not good for you—"

I watched my daughter's face fall in disappointment and I waved at her. "Emma," I called out. "I think your mom just wants you to save it for later, okay? You can pick a fruit."

She nodded. "Alright."

I turned back to Ellie and frowned at her. I'd allow her to stay with Emma for the longest time since her birth this week. She'd spent the last three years in and out of rehab as she tried to be sober again and again. She'd been sober for three months now — the longest period in the last three years. I wanted to speak to her about denying our daughter what she wanted because it came from Jenna but Emma turned from the fridge, a bright red apple in her hand.

"Want me to cut it up for you?"

"Yeah, dad."

"Atta girl," I chuckled as she glanced at me with a smile before turning her attention to Ellie and the apple.

"What've you got going on tonight, Tyler?" Ellie asked.

I looked up at her. "Uh, tonight? Hmm – not much. Hadn't thought much further than dinner. Why, you got something in mind?"

She grinned. "If you were feeling up to it. Some of the tourists and staff mentioned the County Fair tonight."

Emma's eyes lit up. "The fair! I forgot! Daddy, we have to go! Please?" She clasped her hands together and closed her eyes. I chuckled at the cute little begging form she cut in the middle of the room.

"Dang," I said. "I totally forgot about the fair." I couldn't resist. I'd been so busy at the ranch I hadn't had a single chance to get into town. A little change of pace sounded great, especially for Emma. "Alright," I announced, getting up. "We can head into town in a little bit."

Emma squealed with delight and jumped up and down. "Yay!"

Ellie smiled at her, then looked at me. "You know, I don't think we've ever been to the country fair like a real family before. Maybe this is a sign of things to come, yeah?"

"Let's not get ahead of ourselves." I frowned at her. "It's just a simple night out with junk food and carnival colors and so on."

"Ah," she murmured, obviously disappointed. "Duly noted."

"We can go now, Dad?" Emma chirped in, her voice still carrying her excitement.

I nodded. "Why don't you run to the house and let Isabella and Edwin know we're going into town for the night. Then we can get going before the crowds get too insane.

"Okay!" Emma screeched, already halfway out the door.

When she was gone, I turned toward Ellie. "What kind of stunt were you trying to pull there?"

"None, Tyler. I know you loathe the sight of me, and you'll never let us be a proper family." She sighed, putting her hands on her hips and shaking her head. "I'll just go with her," she announced, glancing at the door. "Make sure she doesn't get distracted."

"Um, sure. I'll pull the truck up to the house in a few. Meet me out there?"

"Will do." She gave a little smile before heading out.

I let out a big lungful of air as she left. I didn't loathe Ellie, but I didn't trust her. I'd asked her what she said to Jenna in the bathroom tens of times, but she'd refused to tell me, claiming she hadn't said anything. But for Jenna to pull away so hard and fast, it was obvious that Ellie was hiding something.

I pushed her out of my mind and took a quick shower and got myself ready by throwing on a clean pair of jeans and a white T-shirt. Once I had my boots on, I was ready to go. A quick drive later, I was in front of the house, Emma and Ellie coming out the front door the second I came to a stop.

"Y'all ready?" I asked as they climbed into the front seat, Emma sandwiched between the two of us.

"Ready!" Emma replied, her voice charged with excitement.

"Then let's move!"

The truck's engine thundered as I steered away from the house and toward the front gates of the resort. Moments later, we were on our way, taking the winding road through the forest and into town. Emma was a chatterbox the entire time, going on and on about what games she wanted to play, what rides she wanted to ride, and what foods she wanted to eat. As she jabbered, I smiled while my eyes focused on the road. I was happy to have my daughter excited.

After some minutes we could spot the lights of the fair in the distance and the Ferris wheel rising out of the horizon. The parking lot in front of the fairgrounds was packed with the most pickup trucks I'd ever seen in one place, all at once.

"So much for beating the crowds."

"I hope they're not out of fried chips," Emma said with a smirk.

"Don't you worry about that girl," I said. "And even if they are, you can probably get cheesecake."

I parked in an open space far from the front, and we started to walk toward the blinking lights in the near distance. The soft blue color of the sky was fading into deep oranges and fiery yellows. There was a slight chill in the air, but otherwise, the weather was perfect for a fair. I paid for the tickets, and we were in.

"Where do you want to start, kid?" I asked, mussing Emma's hair. "They got games and rides— and you know the drill."

"I want to play games!" she yelled, her excitement clear in her shining eyes and excited voice. "I want the game where you shoot targets and win giant bears!"

I laughed. "Oh, you clearly know what you want I guess."

"Let's do that then," Ellie agreed. "And then we can take the Ferris wheel up to the top and watch the sunset."

"Sounds like a fine plan to me," I agreed, taking Emma's little hands in my own.

The whole place smelled of hay and then fried food mixed with the mountain air of Taos. Crowds weren't really my thing, but there was something about a good old Texas fair – nothing like it.

"There!" Emma shouted, pointing to the rifle game when she spotted it among all the other booths.

"That's the one!"

We headed to the booth, and after a brief period of standing in line, it was our turn. The game was simple enough. We got to shoot red and white circled targets as they zipped by, and whoever hit the most targets won.

I picked up my toy rifle, and Emma did the same. "Ever shot one of those before?" I asked with a grin, knowing well the answer.

"No. But it's like taking a picture with your camera phone," Emma said, her eyes staring down the sights of her toy gun. "Point it and shoot, right?"

"And where did you learn to take pictures?" I asked with a tinge of surprise in my voice.

"Jenna," she said. "She showed me how to take beautiful pictures. It's so much fun!"

I laughed. "Well, I think it's a funny thing to relate pictures to guns," I glanced at Emma. "But she's right. Point and shoot."

Ellie leaned over a bit, her face scrunched up in a frown. "I don't think it's right to be talking guns with little kids, Tyler."

"From what I heard Ellie, they were talking pictures." I turned to the kid. "Ready, kid?"

Emma held the toy gun in front of her face and closed one eye. "Ready!" she shouted.

The worker behind the booth smiled at us and pressed a button. A buzzer rang, and the machine started whirling. The targets came in from the left and right on three rows, and Emma didn't waste any time taking shots. I grinned, proud of Emma. The girl was surprisingly good for someone who'd never fired a gun before.

Ellie was a different story. She was huffing at my dismissal of her accusation. In her anger, she took aim after aim, the end of her rifle pointing at one target, then another, stressed noises coming from her mouth as she fired missed shot after missed shot.

I ignored her and focused on my target. I knew my way around a gun and with steady hands, I fired the pellets, plinking one target after another. I played as slowly as possible, letting Emma hit as many as she could.

When the buzzer sounded, Ellie took one last shot, hitting a target as it zipped by. "Got another one!" she shouted triumphantly.

"And the winner," the worker announced, "with ten targets hit, is…" He gestured to Emma, giving her a sign to say her name.

"Emma!" she screamed with a big smile.

"Emma!" repeated the worker. "Take your pick!" He swept his hand in front of the array of stuffed animals hanging from the top of the stand.

"That bear!" She pointed at one of the bears on top of the shelf.

"The bear it is!" He plucked it off the wall and handed it to Emma, who squeezed it tightly, a happy smile on her face.

"Well done, girl," I grinned at her. "Let's head on over to the food stalls. Shooting gives me a wild appetite."

We stepped away from the stand, Emma in front of us as Ellie and I walked side-by-side. Emma was in front of us, the stuffed bear in her arms almost as big as she was. Her head swiveled in every direction as several things caught her attention.

"Don't run too far off, Emma," I called, my voice barely rising above the din of the fair. "Stay where I can see you."

"I know, dad," she said, glancing over her shoulder just long enough to speak the words.

We made our way to the food stand area, and the food smelled so good that my stomach wouldn't stop grumbling. I bought some snacks and soda for the three of us, and we found seats on the stands a little off to the side. We ate, talked, and laughed as we watched the people pass by. When we finished eating, we played a few more games and checked out the rodeo, and by the time we were done with all that, the sun was nearly set. We went to the Ferris wheel next, and soon we had walked the entire fairgrounds.

"Dad?" Emma suddenly called. "Do you know if Jenna came to the fair?"

The mention of her name sent a sharp pain through me. It felt like a hand closed around my chest and pressed it. "I don't know, baby."

She nodded, her face scrunched up in a disappointed look. "I miss her. Do you know when she is coming back to the resort?"

Ellie reached toward her and curved a hand around her neck. "I wouldn't get my hopes up if I were you. I don't think Miss Jenna will be coming back."

"She promised me she'll be there for my birthday next month."

"Really?" Ellie called, "I don't think you should expect much."

I looked at Ellie and she could see the anger on my face. There was no way I was going to stand by and watch her keep trying to twist the opinion of Jenna in my little girl's head.

"Emma," I called. "How's Miss Jenna been to you so far?"

"She's been nice," Emma nodded. "She teaches me fun things when she is around. I like her a lot."

"She's still a stranger," Ellie muttered, clearly pissed.

"No, she's not," I bit out, unable to control the anger that simmered, now brought to a boil. "She's a totally dependable woman who focuses on her responsibilities and doesn't go on slandering people to kids behind their backs."

"What?" Ellie gasped, a blush spreading across her face.

"Emma," I called softly, in contrast to the anger boiling in me. "Could you go to the Ferris wheel for a second? Count how many chairs, and please stay in sight."

"Okay, dad." She jogged off with her bear clutched close to her chest.

As soon as she was out of earshot, Ellie stepped closer. "You shouldn't speak about me like that in front of her."

I let my eyebrows rise in mock surprise. "I didn't mention names. What makes you think I was talking about you?" She was immediately taken aback, and she cursed under her breath. "And Ellie, you don't just go around destroying people's images to kids. That isn't proper and I won't stand for it."

"I know, I know," she said, holding her hands up in surrender. "But she's my kid and no one should be taking my place in her life."

"If you're that threatened by a woman showing your daughter love and attention, maybe you're not that good a mother after all."

"You'd love that to be true, wouldn't you?" Ellie said, her tone one of protest. "You can't wait to kick me out of her life."

"And yet you're in her life right now, spending more time with her than I am. I was sceptical before, but maybe it's time I see that I am making a grievous mistake." I stood with my hands on my hips, my eyes locked onto her face. She closed her eyes and clenched her fists, and for a moment, it looked as if she might lose it.

After a moment, Ellie begrudgingly said, "It's not a mistake."

"I hope so, because I would hate to learn that you're poisoning Emma's mind with your unfounded hate. Then we would definitely have a problem, you understand?" I replied. "I know whatever you said to Jenna was a plan of you and my brother. I need to meet the both of you."

"Why?"

I cocked my head to the side. "You know why. Tell him we have to meet. I won't have the both of you going behind my back and destroying my chances with a woman I want."

Her eyes widened and she froze.

"What's wrong? You've seen a ghost?"

She shook her head. "You truly like her? Have you thought about what this means for Emma? For all of us?"

"I have, Ellie. Which is why I need you to tell him to back off her and stop feeding her with half-truths."

I turned around and called Emma. Minutes later, we were back in the car. The drive was silent. Out of the corner of my own eye, I saw Ellie glancing at me occasionally, and I began to wonder what he was thinking. It must have been a surprise for her to hear I was willing to put a lot on the line for Jenna. We were soon back at the resort, and the three of us climbed out after I killed the engine. I grabbed the sleepy Emma and walked through the cool night air into the house and up to her room.

After I tucked Emma into bed, I went to check On my phone to see if I had any messages from Jenna, but there were none. I closed my eyes, trying to stamp out the fear that any chance I had with her was already gone.

CHAPTER 11

- JENNA -

I was off duty for the rest of the weekend, so on Saturday evening I decided to step out of the house and take a walk to clear my head. The park was just across the resort, and I took the path that I'd seen Tyler lead some tourist group the other day. I walked slowly, enjoying the sights and the feeling of clean air in my lungs. Birdsongs filled the air as the sun was setting above the mountains surrounding the trail, casting golden light across the lands. A couple of locals walked past.

It was a good evening for a walk and there were quite a number of people around the park, waving at me and hollering their greetings. That should be expected with the sky so bright and a brilliant blue and barely a cloud hung within its shimmering colors.

I sat for a bit on a stone bench, observing the crowd as they came and went. My mind mulled over Mark and Tyler. Individually they seemed like smart, confident men. So how could both brothers be so pigheadedly stubborn and hellbent on going for each other? I didn't want to be stuck in the middle of their fight, but no matter how much I thought about it, I couldn't figure out how to easily avoid being involved in all of this. When I checked my watch, my eyebrows rose, realizing how much time had passed. It was nearly six. I decided to head back home through a path that cuts through the resort because I enjoyed walking through the trees, and I was thinking of probably having a quick dip in the pool if it was unoccupied as well. . As I turned around the southeastern corner of the park, I spotted someone standing in a little alcove, staring into the pool.

As I drew closer, I saw him clearly — a familiar figure. Tall and strapping, and strongly built with broad shoulders. The sleeves of his shirt were rolled up along taut forearms with jeans and a pair of boots completing the picture.

I swallowed a nervous gasp. *God, what was he doing here?*

My body thrummed, my breath shortening as I stood still, staring at his back. I couldn't get over how damn gorgeous he was, even when everything I felt about him was so complicated. The smart thing to do would've been to turn around, give Tyler his privacy, and take the other path back to my house. But I didn't do the smart thing. I couldn't because I missed him so much, and just the sight of him lit me with a desire to speak to him, to see those flaring eyes set on me again.

I walked until I was close enough for Tyler to notice. When he turned around, I saw surprise flicker in those green eyes that focused on me.

Christ, he was one handsome man. Strong jaw, steely green eyes, and lips that were perfectly made for kisses. My body knew well enough how that would feel. I felt butterflies fluttering in my belly as my mind recalled his kiss. Our bodies pressed together heatedly, our breaths heavy as our lips craved on another. I could still taste that luscious thrill of his lips on mine, still feel our shared breath and the thuds of our combined heartbeats as our lips mated.

Tyler cocked his head to a side, sending those shaggy brown hair over one of his eyes. "Jenna?"

"Hey there," I swallowed quickly, trying to stay calm.

"I thought for a moment that my imagination made you up."

"No, I'm real." I shrugged and I caught his eyes focusing on my moving breasts. A little buzz started under my skin right where his eyes settled. I cleared my throat loudly and his eyes returned to my face.

"Umm," he cleared his throat. "I'm sorry. Did you come to pick something up?"

"No," I chuckled dryly. "Came to clear my head."

He nodded and turned back to the water. "The water has a way of helping clear the mind."

His words were barely audible, and I made my way around to the gate around the pool, opened it up, and stepped into the pool area. There was a little fence around the water to keep away animals with a few lounging chairs for guests arranged around. This place was perfect if you wanted to be alone, with only the trees, sun, and birdsongs as companions. I should have known Tyler also visited this place to clear his head, that was just another thing that we probably had in common.

"Did you say the water helps?"

"Sure did," he nodded. "The way the water moves, it's mesmerizing. Makes you forget how complicated life can be. Full-body workouts like swimming have a way of clearing your head, too. The water is magical like that."

I nodded stared directly at him. He had a worried look in his eyes like he didn't know how to act or what to say around me. I wondered if Ellie even told him I came around, or what she'd have told him I came for. Then the image of him with Ellie and Emma in the fair flashed across my mind.

A mix of pain and anger filled me to the brim. I didn't know what to do right then. My emotions were jumbled into a bunch of different thoughts I couldn't process at the moment; when I came here, I'd sought peace from thoughts of Tyler, not to encounter him in the flesh. I closed my eyes and dragged in a deep breath, when I opened them, I started kicking off my boots and peeling off my socks, setting them down in a small pile away from the water. Then I unbuttoned my jeans and rolled them down my hips.

"Jenna —" he gasped, "What the hell are you doing?"

"I'm taking your advice."

I pulled off my tank top too before sitting down on the edge to dip my feet into the pool. *God, it felt good.* The water was the perfect temperature, warm enough to melt away the tension and weariness in my feet from my walk.

"Oh...damn..." I sighed, shaking my head in mild disbelief at how soothing it felt. I'd missed this feeling for about two weeks. Planning for the fundraising had taken most of my time, and the weekend hadn't given me the opportunity to sneak in there as well.

"Jenna?"

His eyes were fixed on me, flashing with a fiery lust. Good. Let him see what he's been missing out on.

"Wow," I answered with a flirty smile. "You should come in here. Take your own advice."

His whole body was tense with his restraint to avoid staring at my body, and I smiled secretly to myself that I could get that kind of reaction from him. I wore a tight bra, one that emphasized my cleavage in my tank top, so I already knew that my breasts were nearly busting out of my bra. If I actually went swimming like this, they would probably fall out.

The front of his pants tented slightly and every rational thought flew out of my head at that moment, realizing that despite everything, I still wanted him badly.

The expression on his face showed he was confused, though. He stared away, worry knitting his brow.

When he didn't say anything, I spoke up instead, saying, "I spoke to Mark. And he took me to see you, Ellie and Emma at the fair."

"Weaselly shit," he sneered, his angry eyes meeting mine. "I assure you that was just a night out to spend time with our daughter. There's nothing between me and Ellie and there hasn't been for years."

I nodded, still staring straight ahead. "I appreciate you saying that, because Mark seems to think that's not the case. And seriously, it feels good to hear that come from you. At least that's one load off my mind out of the millions I have."

He crouched close to me and put his hand on my shoulder, causing little tremors to race down my spine. "Anything

I can say or do to help get those things off your mind – just let me know. I want to make this up to you, Jenna."

I cock my head to the side as if I was giving the matter some thought. "Actually, there is something you could do."

"Name it."

I smirked as I met his eyes. "Strip off your clothes and hop in the pool with me. We've both got a lot on our minds, and I bet you could do with a dip just as much as I could."

He chuckled. "That sounds tempting as hell."

"So what are you waiting for?" I winked at him and then pushed myself off the edge of the pool into the water. Immersing myself under the surface for a few moments before coming back up, gasping for air and soaked through my bra and panties.

"We should talk, Jenna."

Yes we should. What's really happening between you and Mark? There were questions mixed with worry and fear for the answers boiling inside me, but I pushed them down. I just wanted to be with him right then, give him the chance to rethink his standing before he made his decisions.

"Not now, cowboy."

When he hesitated, I swam to the edge again, grabbed his shirt, and pulled him into the water. Tyler let out a shriek of surprise as he splashed in. His clothes were soaked and heavy, clinging to his hard torso as he breached the surface. Tyler ran his hands over his hair. The sight of him with his hair slicked back gave his handsome face a new look. I'd seen several phases of his sometimes poised or rugged personality, and I found all of that to be sexy as shit. But now in the pool, with his hair back, his eyes shimmering, he looked too sexy, too attractive. The man was stunning, handsome, and built – he was easily the best-looking man I'd ever seen in my life.

"What?" he asked with a smirk. "You surprised I can swim?"

"No," I answered, looking around. "I just think the water went up a foot with you in here."

"You saying I'm fat?" He grinned.

"You're big, that's for damn sure."

"So good big or not so good big?"

I tilted my head flirtatiously. "One would think your ego's not that fragile that you can't take a bit of criticism. You're a confident man with money who rides horses like a pro and looks like a Greek god with an adorable personality. Being a bit big would not... make you less perfect."

Did I really just call him perfect?

A bit of embarrassment slid into my heart, but I dismissed it as he moved through the water over to me, both of us treading only a few inches apart. He smiled at me and waddled back to the edge. Once there, he stood on the bottom and began unbuttoning his shirt. When that was off, I watched as he reached under the water and did the same with his jeans, piling his clothes in a wet pile on the edge of the pool.

I stayed put in the middle of the pool, treading water. Seeing him in only black boxer briefs was doing something to my insides. It didn't help that I knew exactly what was waiting behind that strip of clothing, and his body was so close to mine that there was no hiding the huge hard-on he was sporting, and little flames danced across my body in response. My mind flashed back to his cock driving inside me, and I bit my lip quickly to stifle my groan.

I didn't know what to say, what to think. I only felt one thing right now: pure, unadulterated lust. There was no doubt in my mind that I was into him like crazy, that I'd never felt for any other man what I felt for him.

"Well," I murmured. "I'm interested to see if you're as skilled in the water as you are on the ground."

The words barely left my mouth before I realized there was a double meaning to them. Unsurprisingly, my brain had turned into mush again like it seemed to do around this man all the time. I closed my eyes, considering how bad of an idea it was for us to be together in the pool nearly clothesless. We were in our underwear, and I knew this was going to end up being more than just swimming to clear our heads. But I wanted to be with him. My body just couldn't resist, and if I wanted to fight the temptation, I should've gotten out of the water. But I didn't give a damn about that. Now wasn't the time to hold back and there was no sense in resisting it.

"Oh, you'll see," he winked before dipping under the surface of the water. He swam with total ease, crossing over to the other side of the pool in a flash.

Tyler resurfaced and gestured to me. "Come on – let's see how you move."

"Not like that," I said with a laugh. "Honestly, I haven't really been swimming since I was a kid."

"Doesn't matter. You move well enough, just go under and swim as fast as you can. Such a simple physical activity."

At that moment, there was only one physical activity I had on my mind.

I went under the water though, catching sight of his legs beneath the surface. His boxer briefs clung to his thick quads, and the bulge of his big cock was visible even from my distance. I swam over – not as fast as him, but I pushed myself hard, my legs kicking behind me. When I was near him, I threw myself up, breaking the surface with speed.

"There!" I cried, my voice jubilant. "Not bad, huh?"

Tyler's eyes weren't on me – they were on my chest. An expression of shock was on his face.

A slight breeze grazed my breasts and I glanced down, frowning. My eyes widened as I realized my bra was gone.

"Shit!" I covered my breasts as quickly as I could.

Tyler's eyes ascended to my face, his look was cheeky. "Well, I can't say you didn't give it your all – you swam hard enough that your damn top popped off."

116

I scanned the pool, trying to find it. I saw it a little distance behind me, floating on the water's surface. Tyler didn't say a word as he swam over to grab it and come back to me.

"Oh, my God," I said, a heated blush covering my face. "I can't believe that happened."

"No worries," he said. "But..."

"But what?" I asked as my mind raved over how his eyes fixed on my breasts. I wondered if the same thing in my mind was running through his. I wanted to see him naked too.

"Just asking if you really wanted to put that back on, or...we could do things in a fair way."

"Fair, huh?" I looked at him out of the corners of my eyes. "Now, what do you have in mind, exactly?"

I had a pretty damn good idea, actually. But I wanted to hear him say it. Or do it.

He swam closer to and held my bra just out of reach. With a hungry look in his eyes, he tossed it behind him. Once it was dispensed with, he reached under the water and took off his boxer briefs, his eyes locked on mine as he did so. He threw that away in the same direction as the bra.

"See?" he asked. "Fair."

"Well..." I cut the distance between us, my breasts pressing against his broad chest. "Not entirely fair. Ladies have more to lose in the pool than guys do."

His eyes flashed. "Then go ahead and make things even."

"You know where this is going—"

"Yes," he nodded. "I want you, Jenna."

I looked around. "Here?" I asked, my voice coming out breathy.

"Yes, here, and everywhere Jenna. I want you in the pool, in my fucking toilet, in the bar, in my room, even on the road. I want you everywhere Jenna."

My body blazed with the heat of his rough voice. "What if we get caught?"

He looked around. "We won't."

He was probably right. Chances were, no one was coming in here today. Most people prefer the other two pools that were closer to the park. And even if someone did come here, the thought of getting caught—of doing something so naughty with Tyler—was unbearably tempting.

"Okay," I whispered and narrowed my eyes at him. "Why don't you sit on the edge of the pool?"

He didn't bother asking what. Tyler heaved himself out of the water and onto the edge. My eyes fell on his cock, watching the water drip down the engorged end. He was hard as a rock, looking so appetizing I could hardly wait to get to it.

I ambled closer to him, my face inches from his dick and then I took it into my hand and stroked it slowly. Tyler shuddered. I smiled at him then lowered myself into the water, trailing soft wet kisses along his muscular leg, and then up his thighs. He groaned as my lips inched closer and closer to him until I was at the base of his cock. I flicked up my eyes to look at him as I wrapped my lips around his balls, sucking gently before continuing to kiss up his length. Making slow teasing circles along his head with my tongue, he closed his eyes and let out a low growl.

I didn't stop. My lips and tongue assailed his head, teasing him a little more before opening my mouth and sheathing that delicious cock in my mouth. Tyler growled again, louder this time. His hand reached desperately downward to slick the hair out of my face and give himself a nice view of my mouth on his cock.

I enjoyed the thrill that went through me as I took him further into my throat. I could feel his moans and growls deep inside me and it made me feel powerful. I might not be able to make sense of anything else between us, but this I knew well enough. This shared passion and connection held both of us spellbound. The need to give him pleasure upon pleasure until he exploded into orgasm.

I circled my hands around his base, stroking him up and down as I kept sucking until I could feel the sweet and salty spice of his precum spread over my tongue.

"You want to come for me?" I asked, taking my mouth off him and continuing to stroke with my hands.

"Yes...No," he rasped. He took in a huge breath and looked down at my smiling face. "The truth is that I want to come down your throat. Watch you drink every last drop of me."

I dragged my tongue across his head in a slow teasing lap. "I'd like that. I bet you taste so, so good."

"Wait," he groaned and held my head as I was about to close my mouth over his cock. "There's something I want more."

Before I could ask what it was, he scooted to the side and slid into the water, his waist disappearing beneath the surface. Once he was next to me, he pulled at my waist, bringing my body flush against his before kissing me hard and deep while his hands fondled my tits and teased my nipples.

His mouth devoured mine and I clung to him, every part of me aching for him. I needed him and I needed him now and I could feel the thrill between my thighs as he touched and kissed. His hands slid to my hips, and he moved me over against the side of the pool, facing me. Then scooped up my leg with his left arm, raising it above the surface of the water.

His right hand brushed against my wet core once, twice, sending tremors through my body. And then he slid his fingers into me, moving slowly in and out. My eyes closed, the pleasure so sharp that I could feel things spark in my brain. I groaned, bucking my hips against his hand as his index and middle fingers curled inside me and his thumb made slow circles around my clit.

I couldn't hold back, I threw back my head and moaned, hoping no one heard us, and I felt the urge to cover my mouth and muffle the noises of total delight bursting from my lungs.

Pressure built in my core, rising higher and higher, until it reached a crescendo where I couldn't hold on anymore. I let go, surrendering to the pleasure of his touch. Warmth spread down my spine, around my hips, and between my legs, making me buck against his hand. My hands clenched, my entire body quaking from the orgasm that was rushing over me, leaving me gasping for air.

I was shaking and Tyler was all over me with kisses. He then wrapped his big, tattooed arms around my waist and lifted me. I circled my legs around his hips, feeling his cock grazing my core. He tugged at my panties and pulled them off.

"You ready?" he asked, his eyes glinting.

"Yes."

He aligned himself with my opening, and with a low growl, he slid inside. His girth stretched me open and I moaned again, pleasure overtaking me. I'd never thought being fucked in a pool like this could be so good. But this was everything. The way he held my hips in a tight grip. The way he drove into me, grunting with each thrust. This was raw and real.

Tyler was hurried and needy for me as much as I was for him. I'd never felt so alive. My arms circled around him. He was all that existed for me at the moment. I was wrapped up in the feeling of his thick cock driving in and out of me. Buoyed by the danger, the thrill. It was crazy. And I loved it. Pressure built in my core. I let go, writhing against his hips as I realized I couldn't hold out anymore.

"Tyler!" I called out as I felt my insides begin to spasm around him. . My moans were loud and constant. I was wild and free, and his. *All his. Only his.*

He pulled out, leaving me gasping and then pushed back in, his eyes fixed on mine. I wrapped my legs around him as his cock sunk in deep. His mouth found mine and his hips drove hard and fast into me. Tyler's face was fixed in an expression of hard concentration, those eyes drifting up to mine for a moment every now and then as if he was more concerned with my pleasure than his own.

"You feel so fucking good, Jen."

"I...I..." The words were stuck in my throat, and moans were the only thing I could utter.

"You what?" Tyler asked, still pushing into me. "I wanna hear it."

I swallowed. Every drag of his cock through my wetness drove me toward ecstasy. "I...I want you to come inside me."

As soon as the words left my mouth, I closed my eyes, dug my hands into his shoulders, and burst apart. The orgasm exploded through me, so intense that it felt like I was shattering into the water. I moaned as the waves of my orgasm swept through me, feeling my inner muscles pulse around him. He grunted, thrusting hard.

"Fuck," he groaned. "I can't resist you."

He throbbed inside me and he slammed me against the wall, coming hard. His eyes closed again as he came, hot spurts of his seed shooting into my body. His orgasm spurred mine to new heights and I felt renewed pulses that made my insides clench tight around him. His thrusts slowed to deep and hard jabs. I could barely breathe as both our bodies shook.

When it subsided, he stayed buried deep within me for a long moment. He leaned into me, breathing against my neck. Finally, he pulled out and set me back on my feet.

"Wow," I said. "That was intense."

No man had ever pleased me like that before. Not one had even come close.

"Yeah." He grabbed my face and looked deep into my eyes. "Stay with me tonight, Jen, please?"

I stared at the emotions flashing in his eyes and all I could do was whimper and close my eyes.

"I'll stay."

When I opened my eyes, Tyler had a sexy, wolfish grin on his lips that filled my belly with butterflies. The chemistry between us was so strong, and the feeling was overwhelming. Maybe it could work out between us, maybe we could find a way to navigate these feelings.

LOVE AT PEAK BLISS (MR. STARK)

CHAPTER 12

- TYLER -

I stared at Jenna as she set the table. She'd insisted on dishing up the bacon and eggs breakfast that we'd prepared together. She gave no inkling that anything was wrong, but I couldn't stop wondering what was next after the last night. I was worried. I hadn't felt like that all night, in fact, it was the best night I'd ever had. I sipped my coffee, trying to wrap my mind around how to approach the huge question hanging over our heads.

"I'm thinking I ought to get on the way home now," she announced. "Got a full schedule next week that I should start planning for. The new guests are coming in soon, right?"

I nodded. "Yeah, they are. I should probably go pick up Emma from Ellie's."

"Good." She smiled. "You'll tell her I miss her right?"

"Of course." I sipped my coffee again. "She'll be glad to hear from you. I pray she lets me get time to work."

Jenna shook her head. "No, don't you worry about that. I'll handle the whole plan and mapping out for the tourists?"

"I know. But I still feel like—"

"Tyler?" She raised her eyebrows. "Leave those for me. Spend more time with your daughter."

"Okay," I agreed, feeling chastised and yet at the same time, relieved and worried.

She obviously didn't want to talk about what Mark said to her. She'd changed the topic every time I raised it throughout the night but damn, I couldn't stop thinking about it. Whatever he'd told her clearly bothered her, and yet here she was, in my home where I wanted her. Something didn't feel right, and I wondered why she'd acted the way she did. Should I not have taken her up on the offer to swim or even told her I wanted her until we had the chance to talk things through?

I should have resisted, but that was easier said than done. It would have been hard enough with any other woman half as beautiful as her, standing practically naked in that pool, but with Jenna, I stood no chance.

If there had been any doubt that Jenna was the most gorgeous woman I'd ever seen in my life, the glimpse of her perfect, naked body right in front of me in that pool was more than enough to put that question to rest. She was like a damn dream – curvy hips, round breasts, and an ass that completed the most perfect hourglass shape I'd ever seen.

We also had a connection, something that transcended the sex and bound us tighter than I'd ever been with any other woman. The whole thing excited me, and at the same time, it made me feel ill at ease. This was initially supposed to be a casual fling with no strings attached, but right now it felt far different from that.

Fucking hell. Some part of me wanted to take the easy way out. It would be comfortable to leave things as they were. It was so nice sharing breakfast and having a cup of coffee with her — that was all I wanted. But what if I needed more?

We needed to talk about this. I needed to talk to Jenna about the confusion I felt about our relationship. And about her talk with Mark, I could sense that he knew there was more than she was letting on. But I'd let it drop yesterday, and I didn't know how to bring it up again.

Jenna was cool throughout breakfast, silently eating her bacon and eggs.

"You okay?"

She shrugged. "Yeah, just tired. A long night you know?" She ended the second part of her statement with a little smile.

"Are you sure? It kinda seems like there's something going on." I forked a piece of bacon around one of the eggs and took a bite.

She looked away and shook her head slowly. "I don't know, maybe there's something going on, Tyler."

"What's wrong?" I asked, my heart ramming against my chest. "Tell me."

She sighed loudly and slipped out of the chair and away through the kitchen, resting her back against the counter and crossing her arms over her chest.

"Jenna," I called out after her. "Talk to me."

She turned toward me, her eyes fierce with emotion. "Can you and your brother ever make up?"

"What?" I asked, my confusion clearly evident in my voice and on my face.

"I've tried — I really have – to ignore some of the things Mark said about you, but I can't understand if this bad blood between you will ever go away and I cannot be fodder for your wars. I can't risk that. I just…I need some time to think about what I really want."

Before I had the chance to respond, she strode away from the kitchen. I called out, but she kept on walking through the house and to the living room.

No way was I going to let this go like that. I couldn't think of anything else to do other than follow her and get to the root of this. I hurried after her and caught up in the hallway.

"Jenna," I called out, my voice low. "I need you to listen to me."

I wasn't going to take no for an answer. She let out a full breath before turning around, her eyes still blazing and her lips

126

pursed. It crossed my mind quickly that she looked sexy as hell when she was mad.

She blew out a breath and shook her head. I saw the look in her eyes, it was fear. She was afraid of whatever it was she thought I was about to say.

I turned my head around, before looking back at her. "I don't think we should stand out here in the hall like this."

She nodded and stepped back into the living room, then waltzed over to the couch, taking a seat on the edge. "Fine. Give it to me straight. Am I a pawn to get back at Mark?"

"I think you know the answer to that, Jenna," I answered, crossing my arms as I took a seat across from her. "If you thought for any moment that's true you wouldn't have jumped into that pool with me last night."

The side of her mouth lifted in a little smile. "I guess I knew."

"I never thought our relationship would play out this way. I don't want you to be hurt by any of this, Jenna. It's between me and Mark."

Her eyebrows rose. "But not just the two of you bear the consequences you know," she said. "I have been hurt already by your feud. Emma is affected, too. Which makes this…" she pointed between me and herself, "more difficult."

I glanced aside and nodded. "That's…yeah. We do have to think about her."

"It would have been one thing if we'd just been having an affair with no strings attached like we'd originally agreed on. We could screw, wake up and laugh about it the next morning. But this is different with Mark and Ellie also in the picture. And as much as I'd been dead set on not doing it again…"

"You can't resist me." I grinned as I watched her eyebrows shoot up again.

"Oh," she scoffed. "Someone's cocky."

"Nothing cocky about the truth, Jenna. You can't resist me, and I can't resist you. So we gotta figure out what we're gonna do here."

She nodded. "I know. Sounds like we both tried resisting, but all it takes is for us to be alone and…"

"And we've got our hands all over each other."

"Right."

Silence. It was more than just the physical feelings for me, I understood quite well that I had connected with her on a much deeper emotional level. I trusted her and I wanted her by my side.

I cleared my throat and spoke. "I think this is more than just our physical desires, Jenna. I wonder if you feel the same as I do about you ?"

Her brows furrowed. "The way you feel about me?"

I nodded. "I want you, Jen. I want your body, your mind, every part of you, Jenna. And I want us to try a proper relationship. See what happens."

"I don't think it would be that easy," she countered.

I sighed. "Of course, I know. But we feel the same, right? We could figure out a way to make this work."

"Yes, I want you too, Tyler. But there's still the matter of Emma."

I nodded. "You're right. You want to keep this from her for the time being."

"Yeah. Don't want her to get too confused about anything going on between you and me." She sighed. "Especially if this doesn't work out."

I shook my head. I wanted this to work out well. I watched as she rose and stretched, her voluptuous body curving back, muscles popping and tautening as she stretched. This was my dream woman, here and now. I knew that without a shred of doubt in my mind.

"Jen?"

"Yes," she turned to face me. "What is it?"

I wanted to find a way to stretch this moment, right there, into eternity. "So, tell me something."

She raised her eyes to my face, smiling a little nervously. "What do you want to know?"

"Honestly? I think I want to know everything about you. But I'm willing to start small. One step at a time."

Her smile widened and she twisted a strand of her hair around her finger, her lips pursed in a grin, "Let's start small. Riiiight."

I cleared my throat and then focused on her face. "So how about dinner this evening? In a public place that you choose of course."

Her eyebrows rose. "Are you asking me on a date, Tyler?"

"Yes." I nodded, hoping I wasn't pushing her too much, and to my joy, she answered without hesitation.

"I'll be happy to go on a date with you, Tyler," her smile returned, brightening her face.

"Good."

"I should get going soon," she said. "Maybe do a little thinking about the place I want us to go while I'm at it."

"Same here."

She turned to me in the silence that fell between us. Neither of us seemed to know what to say next, but it didn't matter. It felt like we were finally on the same page and this feeling between us was heading somewhere positive.

"Thank you for trusting me, Jenna."

I leaned forward and kissed her on the lips. The kiss lingered, and the longer it went on, the more I wanted to grab her waist and pull her onto the couch. But I didn't. I let us linger on the sweetness for a moment longer, and a fluttering, delicate sense of the possibility of something more between us settled in my stomach. I wanted more, but would it really be possible?

The shrill ring of the doorbell interrupted us. We pulled apart in a rush as if we'd been caught red-handed, and Jenna gave me a sheepish smile. I hurried to open the door. The moment the door swung open we came face-to-face with Ellie, and I froze.

"What exactly were you two doing in there?" she asked, her eyes moving between the two of us.

A recap of all she could have heard flashed through my head, and I felt a burst of heat spread along my skin. I chanced a look over to Jenna as she did the same, and then I turned back to Ellie and shook my head with a barely subdued scowl.

"I don't think it's any of your business. She works here."

"Hi Ellie," Jenna muttered. "We were just talking."

"Oh, I heard something in there, but it certainly wasn't talking," Ellie said, smirking.

"Don't be ridiculous, Ellie. We were discussing an issue at work," I responded, trying to move around her.

"In your quarters?" she asked.

"Yes. Sometimes it's just more convenient than the office. And as I told you, it's really none of your business."

I made to close the door and she put her foot behind it to keep it from closing. "Do you think I'm stupid, Tyler? It's no secret that you two are not discussing any business. Are you two, like, dating now?"

"No!" we both yelled at once, our eyes meeting for a brief moment before quickly darting away.

"So . . . you're just fucking then," she said, and it seemed that neither of us could find the words to reply. The tension in that hallway was so heavy I briefly considered how much damage a jump from a third-story window could do. "Ellie . . ." I began, shaking my head. I could see what seemed like tears pool in her eyes and for once I actually felt bad about her discomfort. I'd never seen her look like this before. It was as if all this time it really hadn't occurred to her that I didn't truly want her. There were times when I'd felt the deepest guilt for what happened between us. That was why I'd taken it up to help her through her recovery from her drug addiction, but Ellie was still too stressful and immature to be around.

"How long, Tyler? Jenna?" she said, looking between us.

"I—we just—" I started, but just what? How could I explain any of this? "We —"

"We made a mistake. It was a mistake." Her voice cut through my thoughts, and I looked over to him in shock. Why did it bother me so much that she said it? It was a mistake, and yet hearing her say that . . . hurt.

I couldn't tear my eyes away from her as I began to speak. "It wasn't a mistake, Jenna. And we don't owe Ellie any explanation." A little tinge of worry spread into my mind. Ellie could be quite unreasonable when it came to situations like this, and I didn't want Jenna caught up in all of this any longer.

Ellie scoffed. "Mistake or not, it needs to stop now."

I crossed my arms over my chest. "What makes you think you call the shots here, Ellie?"

"Emma? Does she matter to you at all? Or have you forgotten about her because you're more interested in chasing ass?"

I shook my head and exhaled deeply, feeling a churning rage come on. "You lost the right to play the Emma card. I don't know what you think is going on here, but I told you before, it's none of your business."

I could see the waves of disappointment hit her as she digested my words. I couldn't bear that. Ellie had always blamed

131

me for her troubles, insisting that my bitter breakup with her led to her relapsing into her addiction. Most times I agreed with her that I had a part to play, but I could also clearly see she was trying to manipulate me and drive a wedge between me and Jenna, and I was not going to stand by and allow that. I looked over at Jenna who was standing near a flowerpot, her expression barely readable.

I'm sorry. I mouthed to her and she nodded, a little smile playing across her lips.

"You need to leave now," I said, purposefully staring into Ellie's gaze. "I intend to use the morning for more profitable things than arguing with you."

I moved toward the door to hold it open for her to leave, but Ellie paused for a second, and then. strutted into my living room and planted herself on one side of my couch in a relaxed manner.

"We need to talk. And I'm not leaving until we do."

I frowned. "Does this concern Emma?"

"No. She's fine."

"Then we don't have anything to talk about. I still wonder what are you doing here, Ellie?"

"I just said we need to talk." She stared at Jenna across the room and then back at me. "Alone."

I shook my head slowly. I was getting pissed off by Ellie already. I rubbed a hand across my face and grabbed my abandoned cup of coffee, not looking up when I spoke. "I'm busy. We will see if I have time when I come around to pick up Emma next week after her vacation with you ends."

She sighed but didn't budge. "No. Alright now I want to tell you that this is about your daughter."

My eyebrows shot up "And... so then why don't you talk? Whatever you have to say, I'm sure Jenna can hear it too."

She glared at Jenna. "She's not even family."

"Not yet, no." The words were totally out of my mouth before I realized what I'd just said.

"Ty—"

I shook my head at Jenna, indicating that she should not speak.

When I looked back at Ellie, the shock was clearly written on her face. "You can't be serious? Saying something like that? Did you even think about Emma? As a father, you shouldn't be introducing your daughter to someone who you barely even know. Emma could get attached."

"I'm well aware of that, Ellie, but Jenna works at the resort. They can't exactly avoid each other. Get to the point."

She huffed, shaking her head in disbelief. "You barely even know each other. What's it been? A month? Two weeks?"

I looked up to see Jenna quietly slipping out of the room. She probably thought she needed to give us some privacy. I turned back to Ellie, anger boiling in my chest. "I know her better than I ever knew you."

"We spent nearly two years together."

"And yet I never knew the woman you were. The things you were capable of."

"That's not fair. You were the one using me to get to your brother."

"Oh, that's fair. It's never your fault, is it? You slept with your boyfriend's brother of your own free will but I get to take all the blame."

"Because you're a predator!"

My jaw dropped open. "What?"

"Yes! And you'll probably smash her heart into irreparable pieces when you're done with her too. She's a fool if she doesn't see that." She shouted the last statement to make sure Jenna heard.

133

"You don't get to show up at my place unannounced to insult someone who I care deeply about, Ellie."

"She's not even right for you."

"Let me guess. You are?"

"Well…yes. I was."

"I don't think so. Dating you was the biggest mistake of my life, Ellie."

She flinched, but recovered quickly, straightening her back and narrowing her eyes as she spoke. "It won't last."

"Get out, Ellie. I have work to do."

"I'm just trying to protect my daughter."

"Our daughter."

"No, mine."

"What the fuck do you mean by that?"

"I didn't want to do this before." She crossed her arms. "But it's become more and more obvious that you don't care about anyone but yourself."

"What?"

She pulled a white envelope out of her bag and slammed it on my chest. I held the envelope and looked up to see her staring down at me with a defiantly crooked eyebrow.

"What is this?"

Without an explanation, she turned and walked out of my living room. I glared at the envelope, my mind flipping around on what the letter could be. I'd come up about a hundred explanations, but what I didn't expect was a file for custody. . . of Emma.

"Tyler? Are you Okay?"

I heard Jenna's faint voice call from behind me, but blood was pounding in my ears as my panic over the thought of losing my daughter grew. I shot up toward the door and raced out of my house after Ellie. She was headed for the gate. It was good that the former batch of tourists had left earlier after the fundraising and the fair and the new ones weren't coming in until tomorrow. The resort grounds were almost empty, and I could scream at her with no one being the wiser, except Jenna. The gate closed with a heavy clang and her heels echoed their way down across the gravel.

"Ellie, what the fuck is this?" I waved the paper in the air as my legs ate up the ground in pursuit of her.

"You know, it's pretty easy to read. Even an airhead like me understands what's in there. What does it look like? It's me filing for custody."

"I can see that," I grunted through my teeth as I crumpled the paper into my clenched fist. "What kind of games are you trying to play?"

"It's no game."

She continued walking without turning back to look at me. "You don't care about her, Tyler," she hissed. "So as her mother, I'm going to ensure she's kept safe with me. You can now go on fucking your lover without worries about what to say to Emma."

How could someone be such a bitch?

I caught up to her on the landing between the mess hall.

"No way I'm letting you take my daughter away from me," I growled.

She shrugged and then leaned her face closer to mine and whispered, "I'm not sure she's yours."

Well, fuck. I took a deep breath through my nose and threw the paper to the floor. "What do you mean?"

She looked up into my eyes and hissed. "You weren't the only one I was fucking, Ty. Emma's my daughter, she's not yours."

135

Blood pounded in my ears and my heart slammed hard in my chest. "Tell me you're lying, Ellie. You're about to put Emma through hell if we have to drag this."

"You don't care about her either way. You're an asshole."

"I'm an asshole?" I murmured, looking down at her as she straightened the collar of her dress. "This is mad, Ellie. You're mad if you expect me to believe this and let you have my daughter."

"What goes around comes around, so to speak." She seethed. "Enjoy some of the pain you've given others over the years."

"What are you talking about?"

She had a cocky grin, and she was obviously glad that she'd hurt me. Part of me ached to grab her and shake her until she told me the truth. But a larger part of me was just confused, weak and angry.

"You have more important things to focus on, don't you?" She nodded calmly toward the house, and I turned to see Jenna standing on the balcony. When our eyes met, she continued down the stairs but stopped abruptly.

"But you should really consider spending more time with your daughter while you can. As soon as she's mine, I'll make sure you never see her again."

I watched Ellie walk towards the gate and then disappear out of sight down the path to the driveway.

My vision started to fade, to distort, as if I was looking through a fish-eye lens. *No, it's a lie. She has to be lying just because she wanted to get under my skin.*

I closed my eyes and took a long, slow deep breath. I couldn't think, could barely breathe. I turned away toward the house, leaving the crumpled paper in the field. My hands clenched so tightly that my nails dug into my palms. Breathing was hard. Really hard. As if I'd just run a fucking marathon.

Anger and hurt settled like a lead weight deep in my stomach. Ellie had been a mistake, a huge, colossal mistake and in the years when we dated, my goal had been getting back at my big brother for telling me off and laughing at me with his friends. Those were dark days when I was lost in rage with myself and the whole world, and only the conception of a child had given me hope to fight through. It had been only Emma that mattered to me in the world, and it was only for her that I had the ethic and motivation that buoyed me through those difficult times in my life because all I wanted to do was be a good father to her. Now Ellie was sowing seeds of fucking doubts in my mind that the sunshine that had brightened my life was about to be taken away from me.

I refuse to believe that. I wanted to scream, my chest growing tight as bile rose in my throat. It was a mistake agreeing with a custody plan that allowed my daughter to spend two weeks of her holiday with Ellie. I had to find a way to get her out of Ellie's grasp immediately.

"Tyler?" Jenna called out as she hurried toward me. "Oh my god, I heard what she said."

She stepped forward, ready to throw her arms around my neck. But I held a hand out to stop her.

"Don't."

She flinched backward like I'd slapped her, and I felt a sharp pain rip through my heart.

"What?"

I shook my head. "I can't."

"You can't what?"

"I can't do this yet."

"I don't understand."

"Fuck. I can't talk right now," I muttered. I couldn't look into her eyes as I clenched my hands into a fist again. It felt as if the whole world was crashing around me. "You need to go."

"You can't be serious. Tyler—"

"Please," I said through gritted teeth. I couldn't involve her in this. Maybe Ellie was right, whatever I did, I ended up hurting someone badly. My whole world felt shattered at that moment, and I needed some time alone to make sense of it. "Please go."

She stared at me for a long time and then turned around to leave. Sadness and anger warred in my chest as I watched her walk away. I wanted to call her back, wanted to beg her to come to be my comfort, but something inside me was scared I'd just be pulling her into my web of pains and betrayals.

Feeling like the world had just flipped upside down, I turned around, picked up the document and then walked back into the house. I landed in my chair with a loud huff, raking my hands through my hair before smoothing the wrinkled document. I stared at the typed words on it for a moment, then opened my desk drawer and dropped it in.

I was not going to give up without a fight.

LOVE AT PEAK BLISS (MR. STARK)

CHAPTER 13

- TYLER -

I was going crazy. It was almost a week since Ellie had walked out of the resort and I hadn't set my eyes on my daughter since then. She'd refused to pick up my calls, and when I'd gone to her apartment downtown to check on her, the place was deserted. I couldn't stop blaming myself for being careless with my daughter. I should have protected her more. I should have kept her as far away from Ellie as I could.

I'd been foolish enough to start trusting Ellie to allow her the legal grounds to hold my daughter for two whole weeks. Now I knew she was going to do everything in her power this week to keep Emma forever, but I wasn't going to let that happen.

I didn't pay attention to anything on the resort throughout the week. I left the whole activity schedule to Edwin and Jenna. I refused to see her throughout the week; I didn't want to involve her in this, and besides that, I didn't want anyone around me. The only person I'd contacted for help was my lawyer, Dunrad, and I'd informed him to hire someone to help me find out where Ellie might have been taken. I'd been driving around for most of the morning, so when Dunrad's name appeared on the screen of my phone, I picked it up immediately.

"Hello Tyler, how are you doing?"

"Cut to the chase, man. Have you got any idea where they might be?" I muttered as I kept my eyes on the road. I had turned over most of my options downtown already and I hadn't yet spotted any sign of my daughter or Ellie.

"I just may have, Tyler."

"I'm listening."

"I think they might be with your brother."

"The fucker!" I was mad as hell and frustrated on top of that. I should have suspected that he had a hand in this from the very beginning. Mark had several hideouts around town that would have been perfect for something like this. Back when we were kids, he used to disappear for days. Sometimes in the summer when I was around, he'd take me with him and we had fun together. But gone were those days of bliss and companionship between us. Things had gone on from bad to worse as we grew apart.

Bad enough that my own brother is keeping my daughter away from me.

"Where are they, Dunrad?"

I heard him clear his throat nervously. "Why don't you pull over first?" Dunrad asked. "I think we should figure out our next step carefully. You could just wait until the week is over and Ellie's legal hold on Emma ends."

I didn't want to do that. I wanted to keep going, to search every fucking square inch of this town until I found my baby girl and the asshole who'd taken her. I knew he was right but I was far from reasoning at that moment. I'd spent too many sleepless nights wondering where Emma was not to take advantage of this chance. And who knew what lies they'd have fed into my daughter's ears in one week? What if she started to truly believe that I wasn't her father?

"Where are they, Dunrad?"

He could clearly hear the impatience in my voice and Dunrad knew well enough how I disliked being crossed when I was desperate. He also understood the connection between me and my daughter.

"I'm done waitin' around Dunrad," I muttered, shaking my head. "You either tell me or I start knocking on random doors. I'm not gonna stand around when my Emma could be in danger."

"Fuck," he cussed. "I'm sending you the location now, but be careful Tyler."

My phone buzzed, and the map flashed on the screen. "Thank you," I said. "I'm heading out now."

I loaded the location into the truck's map and turned the truck around in that direction.

I followed the map for about ten minutes until I arrived at a seemingly deserted property. I was starting to think Dunrad was wrong when I saw a small trailer on the far side of the property. As I moved closer, I realized it was more a mobile home than a trailer, the lights around it illuminated. Although not a dump, this certainly was no place for my little girl.

"That's got to be it," I murmured to myself. I turned off the ignition and took a deep steeling breath before I hopped out of the truck. The gravel crunched under my boots. The air was sticky-hot. As I made my way to the entrance, I glanced over my shoulder to see there was no one in sight. The whole place was deserted. I was on my own.

The hairs on the back of my neck tingled as I made my way through the park. I felt a rush of adrenaline. There was a haze of panic in my brain of what I would find inside the trailer, but I stifled it. My goal was clear. I'd already visualized what I needed to do depending on what I found when I got there. I had one objective. Retrieve my daughter. I slowed when I got close and did a quick visual sweep of the front. No one. But a lot of smoke was rising out of the chimney of what must be the kitchen.

In the low light, I could make out the hazy gray, flowing across the ceiling like cloudy liquid. No alarms sounded. The house was eerily quiet except for the growing roar of flames. My heart pounded as I put one step in front of the other, with only one thought in my mind. I have to get her out.

As I approached the trailer, the front door opened. I clenched my hands into tight fists as they did, ready to rush at Mark and take him down with a pummeling of my knuckles on his face.

To my surprise, Ellie was holding the door open, looking around. I quickened my pace, my heart racing at the sight of her.

"Tyler!" Ellie rose, her face lighting up as she watched me approach. "You need to leave now."

"I'm not leaving here until I get my daughter, Ellie."

Before I could take another step toward her, another figure stepped out of the entrance. It wasn't Mark – this man was tall and built, his head shaved and a snake tattoo curling up the side of his neck. I could tell by his posture and the way he carried himself that he was put there as protection which probably meant my brother wasn't here himself. He climbed down and crossed his hands over his chest. The man raised his palm, gesturing for me to stop where I was.

"You're trespassing. You need to leave now."

I wanted to yell, to tell him to fucking give me my daughter. But at the same time, I didn't want to scare Emma in case she was in the house. She couldn't know what kind of situation she was in.

"Let me see her," I said, my voice stern and commanding.

"I don't know what the fuck you're talking about." The man's accent was Texan – he was likely one of Mark's contacts. "The only thing I know is that you're trespassing right now."

"You've got my daughter in that house. I wanna see her, make sure she's fine."

He stepped all the way down the steps and stood face-to-face with me. "You need to fuckin' get out or I'll have to remove you myself."

He made an attempt to grab me, and I lashed out, my fist hitting his face. He replied immediately with a swift punch to my kidney. Grunting, I took the blow, absorbing the pain. Didn't have a choice. Ellie screamed and another man rushed out of the house. The guy jumped on me and grabbed me to restrain my arm, but he wasn't strong enough to hold me for long. And when I saw the first man approaching, I knew these assholes were going to do as much damage as possible if I didn't fight back. I growled at the greasy piece of shit in front of me. His face was turning purple where I'd bruised him, and I'd do a lot more if that's what it took to get Emma back.

"I'm gonna fuck you up, man." There was a slight grin on his face as he threw another punch at my belly. *Fuck.* I struggled against the grip on my arms. I couldn't see the guy who was holding them behind my back, but he was slipping.

"Not so tough now, are you?" the first guy sneered, flashing his yellow teeth. "Should have left when I told you to."

I met his eyes, locking him in a hard stare. I was going to hurt this guy. Badly. As soon as one of them made a mistake, I was going to unleash on these fuckers. And I was going to enjoy it. Frustration boiled in me as I pictured Emma inside the trailer, waiting for me, but that I was unable to get to her.

The first guy hit me below the ribs while the second one held me tight. Adrenaline coursed through me, my heart pumped fast, and my muscles flexed against the arms trying to contain me. Still staring the first guy down, I shifted my body weight. The arms holding mine were tense and rigid. I stayed fluid, ready to strike, ready to go on the attack. The first guy's fist smashed into my face again, flooding my mouth with the metallic tang of blood.

The second who was obviously feeling left out of the action, dropped one of my arms so as to punch me in the ribs.

This was my chance.

Throwing my weight forward, I bent my knees and hinged at the waist. The guy holding my arms flipped over my shoulder. I roared, surging toward the first guy, and landed a swift punch to his gut. I didn't have long before the second one returned and I had to make this count. A heady sense of euphoria filled me as I rained blows on the first guy. The second jumped on my back, trying to regain control, but I tossed him over my shoulder. He hit the ground with a groan. He returned again, barreling into me from the side, wrapping his arms around my waist. We crashed into a floor and his body weight smashed the air from my lungs. Gasping for breath, I fought back, but now they had the upper hand and I couldn't take both of them at once. I held my arms up to protect my face while they hit me. Ground and pound.

Just at that moment, the blare of sirens sounded in the distance. The noise grew louder and louder until flashing lights approached from around the corner. Three cop cars, all Patterson PD, raced down into the clearing.

"Hey!" Swift footsteps approached. The cops shouted orders.

I took a few more punches before someone dragged them off me. Damn it. That fucking hurt. Another guard hauled me roughly to my feet, then yanked my arms behind my back and cuffed me. I didn't resist. Just blinked at the blood dripping in my eye and stared daggers at the assholes who I'd fought as the cops slammed them onto the floor and locked them in cuffs.

"Come on," the cop barked, shoving me ahead of him. "Let's go."

I didn't bother pointing out that I had come here looking for my daughter. One of the cops was already interrogating Ellie who kept pointing at me. Anything I said wouldn't have mattered. The metal bit at my wrists and I seethed with rage at everyone. Ellie who was keeping this stupid charade up. Those fuckers who'd attacked me. The cop that was leading me away.

I ground my teeth together, anger pulsing through me, deep as the blood in my veins. The cop led me straight to one of their cars and pushed down my head so I could get in. I'd probably be going to jail tonight, and I didn't care. They could do to me all they wanted. Throw me in the hole again if that was what they thought was right. They couldn't do more damage than had already been done. I was already broken. I stared at the trailer house wishing I'd just catch a glimpse of my daughter staring out the window, but there was nothing.

One of the cops walked toward me and leaned against the window. "Sir., we were told you trespassed, and when you were told to leave, you started a fight. Is that what happened here?"

I stared at the cop for a moment and then looked away from him.

"You'd have to come with us to the station."

I shrugged, not giving a damn. I should have felt something. My knuckles were battered and raw. When I flexed my hands, a part of my brain registered the pain. But I didn't really feel it. It was like I'd been dosed with anesthesia, only I was awake and able to move. It wasn't natural. The gnawing ache in my chest and the heavy knot of dread in my gut was another matter entirely. Those were acute and painful—and unavoidable. Like the mental image of my daughter being somewhere in that house, waiting for Daddy to come for her.

Asleep or awake, that haunted me throughout the week. As did the truth that I was at fault. I had brought this on myself in a way. The last one hundred and sixty-eight hours had been a never-ending nightmare, the kind that leaves you gasping for breath and grabbing your chest until you're flooded with relief because you realize you were dreaming. Except there was no relief. I wasn't asleep. The nightmare was real. And every day it got worse.

I closed my eyes and rested on the chair's upholstery as the police car zoomed out of the clearing.

LOVE AT PEAK BLISS (MR. STARK)

CHAPTER 14

- JENNA -

I hurried into the packed police station. I'd rarely been in here and most times I just drove past, but today it seemed like half the town was stuffed into the bench seats.

I'd gotten Edwin's call less than an hour ago. Tyler had been arrested for assault. The details were hazy, but he'd told me he needed me to come to the police station to help with Tyler's bail…and here I was.

The air was thick and stuffy, the temperature uncomfortably warm. Bella sat next to me, holding my hand firmly in hers. Edwin sat on her right, holding her other hand. He'd called me, Bella and Tyler's lawyer quickly to inform us of Tyler's arrest and we'd all arrived here at the same time. The lawyer was in with the cops discussing Tyler's bail while we waited out here.

I was glad to have them here. Bella's shriveled hands were clasping mine strongly, giving me strength. Both hers and Edwin's composure gave me a sense of calm that I naturally didn't feel.

She and Edwin had been the ones supporting me because I'd been going out of my mind since I got the call. Apparently, Tyler had been avoiding all of us at the resort. We barely knew his movements and his plans throughout the week. When Bella and Edwin started to ask questions about his behavior midway through the week, I'd told them about Ellie's suit, so they knew what was coming and why he was acting the way he did. We knew how important Emma was to Tyler, and we also knew there was a chance he would do something drastic, so we

148

spent time watching him without letting him know. We also considered how we could approach him and get him to understand that we were on his side.

But no one expected to get a call that he'd been locked up for assault. But I should have known Tyler would do anything to find his daughter, I just wished he'd let me help instead of going about this all on his own.

A few minutes later, the lawyer popped his head out of the room and walked up to us. I quickly jumped up and ran to meet him halfway.

"Is he alright? Hope he isn't hurt?"

"No, he's not," he shook his head. "But I can bring one more person into the room with me. So who's it going to be?"

Edwin, Bella, and I looked at one other, and then both of them nodded at me and agreed that I should go in to see him. I followed the lawyer into the room, and Tyler was brought in handcuffed. I covered my mouth with my hand to muffle the gasp that escaped me. He looked unkempt, his hair shaggier than usual with bloodshot eyes and a shadow on his chin. He looked strangely calm — almost numb and I knew immediately that somewhere in his head he was pulling away, constructing defenses.

I hated the fact that he always decides to handle things alone, and I just wished he would trust me enough. He twisted his hands, obviously feeling uncomfortable with the pull of cold metal.

"There's no need for the cuffs with him, is there?" the lawyer asked.

"I'm sorry, just protocol," the Deputy apologized.

"Damn your protocols, officer. You've known this man for how many years now? He's much more a benefit to this community than you'll ever be."

The officer opened his mouth to defend himself, but Tyler patted his arm and nodded at him, an understanding smile on his face. "I totally understand, officer?"

"Michaelson."

"Michaelson," he repeated, nodding. "I apologize on behalf of my lawyer. He can be a little feisty."

The officer nodded and proceeded to undo Tyler's handcuffs. He rubbed against his chaffed hands. "Calm down Dunrad," Tyler murmured. "He's not the enemy."

Tyler paused and his eyes landed on me. A look of pain flashed across his face and something inside me broke. This was my fucking fault. Ellie had been pushed over the edge of jealousy to go this distance because of me and I felt responsible to do everything I could to help him. He wasn't the same without his daughter. Deputy Michaelson directed him to the one other chair in the room, gave a short nod, and then left the room, closing the door behind him.

"Hey." My voice shook. "I want to ask if you're okay, but of course, you're not."

"How are you?" he asked with a smile.

"Me?" I pointed at myself in disbelief. How could he be worried about anyone else in this situation? "I don't know. Okay, but also terrible." I couldn't properly put into words how awful I felt, nor explain the uneasiness in my heart.

"I guess I made the right decision bringing her here," Dunrad chuckled slightly and took the seat across from Tyler. "But enough of that, now let's get to business."

Tyler turned toward him. "What do you have for me?"

"Trespassing and assaulting isn't a good look for you on this case, Ty."

Tyler buried his face in his hands. "I didn't assault anyone, it was just an argument."

"Yeah," Dunrad nodded. "An argument on their property that got physical, with you throwing the first punch. I'd have thought you were smarter than that man."

150

"And I'd have thought you were smart enough to solve this, that's why I pay you is it not?"

I could see Tyler's eyes flash with anger, and I immediately left my chair to put a hand on his arm. He looked into my eyes and let out a long drawn-out breath before putting his hand on my own.

"I'm sorry, Dunrad. I'm just unnerved by this situation. Obviously I didn't anticipate getting arrested when I went to retrieve my daughter."

"I understand. I met with the prosecutor this morning, and they've agreed not to press charges if we say yes to some of their terms."

Tyler shook his head. "I'm not cutting any deal—-"

"Do you want to speak to your daughter again, Tyler?" Dunrad interjected. "Because you can do so today, right now and have constant calls with her while we sort out this mess."

Tyler closed his eyes and sighed. "So what's the deal?"

"Good. Here's where we are," Dunrad began, his tone all business. "The prosecution agreed to drop the charges on your trespassing and assault, but no physical contact with your daughter."

"What bullshit does that mean? You just said they agreed that I speak to her." I could feel the rage buzzing through Tyler and I wrapped my arm around him to calm him down.

"It means no physical contact. You can speak to her on monitored calls, but you don't get to meet her in person for the duration of this custody case. They're making a case for you being a violent man who's unfit to take care of a kid—"

"That's bullshit!" Tyler shifted in his seat, and I wrapped my arms tighter around him.

"I know Tyler," Dunrad nodded. "I believed they baited you solely for this purpose. This fight doesn't look good for you in the long run, I must say. They say they have a witness who can prove this isn't the first time you flipped the lid."

"Fucking Mark," Tyler gasped, covering his face with his hand. "I should have listened to you and waited the week out man. I've failed Emma haven't I?"

"No, Ty," I pressed my lips to his temple. "You were fighting for her. You're a good father."

"I believe you are too," Dunrad added. "We'll try to find our way out of this but for now we dance to their tunes if we want correspondence between you and Emma."

Tyler groaned and looked at me. I could see he was torn between his pride of not wanting to be at the mercy of his brother and Ellie and his worry for his daughter.

"I highly recommend you take this. They hold the upper hand for now, but if this goes to trial, we can crawl back to get her."

"Or they can use the time to poison her mind against her father, and then it wouldn't matter what I do anymore. Ellie is willing to do anything to take Emma away from me. I'm right, aren't I, Jenna?"

My chest felt like it was being crushed. Deep down, I knew he was right. As much as I wanted to encourage him, I couldn't. I stared into his eyes, letting him see my feelings for him in there, letting him know that I cared for him and that he was not alone. I could see how hurt he was that he wasn't able to protect his daughter. Tyler was obviously a man who was not used to feeling helpless and that was how he felt now. I'd need to help him keep his patience while all of this played out.

"Do you want to take a paternity test to confirm if you're her father?"

"What?" He turned towards Dunrad.

"I know it's not what you want, but you can take some time to think about it." He leaned across the table toward Tyler.

"No." Tyler shook his head. "I don't need a paternity test to confirm that Emma's mine. And if you don't mind, I'd like to speak to her now."

152

Dunrad nodded slowly, and I could see the sympathy in his expression. Anyone who knew Tyler would know how difficult this was for him. "I understand you Tyler, but a paternity test that confirms you as the father gives you more legal ground. I'll notify them and get your bail sorted so you can go home. They'll call in here."

He dropped Tyler's phone on the table and hurried out of the room. As soon as Dunrad left, silence settled in the room as we both stared at the phone on the table. I tried to keep my expression neutral—to hide the whirlwind of emotions swirling inside me. Emma was what was important and not the stupid worries that I have boiling inside my head.

All through this week, I wondered if this current situation truly meant the end of us. My emotional side wanted to crumple into a ball and sob. My practical side wanted to reserve judgment until we had a conversation that didn't end with one of us telling the other to leave. And my stubborn side? That part of me was mostly pissed off.

Tyler didn't say anything, just watched the phone with apprehension. I wondered if he regretted his actions now. He was a clearly emotional person at times when it came to people and things he cared about. That surprised me at times because he was so different with business. Level-headed, calculating, and savvy. The man had so many layers to his personality that piqued my interest almost as much as his physical side.

I cast a quick glance at him. Wide shoulders and a broad chest. His large hands resting on his thick thighs, his knuckles bruised and battered from the fight. He had a taped cut on his forehead. He shifted in his seat and that subtle movement was enough to remind me that there was yet another part of me—a part that wasn't sad, or angry, or interested in problem solving. That part resided directly between my legs and it craved him like a drug. The last time we'd been this close the atmosphere had been emotionally charged and confusing, drowning out my more primal, physical responses. Now I was calm and next to him in an enclosed space. I had to fight down the urge to pull over and climb into his lap to smoothen out his rumpled hair, kiss him and assure him that all was alright.

153

It occurred to me that I could. I could make up a quick excuse to reach across to him since we had a good chance of being alone for a while. I'd be risking a hefty dose of rejection, but what would he do if I wrapped my arms around his neck and kissed him? Would he really tell me to stop?

I dismissed the idea as quickly as it came. I knew him too well. Tyler's mind was focused on a single thing right now and sexual advancements were not the way to get through his defenses. Even if he gave in, he'd only shut me out harder when the moment had passed, leaving us both feeling worse than before. And at this point, the fact that I was physically attracted to him was only making this more complicated for me. Doubt warred with the resolve I'd clung to for so long. As much as I hated to admit it, I had to face the possibility that I'd been holding onto a dream that no longer existed. And wanting him so badly just made this confusing.

My head was still in a total whirl of emotion when the phone vibrated on the table. A call. Tyler quickly picked it up I jumped to his side hoping to see Ellie's name on the screen. But it was the unlisted number.

"That's her, ain't it?" I asked. "Which one of us should answer? Me?"

He smiled and mouthed thank you, but shook his head. "No. I need to handle it. This is happening because of me."

I nodded before moving a step back to give him some space. He placed the phone on the table and set it on loudspeaker. My nerves jangled as he answered with one word. "Ellie."

"Hello, Tyler." Ellie's mocking voice greeted.

I could almost see the rage flash across Tyler's face as he spoke. "Where is she? What have you done with my daughter?"

"You mean my daughter?" She chuckled. "Just taking the kid out for a spin. We're having a great time, aren't we, Em?"

"Yeah!" The little voice was excited on the other end and my heart clenched as Tyler closed his eyes and gasped.

"You want to talk to her?" Ellie asked, a hideous teasing tone in her voice. "Here. But don't get any big ideas about telling her things she doesn't need to know. Don't want to scare the kid, do you?"

Tyler said nothing, rage flashing in his eyes.

"Hi, Dad!" Emma said, chipper as ever. She clearly had no idea what was going on, what kind of situation she was in.

Tyler swallowed, obviously struggling to gain control. "Emma! Are you okay? What's going on?"

"Um, I'm fine." She responded as though it was a totally bizarre question to ask. "Me and Mum and uncle Mark are going for a drive. They said you are out of town, so they're going to take care of me for a bit."

Tyler closed his eyes and when he reopened it, I could see he wanted to come out with it, to tell her that she was in danger or that the two people she was with weren't to be trusted.

I shook my head at him and he nodded. Dunrad's words were clear enough. We needed to play the long game on this. He looked like he was lost on what else to say so I stepped up beside him.

I had to say something. "Em, I want you to know that your dad and I love you very, very much.

We're going to see you soon, okay?"

"Jenna!" She called out with excitement. "You are with Dad on his trip?"

"Yes, I am."

She was quiet for a second, then asked, "Why do you sound funny?"

I blinked back tears. I didn't want to scare her. "I just miss you dear."

"Oh! Well, it's okay, Jenna. Mum and Uncle Mark are a lot of fun – they have tons of candy in the car and said I can eat it before dinner. Isn't that awesome?"

"That's…awesome." The sound of the engine in the background was suddenly cut off, followed by a pair of doors opening.

"Okay, we're here! You and Dad are coming back soon, right?"

Tyler took the phone. "Right. We're going to see you really soon. I want you to be real careful and just wait for us to get there, baby. Okay?"

"Okay, daddy."

"And don't forget that I love you. Never forget that no matter what anyone says, alright?"

"I won't dad! Uncle Mark wants to talk now. Bye!"

"Bye Emma," Tyler's voice was gruff with emotions.

I said my goodbyes too, quickly wiping away the tears in my eyes as I heard Mark take the phone.

"Hey, Ellie!" Mark called over the speaker. "Take the kid inside. Got a few more words for my brother."

"Sure," said Ellie's faint voice in the background. "Come on, Emma."

Another door opened and shut, and then Mark spoke. "I bet you thought you were really smooth sticking with him like that," he said, his voice angry. "You're making the worst mistake of your life, Jen, and I'm very disappointed."

"I don't give a shit about how you feel," I snarled. "No good person kidnaps a kid from her father."

He chuckled. "You'd better start giving a damn about how I feel. In case you haven't noticed, I'm holding all the cards here."

Tyler took the phone from me. "What do you want?" he asked.

"It's easy," he said. "I want you to realize you made a mistake – a fucking big one. I know you and I had our differences, but you can't keep trying to hurt me by going after women I care about."

"I didn't go after you with Jenna, Mark. Believe it or not, the world doesn't revolve around you."

"And you expect me to believe that?" He scoffed.

Tyler banged the table hard. "Jenna's got a mind of her own, asshole. And whatever happens you don't touch my daughter."

"Ellie says she isn't yours."

Tyler gritted his teeth. "You know that's a lie!"

"Regardless, I had to get your attention," he commented as if this was just random talk. "And I'm thinking I got it. Now, we're gonna talk, and I'm gonna get some sense into your head. You don't hurt people the way you did to me. You can't just cut someone out when they love you, and I'm gonna make sure you realize it."

A wave of blind rage hit me, and I reached for the phone, but Tyler shook his head. Mark was delusional. Did he really think that keeping Emma away would make me realize that he and I belonged together?

Tyler took a deep breath. "Maybe I did make a mistake," he said, playing along. "Maybe I did screw up hurting you like that. But Mark, this isn't the way to fix things."

He laughed. "I'm not going to be the one to fix things. That's on you, brother. I just wanted you to know you cannot keep doing whatever you please and think others would roll over and accept it."

"Then you have it. I'm here. Tell me what I need to do."

"I'm thinking about it. But for now, just know that I have her, and you're not going to get little Emma back until I decide. Got it?"

"You've made that part clear."

"So sit tight, and we'll be in touch. Until then, think about what you're feeling right now, think about how all this suffering is happening because of you. Bye, brother."

"Don't do anything to her!" I yelled. The line went dead. "He's totally insane."

Tyler nodded. "Yeah, but he's also right…" He trailed off and I wondered what that meant.

"Why would you say he's right?"

"I can't go back to change things I've done. I'm no saint, Jen. I've done things to hurt him, I've done shit. I don't even want to tell you some of the things—" He stopped mid-sentence and his head dropped.

I kept my gaze on him, my heart lodged in my throat. I didn't think I could reply if I tried.

"I know it hurts to hear this," he continued. "It hurts to say it. But I can't be with you. I'm too much of a wreck. Ellie was right, I only end up hurting people close to me. I can't even protect my own daughter."

"Tyler, it's only been a few days. Things are going to get better."

"Are they?" There was an edge to his voice. "This isn't about me just fighting for custody of my daughter. I'm afraid I'm not the man you think I am. I've never been."

His eyes glazed over with pain as he spoke and I had a sinking feeling in the pit of my stomach. Maybe he was right, but in the dim light, I could see the deep pools of his black eyes. I sank into his gaze, searching. In that moment, I found him. Tyler was a wounded animal, full of anger and pain. Ready to lash out to protect himself. But he was still in there.

Maybe he was not faultless or blameless. But he was still the Tyler Stark I met daily. And I had loads of affection for that man. Blind stubbornness wasn't what made me loyal to him. It was so much simpler —and so much harder—than that. It was a connection. I was connected to this man. A connection I couldn't explain yet. It felt like we were two halves of the same whole. Two souls meant to be with each other, and nothing was ever going to change that.

But I knew he was wounded, I knew I couldn't approach too quickly. I had to get past all that anger and fear before I could help him begin to heal and see who he was in the mirror. I wasn't about to give up now and I was ready to be patient with him.

I softened my expression with a small smile. "Well, for what it's worth, I'm really glad to just be here with you."

His shoulders relaxed. "Me too."

Lifting my eyebrows, I held out my arms. "A hug? You didn't let me give you one the last time."

"Sure."

I stepped in and draped my arms around his neck. His body was a solid wall of muscle, but his thick arms were gentle as they wrapped around me. I hesitated there for a moment, savoring everything. His warmth, his scent, his touch. He let go too soon, but I didn't react. I moved back, dropping my arms to my sides.

I would get to the real Tyler behind all that pain and anger. It might be messy, imperfect, and painful, but I wasn't giving up without a fight. I wanted all of the man, and I was going to get him.

For now, we'd focus on helping him reclaim Emma.

CHAPTER 15

- TYLER -

The decision of the judge kept ringing in my head as I walked out of the courtroom flanked by Edwin and Jenna. I was the one found guilty of trying to break a custody agreement and my show of violence meant that Ellie gets to keep the child a bit longer. I walked briskly toward the parking lot, trying to rein in the rage in my head. When I arrived where I had parked my truck, I heard a voice calling my name. I stopped and turned around, my eyes scanning the scene. Dunrad was waving at me.

"Hey, man. You good?"

I nodded. "Is there anything you want to tell me?"

"Ellie wants to speak with you."

My eyes narrowed at the mention of her name. "About what?"

Dunrad sighed. "She didn't tell me. But she says you probably want to hear what she has to say."

"There," Jenna said, pointing ahead. Her fingertip was aimed at a small truck on the far side of the parking lot with the door hanging open and the engine still running. "That's got to be her."

"And she wants to see you alone," Dunrad added, looking pointedly at Jenna.

"Not a surprise. She hates my guts," Jenna scoffed. "There are obviously driving you somewhere. You know it could

160

be a trap, right? They could have some of those shithead guys lying in wait again. Might start a fight and pin it on you again."

Her worry for me was clearly evident in her voice and I walked up to grab her arm and squeezed. "Right. But it's the only chance we've got."

"I'll hang back, but I'll be close," Jenna assured me. "One of the things I know well is how to be around without being seen."

In the rearview mirror, a pair of trucks pulled up – most of them my staff at Peak Bliss.

"I'll talk to them," Edwin offered. "Let them know what's up and lead them home."

"Thanks, Ed."

"You got it, man. Now, go do what you have to do to get your little girl back."

Jenna gave me a quick hug before waving me off. I took a deep breath and walked away from the truck. As Dunrad and everyone else kept telling me, I needed to play the long game here for the sake of my daughter. The fight had cast a bad light on me that I must never allow to repeat. The only sound in the still night was the pebbles crunching under my boots as I approached the car. It was like everyone on the court grounds was waiting to see what would happen as I approached the truck. As I made my way to the headlights, I glanced over my shoulder to see Dunrad talking to Jenna and Edwin. I couldn't hear what he said, but he was surely talking them down from rushing in alongside me. They didn't follow. I ignored the anger in me and took a deep breath to clear my head as I made my way through the parking lot.

For some reason, the stillness reminded me of days with Ellie. We used to sneak around, walking into abandoned parks like this when we were teenagers. I felt a rush of adrenaline as I strolled toward them.

Keep calm, Tyler. Keep calm.

Jenna was right, they could probably drive me off to a place where the men I fought a few days ago   would be waiting to ambush me. As I approached the truck, I instinctively clenched my hands into tight fists as I watched the open door, ready to say no to any suggestion that we drive away from there.

To my surprise, Emma stepped out of the vehicle, looking around with a confused expression. I quickened my pace, my heart racing at the sight of my little girl. But then she saw me, and her whole face lit up. My heart burst in joy and excitement as my legs ate up the ground quickly. There was my daughter within reach, where I could grab and hold her.

"Daddy!" Emma rose, her face lighting up as she watched me approach. Before she could take off into a run, another figure stepped out of the truck.

It was Mark. He quickly reached down and put his hand on Emma's shoulder, stopping her from running towards me.

"Don't run in the dark, sweetie. He'll come to you."

My girl looked up at him and smiled. "Okay, Uncle Mark."

I bit back the urge to yell and tell him to take her fucking hands off my daughter and let her come to me. I bit my tongue only because the last thing I wanted to do was scare Emma. She probably still didn't understand anything about what was happening, and open hostility between us would only upset her more.

"Well, well, here you are brother. Hope you are alright considering the way things went today?"

"Is daddy sick?" Emma's little voice inquired.

"No baby, I'm quite good. Uncle Mark is just talking about business."

"Oh, am I?"

I ignored him and moved toward my daughter, but he stepped in front of me.

"Let me see her," I said, my voice stern and commanding.

"You're seeing her right now, Tyler."

I shook my head. "No. I wanna see her up close, and make sure she's fine. Emma?"

"I'm okay, Daddy," Emma said, her voice small and frightened. "I'm fine. What's going on?"

"It's okay baby," I answered in a tone light enough to allay her worries, then I dropped my voice so that she couldn't hear. "Ellie wants me to play ball and that's why I'm here," I growled, "then she's gonna have to play ball here, too."

Mark crossed his arms over his barrel chest, shifting his weight from one boot to the other as he thought it over. "Wanna say hi to your dad, kid?"

Emma burst into a sprint, running to me as fast as her little legs would pump. I dropped to my knees, throwing my arms around her as soon as she was close.

"Daddy!" she cried. "Where were you?"

"I'm right here, baby. I'm right here."

I wanted to take her, to run out of there as fast as I could. But over her shoulder, I could see Mark. Court guards were around too and plenty of other witnesses. Duncan had told me to play it all cool throughout this custody case. The last time I'd gone rogue, my ass had landed in jail, and that was enough of an incentive to rein in my emotions.

I looked up at Mark, he had a little smirk on his face as if he was daring me to try to pull off an escape. I sighed softly, being charged with kidnapping would ruin all the chances I had of securing Emma.

"Where's Jenna?" she asked as I let her go.

"She's at the resort. You'll see her soon."

"Don't count on that, Emma," a familiar feminine voice called out.

I looked up again to see Ellie step out of the truck, a sneering smile on her face.

163

"What's that supposed to mean?" I asked, confused.

"I want to see Jenna, mama."

Ellie shakes her head. "Just trust me, baby. You can't see her yet and I'll tell you why very soon."

Emma's little face squeezed in confusion. "Are you planning a surprise? I love surprises!"

"Yes," Ellie responded, her eyes fixed on mine. "A big one. It's all part of the plan. Now, you two want to come inside?"

I shook my head. "Whatever you want, we talk about it out here."

"You're not in a position to make demands," Mark sneered.

Ellie reached out to touch his arm softly. "I did you a favor by letting you see Emma in person when I didn't have to. I think that means that you owe me one, don't you?"

I hesitated, looking from Mark to Ellie. I couldn't trust them, but she was right, they didn't have to let me see Emma physically. They only did that because they wanted something, and I was interested in what that thing was, but at the same time, I was wary of dealing with them any more than I had to.

"What do you want?"

Ellie cocked her head to the side. "To solve all of this and find a way to properly get you back with her." She gestured at Emma.

I covered Emma's ears as I frowned at Ellie. "And why would you do that? I thought you said she was not my daughter?"

She lifted her chin. "Do you want to have her again or not?"

I sighed, shaking my head. She had me up against the wall, and she knew it.

Ellie glanced over my shoulder. "I see you left your lover back at the resort. Smart – didn't want things to get messy again, and her presence here would have made things so."

I frowned, not knowing what to say "Daddy, when can we go home?"

"Soon, baby."

"Sooner if your daddy behaves himself," Ellie said to her, her voice sweet like there was nothing wrong at all. "Now, why don't you come inside? We'll sort this out in there."

I rose to my feet, looking around. I didn't see Jenna or the rest. But I had no doubt she was watching, waiting. She'd been like my guardian angel since the arrest. She'd done her best to keep the resort running as well as keep me company, and as each day went by, I was realizing that what I shared with her was much more than physical.

But right then, I couldn't focus on that. All my focus was on my daughter. Since her disappearance, she'd been in my waking and sleeping moments, with my brain stressing on questions like if I was going to see her again. And here I was, Emma's hand in mine. I smiled at her as we walked toward the front door. Mark entered first. Ellie stepped aside, still grinning, making an exaggerated sweep toward the door as we approached, like she was some kind of butler.

The interior of the truck might've been nice at one point, but that had long passed. The upholstery was ruined, the paint was stained and cracked, and the smell of mold was thick in the air. Some chocolate wrappers and a bunch of other trash lay strewn about, a lot of it left by the current occupants, from the look of it.

"Mark," Ellie called. "Take little Emma for a walk I'll call you when we're done having our discussion."

"Okay, Ellie."

"Not a chance," I said, scowling at Mark. "She's not leaving my sight."

"Trust me," Ellie sneered. "You don't want her to be here for this."

As much as I didn't want to leave her under the watch of Mark, I knew there was a good chance of things getting very dirty between Ellie and me. And with any luck, Mark wouldn't be the only pair of eyes on Emma out there.

"Fine." I squatted down and threw my arms around Emma. "I'll be seein' you soon, baby. Don't you worry."

The expression on her face was pure confusion. It broke my heart not to be able to whisk her out of there and back to safety.

"Okay Daddy," she whispered, her bottom lip trembling.

"Don't be scared, okay?" She nodded, and I kissed her cheek. "It'll be okay."

"Come on, kiddo," Mark said, nodding toward a bench on the other side of the parking lot.

She followed him, glancing back at me and my gut tightened as she stepped out of my sight.

"She'll be fine," Ellie told me. "Not sure if I can say the same for you."

I sucked in a breath and faced him, a sneer on my face. "Now what?"

She moved to a chair in the corner of the room, but she didn't sit normally. Instead, she perched and observed me.

"All of this can stop. In fact, you can drive her home with you tonight if all goes well."

"If what goes well, Ellie?"

"I have a simple proposition to make," she announced excitedly. "You agree to it and then we all live happily ever after."

I shook my head. "Whatever you're planning, you're not going to get away with it."

She just smiled a smug smile I wanted to wipe off her face. "Oh, I don't plan to."

I narrowed my gaze at Ellie and when she saw my expression, she chuckled.

"As much as I want to savor this, seeing you here confused, knowing what kind of shit you've been up to, I also want to finish this right now because you truly have been a good Dad to my daughter."

"What do you want, Ellie?" I asked, my voice steely. "What's this all about? You said you wanted to see me. I'm here. Why not go straight to the point now that you have me?"

She stared at me as if I'd grown an extra head. "You hurt me, Tyler. I betrayed Mark for you, only to find out you didn't even care about me before shacking up with someone new. Do you have any idea how that feels? To sacrifice a lot for someone and find out you meant so little to them that they can forget about you so fast?" She shook her head. "Of course, you don't know. You're too busy playing the rich boss with your fucking girlfriend to care about anyone's feelings but your own."

"Ellie," I called out, trying to keep my voice even and steady. "I understand how you feel. And I know—

"You don't know shit!" Her voice came out with a sharp edge, her face twisting into an even more crazy expression. It was clear that she was losing it quickly.

Ellie pointed her finger at me, her hand shaking with anger.

"Easy now," I said, holding my hands up defensively. "Let me hear your demand."

"You hurt me, Tyler. But I'm gonna be benevolent and forgive you. You can drive Emma back to the house tonight and I'll drop all custody case. But." She held up a hand to stop me. "We come as a package."

"What do you mean?"

167

A twisted grin formed on her face. "We get back together. I stay as Emma's mom and your wife. You sack that woman and say goodbye to her while we live happily ever after."

"What?"

"If you refuse me, I'll fight you to the end of the earth to make sure you never see Emma again." She curled her eyebrows up. "Deal or no deal?"

My heart pounded hard against my chest as I stared into her face and realized she wasn't joking. *Fucking hell! Talk about a rock and a hard place.*

LOVE AT PEAK BLISS (MR. STARK)

CHAPTER 16

- JENNA -

Whatever they called Tyler to discuss, it wasn't good news, and it concerned me.

I knew it from the look on his face, and from the tone in his voice as he told me he was okay when I asked if anything was wrong. I wished I hadn't stayed so far away from him when he went to see them. I wished I'd found a way to follow him so I could listen to the whole conversation and know what was going on.

I had an idea of what Ellie would want though, and that suspicion cut deep into me, but I said nothing as we climbed into the truck and drove home. It was bad enough that he was worried about his daughter's safety, projecting my own insecurities onto him was something else altogether.

When the truck rumbled to a stop in front of his cabin, I looked at Tyler's face again and reached out to touch his arm.

"It's all gonna be alright, Tyler. I want you to know that I'm here for —"

His phone started beeping and he pulled it out of his pocket and checked it. His face contorted with a mix of pain and frustration, and I immediately knew who it was.

"Can you wait inside while I take the call?"

I nodded and stepped out of the truck, seething with anger. Is this how it would be now? Tyler was not the type of man who would ever ignore a phone call if the woman who had custody of his child was calling. Ellie seemed hell-bent on screwing him over again and again and eating into his personal space. If she'd never had his full attention, she sure had it now. Now she had the power to interrupt his life at any given time of day. I had no doubt that she would use it to her fullest advantage, too.

I opened the door and flipped on the lights in the living room. I poured out some juice and stood at the window, staring at him pacing the front of the house as he spoke with Ellie. When he saw me at the window, he waved at me and headed toward the door.

"I'll think about it and get back to you on Monday." He murmured as he stepped into the house and then went quiet as he listened. I heard the sound of her voice but couldn't make out the words. There were a few more curt exchanges, and then he hung up.

"How is Emma doing?"

"She's good, I think," his voice broke and then he cleared his throat. "Give me a second."

I nodded as he went into the bathroom. My heart ached for him as I sipped my juice and stared out the window, giving him some time. I heard the water running and wondered how all of this must be tearing him apart from the insides. I wish I could see the thoughts in his head so that I could give him the comfort he needed, say the right things, help him bear some of this heavy load.

I remained where I was standing even after I heard the water shut off.

"You okay?" I asked when he stepped back outside, with my back still turned to him.

Tyler hugged me from behind and kissed my shoulder. "I'm good. Sorry about that. Ellie was calling to make arrangements."

I turned over and faced him. "She's still in love with you."

He looked down. "I'm not sure Ellie is capable of love."

"She surely wants a connection with you."

171

"She isn't going to get that."

"She's smart too. She knows how to get to you."

"She's never getting to me, Jen. Only one person has the keys to get inside this head —you."

That made me smile. Until I thought of other advantages that Ellie had over me. "But there is a deeper connection. You have a baby together."

"A connection without commitment, it's purely a mistake."

The next question popped up in my mind. I had no idea where it came from — a kind of dark masochist side I suppose. "Did you ever consider proposing and marrying her?"

"Jenna…"

"I need to know."

"Why?"

"I have no idea. I just do."

He closed his eyes. "I almost did. When I found out she was carrying my child, I guess a sense of responsibility kind of kicked in. I bought a ring. I planned with Edwin, and it was more like a business deal than anything romantic. I even had the prenup drawn out and all."

"Oh."

"But I didn't. I just couldn't — I didn't love her. Edwin also seemed to have always known I wouldn't go through with it. One day over lunch, he asked me why I hadn't given Ellie my mom's engagement ring instead of buying a new one. The thought had never even occurred to me, to be honest. Mum had given me her ring when I turned twenty-one and told me that it belonged to whomever I eventually gave my heart to. My grandmother's ring was small and simple. It wasn't until I eventually didn't go through with it that Edwin had pointed out the obvious to me that I understood the significance. There was never a question in my mind, given the choice between a small ring that meant a lot to me and a flashy rock, Ellie would rather have had that rock. And

I knew that enough to not give her my grandmother's ring. But I didn't stop to think about what that said about who she was."

"Wow. She sounds like a piece of work."

Tyler chuckled. It was good to hear it after him spending so much time being glum. He took the glass of juice from me and took a drink. "That's partly my fault, Jen. I think I ruined her innocence by seducing her away from my brother."

I wrung my hands together and stared deeply into his eyes. "Why did you do it?"

"It's not something I'm proud of." Tyler squinted and then shook his head, his lips thinning into a line of regret. "My relationship with my father had been quite strained...I was raised by my mother who he was at odds with so nothing I did seemed to get in his good graces — meanwhile Mark was the golden child. I stupidly became jealous."

He closed his eyes in anguish and I placed a comforting hand on his shoulder. "Most kids would get jealous Tyler. You shouldn't beat yourself up too much about that."

"Yeah, most kids would." His voice was gravelly, his jaw clenching. "But most also wouldn't have let the feeling fester and cause such hatred that all they wanted to do was hurt their brother. I got rich off the trust fund my mother left me, suddenly found myself better than Mark at one thing and the first thing I did was go for his woman."

I could see the pain flashing in his eyes and I wrapped my arms around his neck. It was clear that he had bottled up a myriad of emotions over years. I was glad he was letting them out with me, but I was not going to let him beat himself up on things he no longer had control over. "We all make mistakes, Tyler. But we all just have to apologize, forgive and forget and move on."

He nodded, his hand caressing its way down my body, stopping right on my hips. "I wish it were that simple, Jen." He looked right into my eyes as he spoke, letting me see all the pain, fear, and confusion in there. "Whenever I'm not with you, I wake up at night scared that I am recreating the same mistakes with Emma, having her caught in this fight with her mother..."

173

His voice trailed off. At that moment, I was ready to do anything to alleviate his pain, even a bit. So I did the only thing I could — I kissed him. Tyler froze for a moment and my heartbeat drummed rapidly in my chest.

"Jenna," he rasped, voice low and needful. I could feel his body heat, smell his faint cologne and my skin tingled with anticipation.

"Tyler." His name came out in a whisper. My body was practically vibrating with excitement–lust, nerves, the thrill of seeing the lust shining for me in his eyes. I smiled at him, my heart beating fast. I wanted this moment with Tyler, just him and I — a reminder of what we felt for each other despite the heavy cloud hanging over our heads. In this moment I had the power to wash away all the nastiness with Ellie, even if it was just for a while. I could make him feel better, grant him ecstasy instead of anxiety, bond with him in our bodies and our hearts.

He traced a finger up my arm slowly, up to my shoulder, over my collarbone, up the side of my neck, and the shell of my ear.

Then he leaned in and murmured, "I'd never be able to resist you, will I?" His lips hovered above mine, our breaths mingling, growing shallower. "Even when I'm scared and worried, you're always there in my mind, that ray of sunshine that burns away the shadows, that gives me a glimmer of hope. I haven't been able to stop thinking about you, Jen."

My voice caught in my throat. "Me too," I breathed, trembling. "I think about you nonstop. I'm terrified of losing you again."

He brought his other hand up to cradle my cheek, slanted my head back to expose my neck to his lips, and softly kissed the skin below my ear. I trembled, arching to press into his hard body, but he pulled away, taunting me as he lavished me with tiny kisses and nibbles down my collarbone, his mouth followed the low neckline of my dress down to my breastbone and nipped gently at the curve of my breasts.

My nipples had hardened underneath my dress. I wasn't wearing a bra tonight, and the texture of the fabric tickled and teased against the sensitive skin as Tyler trailed around, exploring. I planted my palms on the wall, dizzy with lust, desperate for something, anything.

"You have no idea how badly I want this," he said, his voice warm and velvety. "Want to touch you again. To feel you"— he straightened up from nuzzling my chest to look me in the eye— "to kiss you again." His irises gleamed dark in the low light of the room, darting around my face. I was so turned on that I could hardly breathe.

"I want you too—"

Before I could finish the words, his lips slanted over mine. I melted into the kiss, groaning as his torso pressed firmly to my body, and his hard length pressed against me. I opened my mouth, letting my tongue sweep along his lower lip before diving in further. I locked my arms around his shoulders, wanting to be as close to him as humanly possible. I smiled against his mouth as he stifled a moan, deepening the kiss. His hands swept down my body gripping my ass hard. I whimpered at the thought of having his thick hard cock inside me again.

As if he could read my mind, he bent slightly and lifted me up, pinning me to the wall. I

crossed my ankles around his back, our kisses turning ever more urgent, and bodies grinding against each other in a rush as we hurried to get our clothes off.

"Jenna," he gasped between kisses. "Baby—"

"Tyler—" I wanted more. I need more of him. I wanted everything. "Need you, now. Please."

"I'm yours," he said, slowing the feverish pace of his lips as they brushed against mine. "I'll give you what you need."

He pulled back slightly, and his fingers pressed into my thighs, little fluttering touches climbing higher and higher until he reached the hem of my dress and pushed it up to reach my panties.

"Fuck Jenna," he took in a sharp breath, fingers tracing along the thin strap of my panties to the top of my thigh, giving me goosebumps.

Tyler pulled at my panties, tugging the G-string down my legs until I was bare from the waist down, exposing my wet aching apex. A whimper escaped my throat and the heat bursts between my thighs. I stepped out of the panties, and he flung them on a nearby couch. Then he parted my thighs with his large palms, and he slowly dragged his longest finger from my belly button down to the small patch of silky curls. His fingers disappeared between my legs, flicking against my center—oh, my God–the tip parting my folds, searching for my clit and swirling hot circles around the sensitive bundle of nerves.

A moan slipped from my throat. I laced my fingers behind his neck, holding on for dear life. My back was arched, and I was panting, already on the edge, needing more and Tyler knew it.

"So wet," he cooed, inserting two fingers. "So soft." He slid them in and out of me. "So tight." He flicked and circled the pearl of my sex, and I could feel my orgasm just out of reach.

"More," I blurted out in a wild screech. "More."

Tyler groaned into me, his broad chest heaving as he watched me. Leaning down, he swung an arm underneath my knees, cradling me against his chest. I began tugging at his clothes, wanting to get him naked. He carried me over to the couch and set me down gently next to it, then set about peeling off his shirt as my fingers flew to the top button of his jeans. I quickly unzipped him, and he grunted as I gripped his thick, rigid cock.

"Jen," he said, voice strained and breath coming fast and erratic, "Jenna sweetheart, are you ready…"

"Mm-hmm," I hummed, nodding to let him know just how much I needed him inside him right now. Wide-eyed, I let out a little squeak as he turned me around briskly, bending me over the couch. My elbows landed on the soft seat, and Tyler spread my legs, positioning his rock-hard cock against my wet entrance. I could feel his warm, broad chest against my torso as he leaned into my neck and nipped at my earlobe.

"I need to feel your sweet body," he murmured, kissing my neck and pressing into me from behind.

"Yes, baby."

He pushed in. The angle was deep, the friction unbelievable when he started moving, and I closed my eyes and whined in blinding pleasure as he reached a hand around my front to bring his fingers to my clit. I was throbbing with the need for release, already on the precipice as he rubbed tight circles around my sensitive sweet spot, rocking his length into me with deep, slow strokes.

Everything else ceased to exist at that moment. No fears, no pain, no worries — only two of us and our wild pleasure, mixed with the urge to give each other as much as we could take. I wiggled against him, grinding my ass into his strokes, letting him bury himself deep into me each time.

"I want you to come for me, Jen," he huffed.

"Yes," I whimpered, an exciting pressure quickly rising. He need not say much as the feeling of him driving hard was already pushing me over the edge. "Yes, Tyler, yes I'm coming–"

My orgasm hit me, a scary surge that burned through my body like wildfire, setting my whole body in a tingling blaze.

"You feel so good, Jen. Yeah, come for me, babe. You're so perfect–"

"I want you forever, Tyler!" I screamed as he fucked me with a force that sent my climax careening through me. He came too, grabbing my hips and groaning before collapsing next to me on the couch.

"I truly wish we could have forever, Jen," he whispered, kissing my forehead softly.

By the next morning, all the satiation our bouts of fiery sex had instilled was already starting to dissipate. Our sex had always been mindblowing, but there was some other element to it throughout the night, something that felt like he was saying goodbye, and that scared me. I was on an errand downtown getting supplies for the resort when I called Mark and asked to meet in a pub. I needed to find out what Ellie had said to Tyler, and why he had said he wished we could have forever.

What the hell was I doing? I wondered as walked across the road towards the pub. I shouldn't be seeing him. I considered going back home, leaving Mark without saying a word, but curiosity was eating away at me. I wanted to know what was discussed at the court parking lot. I needed to do this. Fuck it. I walked to the door, took a deep breath, and pushed it open. The colored lights cast a red glow across the hall where a number of people settled on stools around small round tables. Patrons close to the door turned to look at me and immediately pivoted back to their half-filled bottles lined up on their table.

My heart was racing as I walked straight in. When no one came towards me, at first a sense of relief came over me. I was just about to turn and leave when the waiter stepped up to me.

"Can I help you?" She squinted, and then her eyes grew wide. "Oh, my. Jenna. I'm sorry I didn't recognize you."

I forced a smile. I was suddenly panicked and wanted nothing more than to leave. "Is Mark here?"

Please say no. Please say no.

"Yes. He's in that corner." She pointed. "He said he's waiting for someone. That should be you, I guess?" She smiled warmly and stepped aside. "Come in. Feel free to join him."

"Thank you, Theresa."

I walked toward the corner she'd pointed, my mind still reeling with worry that this wasn't right, and his voice swiftly interrupted my internal debate to flee.

"Jenna." Mark was halfway off his seat as he spoke. "Is everything okay?"

178

I nodded.

"Is my brother okay?"

That pissed me off. "He's fine."

He strode to me, rattling my already shaky confidence. For a second, I thought he was going to hug me. But when I folded my arms across my chest, he seemed to take the hint.

"Your call was a pleasant surprise. I've been really worried with the court case and all how you were really faring—"

"I'm quite good, thank you. I don't think I need your worries." I wasn't going to give him any credit for worrying about me or anything like that, not after aiding and abetting Ellie in her plans.

He nodded demurely. "I understand, Jenna."

I saw a light flick in his eyes that looked like regret, but it quickly disappeared. I stared at him, noting the similarities with Tyler his face. He was a handsome man. I used to find him quite charming as well, which was ironic considering the situation we've now found ourselves in.

"Come on. Let's sit." Hesitantly, I followed his gesture and settled in the chair opposite his. "Coffee?"

"Sure."

He poured us both steaming mugs and shifted his plate of biscuits across the table. I stared into his eyes, remembering the times he and I would sit at one of the tables in this same pub, talking while we drank coffee and ate snacks. It all seemed so long ago now, faded into memory. It was pretty obvious that I didn't love Mark, but I'd liked him, and respected him. It had been enough to sustain the relationship, but it had lacked the burning passion I shared with Tyler.

"So. How are things at the resort?"

"Fine."

He nodded. I shut my eyes briefly and shook my head, frustrated with myself. I'd called him to come, yet I was shutting down any conversation he started. It was all because I didn't know how to start this conversation with him. I didn't know how to ask him if Tyler was truly planning to leave me, so I kept silent and sipped my coffee.

A few minutes later, he tried again. "Remember when this used to be our favorite spot?"

The memory of me sitting across from him, laughing as we held hands across the table. It felt like that was so long ago now, and I wasn't the same person I was with him.

"Yes. It isn't mine anymore."

More nodding. Then a few minutes later. "Are you and Tyler serious?"

That hit me hard. It wasn't the question I expected. I took a moment to think about it — Tyler and I might never have discussed it out loud, but our feelings for each other were clear enough. "Is it serious enough for you if I call him my boyfriend?"

A look of shock and regret crossed his face. "That serious?"

I nodded. This was the most serious relationship I had ever been in. "We are."

Mark smiled softly. "I'm happy for you. I hope it works out."

"There'll be more chance of it working out if his brother wasn't conspiring to take away his daughter over some stupid vendetta."

Mark's smile wilted. He closed his eyes briefly, nodding as if it all made sense finally. He took a deep breath and let out a loud whoosh of air. "I made a lot of mistakes in my life, Jenna. Did things I'm not proud of."

"Like kidnapping your brother's daughter just to get back at him."

He nodded. "Yes. Like that. But he hurt me. He took something precious to me—"

"And now you've taken something precious to him. So where does the cycle end?"

"Uhh—" He opened his mouth and then closed them again, shaking his head as he looked away from me into his cup. "For fuck's sake."

I saw the opening, and I decided to take it. "You know, he opened up to me. The things he did to you, he's not proud of them and he only did them because he was jealous of you."

"What?" Mark's jaw dropped.

"Yeah," I nodded. "He said you were the golden boy your father preferred so he wanted to best you at something."

He closed his eyes and went still for a long moment and when he opened them, the expression in them was unreadable again. "Is that why you called? You wanted to tell me this?"

I shook my head. "That's not it, Mark." I cleared my throat and leaned across the table. "I want to know what Ellie and Tyler discussed yesterday."

"No." He shook his head vigorously. "If Tyler wanted to, he could have told you."

"Mark," my voice got louder and more authoritative. "Answer the damn question. What did they talk about?"

He looked down, worried, but I knew him well enough to judge that he was being honest when he spoke next. "Ellie gave Tyler the choice of taking her back if he ever wants to get custody of Emma. He's to make his decision and get back to her soon."

It felt like someone had sucker-punched me in the stomach. "No."

"That's it, Jenna. Ellie wants—"

I stood up, the world spinning around me. I couldn't tell up from down and I stumbled out of my seat, but I kept moving.

"Jenna!"

"I shouldn't have come. This was a mistake."

Everything from the last few days was bubbling to the surface. It felt like there was a tsunami coming, and I was about to get sucked under if I didn't run for it. So I did. I took off like a bat out of hell running out of the pub. I flew past the tables, flung open the front door, and bolted down the road toward my car.

My eyes burned, my throat felt like it was closing, and my chest constricted. I started the car. I was so intent on getting away as fast as I could, that I wasn't even paying attention to where I was going. It was until I turned off the ignition in front of my own apartment that I realized where I'd driven.

I wanted to scream. A vile guttural sound of frustration climbed up my throat. I'd been a fool to think what I had with Tyler was going to end with a happily ever after. There was too much confusion, too much baggage hanging over our heads for this to have ever ended well, and I should have known it. I should have realized it quicker before I fell in love with the man.

I rushed into the house, weeping as my heart shattered into smithereens.

LOVE AT PEAK BLISS (MR. STARK)

CHAPTER 17

- TYLER -

"Care to join me anytime soon, Tyler?"

I stared up at Dunrad's inquisitive face, capped off with an eyebrow raise. We'd been here since lunch, trying to come up with different strategies and a list of witnesses to tighten our case in court. But for the past five minutes, my mind was a fucking mess. I was unable to concentrate, as I stared with shock and unbelief at the damned text from Jenna.

I found out Ellie's request, Tyler.

I can never stand between you and an opportunity to regain Emma — I don't think what we have is worth that.

I want to tell you that I won't be returning to the resort. I am still available to help with anything I can.

Jen.

Shifting in my chair, I ran my thumb over the screen, turning the thought over and over in my mind. She'd said what we have wasn't worth it — she was wrong! I was caught in a world of helplessness at that moment, and I definitely knew that I'd have given a million things up just to have Jenna — Heck! I had to find a way; I was not going to let Ellie's machinations soil every good thing I had with Jenna.

"Tyler," Dunrad called. "Whatever you're looking at on that phone is obviously a hundred times more engaging than what I'm spouting here. And you're not sharing."

I shook my head. I was done with this meeting. Most of the day, all I could think about was her anyway. All I wanted was to see Jenna. Smell Jenna. Sleep next to Jenna. And now at the thought of never having her again, my heart felt like it was being crushed under the heaviest sort of weight. I cannot bear a few days without her, let alone a lifetime.

The fact that she was ready to sacrifice what we had just to help me gain my daughter only strengthened the affection I had for her. She was my anchor, the one thing that kept me sane through all of this, and now I realized she'd become much more than that. It wasn't just the physical need between us. I'd miss her humor, her smiles, her laughter.

My life had been full of mistakes, and letting her go was another one I wasn't ready to add to the list because I wasn't sure I'd be able to recover from that one.

I love her.

"I'm leaving," I told Dunrad and hurried off. Without thinking, I grabbed my jacket and headed down to the parking lot, ignoring his confused calls. I hadn't texted or called Jenna first, so, driving to her place was a risk. But I couldn't take the chance of her telling me not to come. I had to see her, had to convince her that I would get Emma back without having to give in to Ellie's demands.

It was Jenna I wanted. Always Jenna.

Halfway to her apartment, the rain started falling. After I parked the car, I had to run in the pouring rain to her door. I pressed the buzzer to her apartment.

She sounded groggy. "Hello?"

I closed my eyes because I'd been scared I wouldn't hear that voice again. "Jenna, it's me."

"Tyler...it's late."

185

I leaned my forehead against the wall. "I know, but this can't wait."

Without saying anything further, I heard padded footsteps and then she opened the door. She stared at me for a moment. My hair and jacket were soaked; I must have looked like a drowned rat. I didn't know whether she was going to kick me out or tell me to come inside. It was her call to make. I had no right to push after the mess I'd brought her into, but I'd regret it for the rest of my life if I didn't try to show Jenna that we could make this work.

I took her in; she was completely natural in a thin, white nightshirt and I could see her taut nipples through the material. Her hair was let down, framing her face while several tendrils were scattered all around her head. She looked so gorgeous, even with her hair a matted mess, and I wanted nothing more than to pull her into me and feel her warmth.

"Oh, God. Come in. You're soaked."

Thank fuck for the rain. I needed any reason to get more time with her at this point. She closed the door behind us.

"Here. Give me your jacket, I'll put it in the dryer."

I peeled off the jacket and handed it to her. "Thank you."

My dress shirt underneath it was still dry. Maybe I should have stood outside for a while longer, maybe that'd have increased my chances of staying with her.

She disappeared for a moment. I looked around, my eyes fixing on the painting hanging on the walls. The home looked like her — pretty and tidy with a U-shaped pink couch circling a little glass table. There were a few things sitting out that hadn't been there the last time I came. A photo of me and her on the resort now sat on the mantle and there were books and a few knick-knacks on a small bookshelf.

She came back outside with a towel. "For your hair."

I scrubbed the towel through my hair to catch the loose droplets while I watched her walk to the fireplace and increased

186

the heat, and then she walked into the kitchen and returned with a steaming cup which she handed to me.

There was no way I let her go. I thought as I looked into her eyes. Just standing near Jenna again filled me with peace deep in my gut. No matter what Ellie did, I was going to find a way to hold on to my girl and my woman.

"How's it going with Ellie and the custody? Any news?"

I knew she was stalling, but I decided to answer her all the same. It warmed my heart that she cared so much about Emma, even if her running away from me was another outcome I needed to fix, and fast. "Dunrad thinks we can get her to admit in court that her allegations about me not being the father was false and then on a call today, we agreed to get Emma DNA tested within the next week."

She nodded and looked away from me. "Hope that coffee is good. Are you comfortable with the warmth from the fire?"

"No, I'm not. Nothing isn't okay."

Her eyes flashed. I stood up and took a step toward her, but she took a step back and shook her head. "I don't know what to say, Tyler."

I looked into her eyes, pleading. "Say you won't leave me."

She looked away. "Tyler...everything is so uncertain right now. I'm so confused, and you cannot give your daughter up because of me." There was a deeply haunted look on her face, I wasn't so sure what was going through her mind, but I stepped up and wrapped my arms around her. She struggled in my arms at first. "You can't give her up, Tyler."

"I'm not, Jen. I'm not giving you up too. I'm fighting hard for the important women in my life—you and Emma, can't you see that?"

Her eyes seemed to come into focus. I watched as they filled with tears and then she melted into my arms. Her full weight leaned on me as I tightened my hold around her, and I relished in feeling her. This might be the last time I got to hold her, and that broke my heart all over again.

"Tyler, I'm scared that if you choose to stay with me, you'll lose everything and then this feeling between us would gradually grow to become resentment —"

"Shhh, baby. That can never happen, Jen. I want you, I need you."

"I don't think that's enough, Tyler. Trust me, I wish it was."

She made a gut-wrenching noise and then her body began to shake, tears streaming down her beautiful face. It physically hurt my heart to see her like that. I could hear that sound of pain coming from deep within her, it was how I felt when I'd read her message. Like someone had cracked open my ribs and gripped my beating heart in their hands only to nearly squeeze the life out of it.

There was no way in hell I was letting her go. I held her as tight as I could for a few minutes while we stood in the middle of the room.

"Come on, let's get on the couch."

Jenna didn't protest as I helped her into the seat, she simply settled beside me. The first few moments were quiet while I rubbed my hand on her arm to comfort her. When her crying finally subsided, she kept her head on my shoulder and her eyes closed. I hated that this was all my fault. I'd fucked things up between us royally. Not only had the situation with Ellie thrown a wrench into our relationship, but I had almost started to consider actually letting Jenna go. The truth was crystal clear to me at this moment, giving in to Ellie's request was only going to put me in misery for the rest of my life, and that would obviously affect my relationship with my daughter also.

Taking Ellie in wouldn't be saving my daughter. It would be suicide as I'd be risking a higher chance of losing my daughter forever just because I wanted to have her close. I would be resentful of Ellie for forcing a relationship, and who knew what that would do to Emma in the long run? It would be a colossal mistake.

Stroking her hair, I finally broke our silence. "I'm sorry. This is all my fault."

She shook her head. "I'm the one who asked. I had a bad feeling and went to see Mark. What was I expecting Ellie would have requested? I should have trusted that you had it under control."

"You should have, but it's only natural. You're trying to make sense of everything going on."

"I guess..."

"What exactly did Mark tell you about Ellie's request?"

"He said Ellie gave you the ultimatum of getting back with her, or else she'd do everything in her power to keep Emma from you."

That much was clear. "I never said yes."

"You would have," she wiped her eyes with the back of her hand. "Or you would regret not agreeing in the future."

I shifted in my seat so we were facing each other. "Whether I have a daughter with her or not, even if I had not met you, there is no way in hell I would be getting back together with Ellie. She's not the one for me, and it's taking her far too long to see that."

She stared at the floor. "But she has Emma now, that changes everything."

"Jenna, look at me." Her head lifted, and her eyes returned to meet mine. "The real mistake would be letting Ellie back into my life. We never shared anything strong enough to sustain a relationship. I was lucky to have smartened up and not made the mistake of marrying her once. Now I will make the same decision as back then because I've experienced what a true relationship should feel like. I know how a man should feel about a woman he wants to build a life with. Ellie and I are not getting back together, no matter what."

"What if she makes good on her promise to keep Emma?"

My next words came out slow, with careful consideration. "I think we'll eventually wear her out in court. I'm not giving up on getting my girl back, and I have the best lawyer money can buy."

"And if she wins in court?"

I looked at Jenna and sighed. "I know what you mean. My mind is spinning out of control, and I know nothing is given, nothing is sure. But there is only one thing I'm sure of right now. Do you know what that is, Jenna?"

She was staring into the fire, but lifted her eyes, looking up at me through her dark eyelashes. "What?"

"I want you. I want to be with you. I've fallen heels over fucking head for you, and one thing I'm sure I need to know is that you aren't going to leave me."

She cracked a small smile. "I think the saying is head over heels, Tyler."

"I don't care." I wrapped my hands around her waist and locked them behind her back. "Tell me you aren't going to leave me over this."

"We don't know what's going to happen, Tyler."

"I know what I want."

"Tyler…things can change."

"I need you, Jenna. I've never said that to another woman in my life." I leaned my forehead against hers and whispered, "I need you."

She nodded. "Okay."

Taking her face in my hands, I lifted it, so my eyes met hers. "Kill all your plans on avoiding me."

"I wasn't really planning on doing that."

I flashed her a look that called bullshit.

"Fine." She rolled her eyes. "I was planning on totally avoiding you, but you've made it clear that's not allowed."

I leaned in and kissed her on the lips. For the first time since I got her message, the world seemed to stop spinning for a moment, and I finally felt like I could breathe.

"Do you want to stay tonight?"

I grinned. "Try to get me to leave."

"Alright then, can we just go lie down?"

I examined her face before responding, "Sure."

Despite our talk, a cloud of hesitance still seemed to hang over our heads as we headed into her bedroom. As I unbuttoned my shirt, Jenna was just sitting on the bed, watching me. I loved the fact that she was so enthralled with my undressing, but to be honest, it was a little odd and uncharacteristic for her to just be staring at me like that. She was definitely not herself tonight.

Throwing my shirt on the chair, I said, "I think my head my head's gonna burst from thinking too hard in finding a way to make you feel better."

She smiled, stood up, and walked over to me then slowly traced her index finger over my heart. "The fact that you came means so much to me. I don't think I ever really expressed how much I'm into you."

"You mean so much to me. You are my anchor, Jenna. Nothing I can do feels truly adequate in expressing how I feel. I feel like all is well or at least its going to be whenever you're with me. Even when we can't physically be together ultimately knowing you're there for me and that you have my back is what's getting me through."

"You're saying a lot of things to make me feel better."

"I'm just being a gentleman. You've had a tough evening. I know the perfect remedy to make you feel better without words."

"Of course you do."

"It's my duty, and I take it very seriously."

"Hmm," her lips curled. "I think I now know what would really make me feel better."

"Name it."

"You, not being a gentleman." Her voice was a soft whisper.

I was relieved to hear a flash of my girl come back. The corners of my mouth twisted up while my cock hardened at the thought of what her statement meant. I didn't take my eyes off hers as I leaned closer and whispered in her ear. "It would be my pleasure to leave the gentleman at the door."

She continued to smile at me when she asked, "Will you shut up and make love to me?"

"Was there ever a question about whether that would happen right now?"

"No, but I want to take it slow tonight. Savor it."

"I can do slow." I was going to show her with my body exactly how much I loved her, that there was nothing we couldn't get through as long as we stayed together both literally and figuratively.

She hummed as I kissed and caressed her waist and hips, stroking her body and running my hands underneath her nightshirt. Her lovely breasts fit perfectly in my hands, and she let out a light moan as my thumbs circled over the hard, rosy nipples.

"Tyler," she whined softly, arching and pressing into my hardened cock which was pushing desperately against my pants. I shuddered, our bodies pushing against each other. She was still wearing her nightshirt–and although I relished the way we were grinding into each other, I needed to feel her naked body under my fingers, against my skin, around my cock.

"Let me take this off you, baby," I said with a kiss under her ear, pulling up her shirt. She lifted her arms, and I pulled the cloth off, revealing the sexy pair of breasts that I had been fondling a moment earlier. I let out a heavy breath, admiring her beautiful body.

Then she surprised me. Her eyelids went a little low, lashes fluttering, then she said, "You're in my bedroom, now. I'm in charge."

The sound of that was intriguing. I watched the little smirk play her lips as she pressed a palm against my chest, guiding me to the bed. I backed up, letting her push me down so I was seated, leaning back with my elbows supporting me, pressed into her bedspread.

She stood in front of me, her eyes narrowed at me as she bit down on her lower lip.

"I see," I said, amused at how she was taking control. "So, you want to have your way with me?"

"Maybe," she shrugged coyly, rolling the bottoms of her nightwear. Her hair fell over her shoulder, and I watched her peel the leggings off, revealing smooth white panties. My heart pounded hard, lust racing through my veins.

She tugged at my waistband, and I lifted my thighs as she pulled my pants and briefs down to my knees. I was hard as a rock, the tip of my cock tingling, needing to touch her so badly I could barely stop myself. She reached for my shaft and rubbed her thumb around the head, making me jerk toward her with need. I lifted a hand from the bed toward her breast, but she squirmed away, denying me.

"No touching," she said, playfully. "Not until I say you can."

"So you want to tease me?"

She shrugged. "Maybe. And it's my call tonight."

"Yes, ma'am. You're in charge."

She resumed playing with me, letting her fingertips trail down my shaft, then sliding down to cup my balls, rubbing them gently. I gasped, my breathing shallow, as I waited for her to do her bidding, desperate to feel her touch—and to touch her back.

"Oh, fuck," I grunted when she started working my cock with both her hands. She grinned at me and then she leaned down to lick the tip. She grinned and took me into her mouth and I desperately reached for her hair. She immediately pulled off me with a lewd pop.

"I said, no touching."

"Huh? Ok," I agreed, needing more and yet feeling a thrill at being denied. She was turning my insides out with this teasing game, and I had to admit, I liked it.

"Good." She leaned back up to pull off her panties, and then climbed onto the bed and straddled me, pushing me down further until I was lying flat.

"Let me taste you," I said, hungry for more touch, more sensation, more of Jenna.

"OK," she said, scooting forward on her knees so that her apex was above my mouth, "but remember. No touching until I say."

I grinned at her. "I'll try."

She lowered herself down, her soft curls tickling my nose as I lapped a stripe along her entrance. "You taste so fucking good, baby," I murmured against her wet core.

She moaned softly, adjusting her body so that I had a better angle, and began rocking against me as I tongued at her clit, her lips, her moist center.

"Yes, I like that," she breathed, "feels so good–Tyler!"

Her legs shook as I licked her, and I couldn't wait to touch her any longer. I flicked a finger through her sweet, wet passage, sliding it between her walls, and this time, she didn't stop me. Then I added a second finger, searching for the spot that I knew would make her scream. I felt her tightening, pulsing, edging toward release. Then I pulled my fingers out. She looked down at me and made a little noise of frustration. I knew she had been close.

"Still don't want me to touch you?" I asked, licking softly at her clit again, but not enough to give her what she wanted. Whimpering, she shook her head, trying to stay in control. I nibbled her clit softly, making her squirm.

"How about now?" I teased. She huffed a little, brows furrowing, shaking her head again. One more lick.

"Touch me! Touch me please, Tyler, please baby, please..."

"Please what?"

"Please touch me...."

"Good girl." I sucked her clit and inserted my fingers inside her again, pumping and curling them forward until she was crying out, pussy fluttering against my mouth as she came like I knew she would.

"Fuck," she breathed, shaking as I lapped softly, bringing her down from her orgasm gently.

I needed to be inside her. I had waited long enough. I grabbed her ass cheek, squeezing it and moving her back until I had enough room to sit up against the headboard, peeling my pants off the rest of the way. My hard dick bobbed as I scooted back and pulled Jenna with me. She climbed on top of me, her nipples tickling and scratching my chest as she settled astride me.

"Now, I want you to ride me, baby."

"Yes, Tyler," she nodded, lowering herself down to surround me, slowly– each inch that slid into her agonizingly sweet. She was so tight yet pliant; soft and hot — so perfect that I might lose my mind if she moved any slower. I grabbed her by the hips and pushed her down. She let out a moan and I grunted as I finally pushed deep inside her.

She looked into my eyes and smiled, and then began to rock–up, then down and back, her tight walls gripping my cock perfectly, making me crazy.

"So wet, so perfect," I groaned, holding her waist as she ground against me. I looked down at where we were joined, watching my cock disappear inside her over and over. I was so close yet trying to keep it together for Jenna. "God, you feel so good, baby. Like we were made for each other."

"Yes baby. It feels so good. Want you to–oh!" She let out a little squeal when I leaned forward to tease and bite her nipples lightly, one after the other.

"Oh, I love you, Tyler. I fucking love you!"

At that moment, I knew — this was the woman I wanted to spend the rest of my life with. The woman I loved. The woman who could make me feel better than anyone ever had.

She pulled back, letting out a high, breathy moan as her fingertips dug into my shoulders. Her pussy clenched around my cock as her orgasm overcame her. I took her chin into my hand and brought her mouth to mine, kissing her hard and rough, feeling her come around me again. I bucked up into her, fucking her through her orgasm, watching her face contort as waves upon waves of climax rolled over her. I finally let go, spilling inside her, groaning. I was panting, my body sticky with sweat and my groin slick with our juices. I held her against me as we caught our breath.

When I got Emma back, I'll finally have everything I wanted, and there was no way I was giving one up for the other. Nothing could tear me away from her.

"I love you so much, Jenna," I said, still shaky and breathless.

"I'll love you forever." She sighed softly in my arms, pressing soft kisses to my chest, and we curled up together in her bed, falling asleep while listening to the rain coming down hard against the window.

LOVE AT PEAK BLISS (MR. STARK)

CHAPTER 18

- JENNA -

I jumped from the truck and shut the door, ignoring the small crowd of people peering as Dunrad, Tyler, and I walked up to the double doors of the courtroom. Halfway through the courtyard, a car drove into the wide circular space. When the sound of his engine died, I could see a few people whispering to one another so I turned around, and caught sight of Mark and a few other men disembarking.

I sighed. We've not talked since the day he told me about Ellie's request — he'd called me a few times, but I didn't answer. I wasn't sure I knew what to say to him and I'd been too focused on enjoying my time with Tyler that I'd decided that I wasn't going to allow incursion from anyone from the other side anymore.

The last week with Tyler had been bliss. There was a warm feeling bubbling inside my chest–not only at that moment, but at every moment these days–and I couldn't deny the other warm feelings that Tyler's body seemed to leave me with every time. All of my skin tingled with excitement whenever he was near. I could even sense his presence a distance away before I saw him — it was like he'd laid claim to me. Every time we were together, it was the best I had ever felt.

Could this kind of feeling go on like this forever?

The only piece missing was Emma, and though at first I'd blamed myself that Ellie had taken her away, Tyler had been adamant that the blame was placed on Ellie alone. It was her jealousy and spite that kept Emma away, not anything I'd done. It

198

was hard to swallow, but Tyler's belief that we would get Emma back made it easier to believe everything would work out.

We settled in the courtroom sometime before the procession was supposed to start. Tyler and Dunrad were huddled together, with the lawyer seemingly going over some final details. I was nervous and wanted to catch some breath before we started, so I slipped out silently and began walking to the ladies' room, ready to put some water on my face and calm myself. I turned out of the entryway and rounded the corner into the hallway, then froze in my tracks.

Mark was standing right in the middle of the hall, with a steaming cup of tea that had chamomile–I could smell it from where I was standing. He also had a small plate of cookies, fragrant with vanilla and cinnamon.

"Hey, Jenna," Mark said.

"Hey," I echoed.

"Erm! Jenna, this must be some kind of providence. I wanted to talk to you…"

I frowned. Something seemed off with Mark. His eyes were bloodshot, with huge dark circles under them. He looked around furtively as if he didn't want to be seen with me.

"Can we take a walk?"

I nodded, feeling uneasy about how uncomfortable he seemed. What was going on with him? He was clearly very worried, that much was evident in the worry lingering on his face. He was also unnerved and that showed in his out-of-sorts messy hair, and the wild look in his eyes.

"What is it you wanted to see me for?" I blurted out as we turned the corner away from the sight of anyone who could be walking toward the courtroom.

"Jenna, I called you this week. Several times as well, but you didn't answer."

"Because I didn't want to. We're on opposite sides of this case, it wouldn't have been appropriate." I crossed my arms over my chest. "I suggest you get to the purpose of this discussion quickly. I want to get back into the courtroom."

"What you told me in the pub...I've not been able to stop thinking about it since that day..."

My heartbeat picked up, sensing this was important somehow. "What I told you? About what exactly?"

We had reached a set of chairs in the eastern corner of the courthouse. Mark sat down and patted the spot next to him. "Here, want some of this?"

I stood still, staring my displeasure at him. "I don't have time to sit and share snacks with you, Mark."

"Please? It's important." He gave me a small smile and didn't say anything else as he stretched the plate of cookies toward me.

I sighed, resigned to listen to what he was about to say. "This had better be good." I sat and took one, nibbling on the sweet cookie while Mark cleared his throat and stared intently at me.

"Jenna," he muttered, adjusting in his seat to face me. "I'm worried that I am creating the same cycle of pain that caused me and Tyler to be hurt."

I put the cake down, my full attention on him now as I watched his eyes flare with what seemed like regret. His worries resonated with me since Tyler had voiced the exact same concern. "So why don't you put an end to it?"

"It's not that simple. On the other side of my worry is a belief that he deserved to go through some pain. You told me he said he was jealous of me? Well he had nothing to be jealous of. Our father was a dick and I had to endure a lot that Tyler didn't see to keep his favor. Meanwhile, Tyler only saw the successes and our father passing him up, and took that as a reason to destroy my love life. He doesn't realize he's been the lucky one — even with you."

It was true. When I dated Mark in the past, I hadn't been this happy, this free, and ready to throw caution to the wind.

Except now that I was with Tyler, every day with him felt perfect. It felt like I was going to explode with excitement any moment. I loved Tyler — and I didn't feel a third of that for Mark. It shouldn't surprise me that everyone was onto me about my feelings, hard as I had tried to keep it from people at the resort, but I knew the majority just needed to look at my face to find out that I loved Tyler.

Still, it was uncomfortable for it to be insinuated by my ex, who was also supposed to be my brother-in-law should Tyler and I decide to tie the knot.

But this wasn't the time to give the weird relationship a thought.

I swallowed and nodded at Mark. "Most times the things we miss out on are the things we think we need the more. Both of you should be looking forward to reconciling, not fighting. I don't think you're a horrible person, Mark, just misguided. I wouldn't have been with you as long as I had been if I thought you were irredeemable."

He blew out a long breath, not looking convinced. "I think that train sailed when I took his daughter, Jenna."

I shook my head and shifted closer to him, putting a hand on his wrist and looking deep into his eyes in a tentative but comforting way. "You'll never know if you don't give him a chance."

"Is it worth it?" He asked slowly. "Is he worth it? He only seemed to be hell-bent on getting what he wants, no matter who stands in the way."

My eyes rolled involuntarily. "Tyler is the last person in the world who would do something to force me or anyone into anything."

What I had with him was pure thrill and excitement, and I've seen him in his purest form to know who he was.

"If he's your lover," Mark swallowed, struggling over the part where he had to acknowledge that I am insinuating I belonged with Tyler. I guess it could be that painful. "It's easy to overlook things with your lover, since it's such a new, exciting thing. You might be overlooking things like warning signs, or clues that your limits aren't being respected."

"He's a good man," I said, feeling defensive of not only Tyler, but myself and my choice to be with him. "He's a wonderful man, actually, and he's fighting as hard as he can to get Emma back."

"Good men don't go out of their way to do things that hurt people, Jen."

"Everyone makes mistakes, Mark," I piped. "Even good men."

"But then they know well enough to apologize and make amends." Mark's dark green eyes bored into mine, flustering me and giving me no time to be tactful or diplomatic.

"Hey," I said, feeling a warmth rise up inside me. "Both of you are incredibly stubborn to a fault. That's one thing in which you guys are undeniably brothers."

He nodded his head. "I guess we inherited that from our father. Maybe we inherited his mistakes too. Tyler and I surely grew up in a difficult situation after our parents divorced."

"And that is why trading vendettas isn't going to help anyone, believe me — think of Emma. You're both repeating his mistakes without realizing it. She's your niece, don't you care what all this conflict will do to her?"

A regretful look flitted across Mark's face.

"What is it Mark?"

"Speaking of Emma," he said, "she misses you and her father terribly. I heard her crying in a corner the other morning. She's barely eating, and we can barely get her interested in anything any longer. It seems the novelty of staying with her mother has worn off, and no matter what Ellie tells her, she knows that Ellie is keeping him away."

My heart clenched with pain. "She needs her father."

He nodded. "Ellie truly loves her, which is great! But I know that she is not yet ready to take care of a child. Her choice to try and take Emma wasn't because she believes she's a better parent than Tyler, and that was wrong of her to do," Mark said, sighing. "I must do something about it."

What is he getting at?

His phone beeped and he stared at the screen. "We have to get back now, Jenna." He stood and made to leave.

"What are you going to do Mark?" I asked, point blank.

A loud scoff made its way out of his throat. "I don't know yet to be honest."

He hurried off and I followed him. "You can still make this right, Mark. If you want to see that Tyler can forgive you and you two can make up — it starts with this."

He nodded to me, but he didn't say anything, as we'd arrived at the courtroom already. The courtroom air was thick and stuffy, the temperature uncomfortably warm. I sat next to Bella, holding her hand firmly in mine. Edwin sat on her right, holding her other hand. I felt nervous and afraid at the same time. Sitting in a courtroom waiting to hear the fate of a little girl whose choice was as obvious as anything. You'd think her opinion should be what mattered most in this situation, but things don't always work that way.

I was mad. Furious, in fact. I was hurt and angry and frustrated. I'd been there every day to see the hurt and pain in Tyler's eyes, and now Mark had confessed that Emma misses her father. *Why did this have to happen?* It felt like a bomb going off, ripping the lives of both father and daughter to shreds. If I had stuck with my initial decision and I hadn't been in that room with Tyler the day Ellie stormed in, none of this would have happened. He'd still be with his daughter, and Emma wouldn't be facing a lifetime of pain and regret if the verdict went the other way. We'd all be living our normal lives. Not sitting in court, waiting for a judge to tell us how bad the future was going to be. I shifted on the hard bench, but there was no getting comfortable. Bella squeezed my hand and I squeezed back.

I closed my eyes, wishing that things worked out the right way. Mark and the men who worked with him were seated in a line on my left, one of them still had his jaw in bandage. Mark couldn't seem to sit still. I watched his leg shake and wondered if it had to do with what we discussed before we came in here.

What was he planning to do?

I looked at the front row where Tyler sat with Dunrad. He hadn't looked back, not even once. Dunrad had told me that the only way to win was by convincing the judge that Tyler was a better fit for taking care of Emma than Ellie. But I also knew there was a chance the judge would impose a different verdict because Ellie's legal team had insisted that Tyler was violent and regularly went out of control. Mark had been listed as a witness to properly corroborate that with his history. I'd been silently praying, pleading, hoping the judge would see beyond their testimonies. To give Tyler a break.

We listened to the details of the case, and sat through the prosecution's statement, followed by the defense. There were some explanations of the law and how it had been applied. The prosecution had given the reasons Tyler deserved to lose Emma's sole custody.

My blood boiled as I listened to the prosecution cite the fight as an example of Tyler's hotheadedness and tried to create a picture of him not having the personality and temperament to care for a child. I was glad when Dunrad refuted that by arguing that he did it because he was separated from his daughter.

Both sides outlined their arguments and they called a few witnesses. And now it was time for Mark to speak. He was called to the stand.

The ginger-haired prosecutor walked up t0 him. "Mr. Harris, do you know the defendant?

Mark's eyes hit Tyler from across the courtroom before he turned to the lawyer. "Yes."

"And what are you willing to tell us about the defendant and his temperament?"

Mark looked across toward me, and his eyes stayed glued on me for a few seconds.

"Mr. Harris, did you hear the question? What can you tell us about the defendant's temperament."

"He's a good man," Mark muttered, and a gasp went through the room.

"What did you say?"

"Tyler is a good man who loves his daughter. He's always done that. He's willing to give her the world and he's ready to go through all kinds of trouble to do it."

"Do you think his volatile temperament is the best thing for his daughter?"

Mark shook his head at the prosecutor. "What I know is that he's the best thing for his daughter."

More gasps went through the crowd. Every statement he made filled my heart with hope. He spoke about Tyler, and how kind and caring he was. He spoke about how he was sure Emma loved her father. When he was done, the whole place was in a hush.

After a few more arguments by the lawyers, the judge was ready to declare his decision. "There is no evidence before the Court to disqualify either parent from being awarded the Custody of the child. But the fact that she had been in custody of the defendant since she was a baby substantially favors the father. The absence of any evidence of plans and proposal for her future education is against the mother while the evidence given by the respondent of his plans and proposal for her education is in his favour. Accusations against his character and temperament to care for the kid have also been proven null and void. In the circumstances, this court decides on primary custody with care and control and responsibility for education to the respondent will be most appropriate..."

The judge continued speaking, but the rest of the details of his words were lost to me.

Tyler won.

They were giving him Emma's custody. By the time I realized I was crying, my cheeks were already wet with tears. Bella still held my hand, her grip sure and steady as she smiled at me. Edwin had thrown an arm around my shoulder, hugging me tight.

Oh god. Emma was coming back home.

As the court dispersed, I rushed to Tyler and put my hands on his shoulders, forcing him to look at me.

He frowned when he saw my face. "Are you okay?"

"Yeah," I giggled. "I'm fine. I'm fine."

He looked me up and down. "Are you?"

"I'm good. These are tears of joy."

"Let's go pick her up," he beamed. "She's outside."

We stepped outside the courtroom and saw her entrance to the hall. Dunrad was standing in the center of the hall. Emma was next to him, a big smile on her face.

"Emma!"

Tyler and I called her name at the same time, rushing down the hall together toward her.

"Daddy! Jenna!" she said as soon as she saw us.

We hurried across the room, Tyler dragging me across as I ran, trying to keep up with his long legs. My heart felt full of a joy that I could not explain.

"She's alright," Dunrad assured us. "Brought her here as soon as I could."

"She'd better be fine," Tyler said. He hugged Emma hard before looking her over to make sure she was truly fine. It was my turn next. I wrapped my arms around her little body, burying my face in her hair.

"I missed you, Daddy!" Emma exclaimed, her eyes excited. "I can go with you to the resort now?"

"Of course you can baby."

"They handed her over without fuss," Dunrad told us, dusting his hands on his pants. "In time they'll like to sit down with you and discuss some stuff. They're outside now, though."

"Nothing to discuss," Tyler barked. "It's over."

I placed a hand on his arm. "I think it was over quicker because of what Mark did in there, Tyler."

Tyler raised an eyebrow as he thought about it for a few moments and then he sighed. "They took her away, Jen."

"And now she's back with us. Easier because of Mark."

"She's right you know?" Dunrad added.

Tyler ran a hand across his face and shook his head and I looked at Dunrad. "Maybe we give it time...?" I nodded at him and he took the cue.

"We need to get her out of here," Tyler said. "I don't want her to set eyes on them."

"There's a back entrance," Dunrad announced. "We can leave through there."

We hurried down the hall. Tyler carried Emma, holding her face against his shoulder as he held her tight. My heart beamed with joy seeing father and daughter reunited.

We hurried around the courthouse and Tyler dropped Emma in the backseat of the truck, tightening her seat belt before he closed the door. He turned toward me, and I could see there was something in his eyes. Something he wanted to tell me.

I took his hand and stepped closer to him. "What is it? Talk to me?"

"I love you, Jenna. I love you like mad."

I grinned. "I love you, too."

We kissed in the middle of the parking lot before he opened the door and we climbed into the truck and he turned away from the courthouse.

LOVE AT PEAK BLISS (MR. STARK)

CHAPTER 19

- TYLER -

One week later…

The last few days had flown by. Jenna and Emma and I had settled into a routine on the resort. Whenever one of us adults was busy, the other two spent most of the day together either studying, doing resort chores alongside, or helping with homework. And then we usually met together around dinnertime. After that, we played games or saw movies with Emma before she retired for the night. And then Jenna and I spent the night together.

The week was busy as hell for me because I'd ignored most work during the custody battle. I personally took an interest in the new batch of tourists. I took the groups out on hikes and trips around town, not to mention horseback rides and other activities.

By the time most of the groups started to go back to the city, I was wiped. I let the other guys handle the few tourists left at the resort on Friday evening, giving myself the evening free because Jenna had asked for it.

I was in my office, sipping on some coffee and going over some numbers at my desk when Jenna and Emma showed up.

"Hey, Dad!" Emma shouted as she ran into the room, her little feet pattering on the hardwood floor as she ran to my fridge and opened it.

"Hey, kid," I greeted.

"Now Em," Jenna said as she entered behind her, shutting the door. "You know we're eating dinner in a little bit, right?"

"I know, I know," Emma said, her face buried in the fridge. "But I'm starving. Can I have a snack or something?"

"You can have whatever you want, as long as it's a piece of fruit."

"What about a slice of pecan pie Bella gave us?"

"Is that fruit?"

"No."

"Then we're saving it for later, okay?"

"All right."

I couldn't help but grin. Jenna had turned out to be a pro with Emma – she was stern and in charge, but never overbearing. Over a short period of time, she'd managed to establish herself as a friend and authority figure to my daughter and that impressed me more than I could say.

Emma turned from the fridge, a bright red apple in her hand.

"Want me to cut it up for you?"

"Yeah."

"Pardon?"

"Yes, please."

"Atta girl," Jenna praised. She glanced at me with a smile before turning her attention to Emma and the apple.

All the nights this last week had been so hot. I cherished every chance to spend time alone with her and even though we spend nights together that didn't mean I wouldn't be thinking about her like crazy. Whenever my mind would drift during the day, I'd imagine the two of us in my room, in the pool, anywhere and everywhere with Jenna's shapely legs wrapped around my body, my cock buried in her, her face twisting into beautiful agony as I brought her to orgasm, and she screamed how much she loves me.

I loved her so much it almost hurt, and I wanted us to move to another level in this relationship. But then I'd think about our conversation about how we weren't going to force things, but let it happen at its own pace. The pace, though, was a little too slow for my tastes. Every time I'd spot her around the property, just the sight of her was enough to get me thinking about how much I wanted her, how desperately I needed to have her permanently. I wished I could spend the days in her arm, basking in her smile and good nature and of course have her naked and underneath me, pounding her hard, her tits bouncing, her full, curvy body squirming as I made her come. I wanted her heart, body, and soul — all in equal measures.

I shifted where I sat, trying to put all that out of my head. But damn, was it tough.

"Em, want to go help Bella prepare cake in the kitchen?" Jenna asked, snapping me out of my daze.

Emma's eyes lit up. "Yes! Daddy, I have to go! Puh-lease?" She clasped her hands together in a cute little begging way.

"Sure, that's fine," I said.

Emma squealed with delight and jumped up and down. "Yay!"

Jenna smiled at her, then looked at me and I immediately knew something was up. Something that could not wait. She wanted Emma to join Bella so she could have time to talk about it.

"Why don't you run along now. Let Bella know we'll be in for dinner soon."

"Okay!" Emma screeched, already halfway out the door.

She was gone, and Jenna and I were left alone. Part of me wanted to lock the door and rush her, putting my hands on her hips, pulling her out of her clothes, and bending her over the desk as soon as fucking possible, but I knew something more important was up, or she'd have waited.

"Somethin' up?"

"Just...going for a walk. Getting some fresh air, wanna come?"

It was a strange request, considering we usually had our time later in the evening, but I played along. "I'd love to." I put a hat on my head and tugged it down by the front of the brim, following this up with another slight smile. "Let's move, then."

She opened the front door and led the way. As we stepped out, I placed my hand on the small of my back, guiding her. It might've been nothing more than a little contact, but it still felt good, reassuring, that she was here, and she was mine.

Jenna and I walked in silence for a time, watching the sun beginning to set over the trees, the wild oranges of its light fading into a whiteish blue.

"Great evening," I said. "Kinda warm, too."

"Yeah, perfect for reconciliation, don't you think?"

I stopped short. All through the week, Jenna had kept drumming into my ears how Mark had made a U-turn to help our cause in court and that I should have a conversation with my brother. I'd brushed off her pleas, finding one excuse after another.

"What do you mean, Jenna?"

"Tyler?" She sighed and placed a hand on my arm. "I invited Mark here."

"What?"

The idea of my brother hiding somewhere on the property was enough to get my blood boiling. I didn't know if I could trust him, and I wanted to wring his neck, maybe sock him across the jaw for good measure. He'd put me through hell. You don't threaten a man with his daughter – simple as that.

213

"You alright?" Jenna asked when we stopped in the middle of the field.

"Where is he?"

"I cannot tell you that until you calm down, Ty," she murmured softly. "I need you to stay calm."

"He threatened me with my daughter, Jen!" I sputtered. "They were planning to steal Emma away from me."

"And then he had a change of heart and spoke for you. How long do you want to keep this feud going?" She wrapped her arms around my waist and looked up into my eyes. "Please? For Emma? What are you going to tell her when she asks to see her uncle or her mom?"

The warmth in her eyes was burning away the cold anger inside me quickly. She was right, I needed to do this for Emma. She's asked twice this week if her mom and uncle would be coming to visit soon.

"Just see him, and talk calmly, please?"

"Okay," I was wearing my anger on my face, and I made a conscious effort to push it out of my system. "I'll speak to him, but I'm not promising to forgive him. I'm fine." A little white lie, but she was stressed enough about the situation. No sense in letting my feelings put her more on edge.

"Thanks, Ty," she said as she led me toward the shed at the back of the house. "He's waiting there. I'll try to keep my nose out of personal business from here on out. Just, you know, I think he misses his brother too and wants you back."

"Okay," I blew out a breath. "I'll go see him now."

"Good," she said. "I'll wait for you at dinner."

"See you then."

Jenna turned toward the stairs in front of the house and was gone, a smile over her shoulder as she stepped out of sight.

I took a moment to collect myself and mentally steel my mind for a chat with Mark, and then walked to the front of the shed, looking furtively around as if it would allay all my fears and worries. It didn't. When my brother finally stepped out, I was shocked. Part of me had thought–or maybe hoped–that he wouldn't really be there. That he had tricked Jenna, and the painful confrontation I feared would be postponed.

He stepped toward the light looking drawn and tired, with obvious dark circles underneath his eyes. I had seen that look before when he would return home after working several shifts. He must have been losing sleep over this, just like me.

When he walked up to me, I had to fight an innate instinct to punch him. It was what I would have done any other time, but somehow, things were different right now. Awkward. It felt like there was so much baggage between us, and I couldn't dislike him the way I used to. His turnaround to defend me in court was the biggest shock I had in my life, and it was more so because the words didn't feel fake. He'd been genuine when he told the court he respected me, and that I was about the best man he'd ever known, and as pissed off as I was about everything, his testimony had turned the tide of the custody battle.

He cleared his throat. "Can we speak privately? I know your tourists and… well, I know everyone's there. But I'd like to talk, just the two of us. If that's alright with you."

"Yes," I said, hoping he couldn't hear the frayed nerves in the tone of my voice. "We can stay out here."

He nodded, and looked off to the side, playing with what seemed like his truck keys. Then his gaze returned to me, with a pleading expression on his face. "Tyler, brother… I owe you an apology. My behavior was abhorrent, and I need to be accountable for that. When I found out that you were dating Jenna I lost my head, but I should never have allowed anger to get the better of me. The damaging behavior I displayed was inexcusable." He inhaled a heavy breath, pursed his lips for a moment, then continued. "And I'm sorry for hurting little Emma. In the days I spent with her, I realized how great a father you were more than anything. I'm sorry for holding to this stupid feud for so long."

Hearing him say those words with sincerity made my heart thump. I'd never thought I would hear an apology come from Mark, ever. I didn't know what to say.

"I miss you, brother. Very much. I've realized in these past few days that I love you more than anything in the world, and even though I still wish things were different, I don't want to lose you, or my niece. I want a chance to make things right, to be there for you and to support you. Will you give me that chance, Ty?"

Relief washed over me, and I nodded up and down emphatically as my chin wobbled. It was like the pain I had been feeling from being estranged from my brother had felt like a heavy weight on my chest, and that oppressive feeling was lifting with every word he spoke. It wasn't like me at all, but somehow his heartfelt confession had the backs of my eyes burning with unshed tears.

"Of course! I'm sorry too, brother. I'm sorry I was such a dick that I was looking to hurt you."

"Shhh. I forgive you, it was all a big misunderstanding. I get that now," he muttered, wrapping his arms around me.

I hugged him, feeling complete in my brother's strong embrace, feeling the safety and security a hug from him had always provided when we were much younger. His bushy beard scratched my forehead as he squeezed me tight, comforting me while I cried into his shoulder. I heard him sniffling too and realized how seldom I had heard my brother cry growing up.

"Mark, where's Ellie?"

He stammered for a moment, before saying, "Ellie still needs some more time. Let's be patient with her, ok? She'll get used to the idea soon, I'm sure."

He didn't sound sure, but I nodded anyway, agreeing to give the mother of my child the space she needed, trusting that Mark knew her better than I did. Jenna had been right, there was no way forward other than to make peace because I didn't want my daughter to grow up in a family of strife and tension like Mark and I had.

"Do you want to come inside?" I asked, looking at his twinkling eyes framed by the faintest crow's feet. "That is, if you're comfortable?"

He took a deep breath and exhaled slowly. "Yes. For you and Emma, I will."

I nodded, and we walked into the house together to find Jenna, Emma, and Bella waiting in the large hall. They were sitting on a long bench, and Jenna was leaning against the back of it, arms folded. When my brother and I walked in, Emma stood up straight, running across into his arms.

"Uncle Mark!"

"Hey, Emma," he hugged her close. "I've apologized to your dad, and I owe you an apology, too. I should have allowed you to come back home sooner."

Emma swallowed, her expression subdued. "Thank you. It was fun staying with you, I just wanted to come home to my dad and Jenna."

"I know kid, I know." He patted her hair softly, smiling at her. Emma smiled back at him and my heart burst with joy. I almost felt bad for denying them this since the custody battle. I wasn't ready then, but it seemed I was now.

Mark turned toward Jenna and chuckled. "Look, I'll be straight with you, because we know each other. I am still not sure how to deal with seeing you with him. But this is clearly out of my hands, and I'm not going to let my discomfort with the situation cost me my relationship with my brother. I would like to thank you for all you've done for this family though, and I'm happy for the both of you."

Jenna smiled. "Thank you, Mark," she said, stepping up to give him a kiss on the cheek. "I hope you know that I'm happy with him. Really happy."

He nodded and looked toward me. "That's the only thing that matters to me," he said. "Both your happiness." His tone suggested he was still trying to convince himself that this was the new reality, and he was going to have to accept it.

"Thank you for that, brother. Knowing I have you by my side would mean the world to me."

"Well," Jenna chirped happily. "Thanksgiving is only a couple of weeks away. So, I'm thinking we've got to plan something huge for that day. How about we all get together next weekend?"

"A big party?" Emma's eyes widened. "Will you be there, Uncle Mark?"

"Sure I will, kiddo," he winked at her.

"Will my mom be there too?"

I sighed deeply at the mention of Ellie, and Mark caught me.

"Baby steps," he whispered and winked, and I felt more hopeful than ever to see my brother's old, charming self. He was the one person who understood Ellie no matter the circumstance and I was glad to have him as the reliable liaison between us and Ellie. I needed her to join to make this family complete and give my daughter everything.

"Baby steps," I agreed.

Today had gone so much better than I had anticipated, and I was on cloud nine as I watched my brother joke around with Emma while Jenna stayed beside me.

Nothing could shake my optimism now.

LOVE AT PEAK BLISS (MR. STARK)

CHAPTER 20

- JENNA -

I curled up on a couch in the corner of the library, a cup of whiskey at my side, and some random novel I picked from the shelf in my lap. The room was nice and quiet, a far cry from the lounge where the tourists were hanging out, having cocktails and conversation after dinner.

Part of me felt I should join them, and be a little social, but I was tired. After long arduous hours of planning our huge Thanksgiving party with Bella, all I wanted was to relax. Sipping my whiskey and staring at walls lined with books with colorful spines.

From my seat, I could also look out through the huge windows onto the property where clouds had covered the evening sky, and light rain started to fall. It was perfect. Nice and cozy and relaxing – just what I wanted to finish off the day here, with my own thoughts.

Emma had already gone to bed after a long day with her uncle Mark. — those two had grown very close over the past few days. Tyler had been out all day, traveled with a group to New York for a kind of conference on tourism.

I missed him so much. Our love for each other had seemed to grow more each day and now I was so torn, so conflicted. I wanted him like crazy and I wanted to move to the next level in this relationship, but we'd agreed to let things progress naturally. I wondered if I should give him a hint — let him know I was up for more, that I want things to become kind of more permanent between us. Hell, that would be a ridiculously stupid thing to do. *What if he was not ready for more? What if I spook him into a retreat?*

And why did he have to be such a perfect guy? Not just any kind of nice guy either. He was the strong type, the one who'd do the right thing no matter the cost. He cared about his family and his ranch and had a big heart on top of it all. So not like the men I'd been with in the past.

I knew without doubt that he was the one I wanted, but what if he'd never be ready? What if all this was just setting me up for the biggest heartbreak ever?

I picked up the book, trying to focus on the words and put the fears out of my mind as I sipped my whiskey.

"Interesting book?"

I glanced up, spotting Tyler standing at the entrance of the library, leaning against the door frame with a sly grin on his face — the kind that I could not resist.

I jumped from my seat and ran toward him. My heart started beating out of control at the sight of him. Oh. My. God. He was dressed nothing like I'd ever seen before. Just a black polo shirt that fit his chest like a glove, displaying those impressive pectoral muscles. He also had on a pair of dark jeans. His hair was slicked back off to the side in a way that made him look younger. And he was wearing glasses.

Damn! This looked worked for me. A little too much perhaps.

My body reacted more with every step he took toward me, the force of his woodsy signature scent nearly knocking the wind out of me. Tyler pulled me into an easy hug and buried his mouth in my neck.

"I missed you so fucking much, Jenna."

The strained sound of his words against my skin was enough to do me in. The night hadn't even started, and my panties were already wet. I was ready to pull him down on the couch and have sex right there.

He pulled off his glasses, his eyes searing into mine before they trailed down my night dress to my cleavage and back up again. He took a fistful of strands of my hair and gently sniffed, whispering seductively in my ear, "God! This smell…"

I wrapped my arms around him. "I missed you too, Ty."

His lips slid to my neck, and collarbone and continued the journey lower. I could only feel his chest against mine and his breath against my lips as he said, "You're driving me crazy. All I could think about on my way back was how much I needed to touch you."

Bending my head back, I held his head into my chest as he ran his tongue slowly down my cleavage, moaning over my skin. He pulled the top of my dress down, exposing my breasts, and took my nipple into his mouth, sucking so hard that it caused me to squeal. The muscles between my legs were pulsating with need.

"It was all I could think about too."

Panting, he buried his nose in my neck and placed his hand over my heart. He pulled me closer to him and cupped his hands around my cheeks. "I'm carrying you to the room now."

I giggled as he lifted me over his shoulder and rushed to the room. Once the door closed behind him, he wasted no time going for the ties on the front of my dress. I groaned as he pulled off the material and ran his hands across my bare skin. Pushing me back to lie on the bed and kneeling between my legs, he placed his palm between my breasts, slowly moving down my belly to the lace panties. His fingers traced the edge of my panties, causing the muscles of my abdomen to clench with every movement as I tried to control my breathing.

I pulled him to me and slid my tongue into his mouth, groaning as his palm pressed against me. Our lips frantically sought each other's; the kiss long and deep with urgency with every inch of skin uncovered. I pulled his polo from his pants and explored the smooth skin over his ribs, the taut muscle at his hips, and the soft trail of hair urging me down his navel and lower. Wanting to tease him the way he was teasing me, I ran my fingers across his belt and to the hard shape of him beneath his pants.

"Damn," he groaned into my mouth. "You don't know what you're doing to me."

"Show me," I whispered back. Seeing the lust in his eyes spurred me on. "I want you to fuck me."

He moaned and bit his lip, his forehead pressed against mine as he shivered. His hands shook as he gripped my panties in his fist. I wanted him to rip them. The raw passion between us was wild and I didn't want him holding back. As if he could hear my thoughts, he tore them from me, the pain of the fabric pulling across my skin only adding to the pleasure.

I pulled my leg forward and pushed him back and off me. Sitting up, I shoved him into the bed, and straddled his lap. I yanked his polo off and threw it across the room. I was lost to everything but him and this. The feel of the air against my skin, the ragged sounds of our breathing, the heat of his kiss, and the thought of what lay ahead. I frantically undid his belt and jeans and managed to get them down his legs. His cock popped free, the tip grazing my wet heat. I gasped, closing my eyes and slowly sliding down over him.

"Oh, God," I groaned, the sensation of him sliding inside me intensifying the eros.

Lifting my hips, I began to ride him, fast and hard, each movement feeling more intense than the one before. His hands grabbed my hips roughly, fueling my lust. His eyes closed and his moans muffled against my breasts as I bent over him. Moving his lips across my breast, he pulled one hardened nipple between his teeth.

I gripped his hair tightly and moaned. My body was so in tune with his, it reacted to every look, touch, and sound from him. I both feared and loved how he made me feel. I'd never lost this much control with any other man, but when he touched me like this, I happily threw control out the window.

"I can't have enough of you, Jen," he murmured, his breath short and jagged.

I pushed on his chest and stared up at him and bared my teeth at him, slowing my movement into an agonizing "Really?"

"Yes, really." He lifted me off and roughly threw me down onto the bed. Pushing my legs apart he thrust back into me. Pulling himself onto his knees, he picked up one of my legs and placed it over his shoulder, forcing his cock deeper inside me.

"Is that how you like it?"

"Not enough." With my elbows pushing off the bed, I lifted my hips off the seat to meet each motion of his hips. "I want it harder."

"Yeah?" He lifted my other leg to rest across his other shoulder. Reaching out, he gripped the bed's headboard and used it for leverage to deepen his thrusts. The change in angle caused me to gasp, as the most delicious sensations spread throughout my body.

"Oh, God, yes."

"Fuck," he murmured as he turned his head slightly, kissing my legs. Our bodies were glistening with sweat, and our groans filled the room. The dim glow from the bedside lamp emphasized every carved indentation and muscle of the man above me. I watched him in awe, his body straining with the effort, his hair mussed and sticking to his damp forehead, the tendons in his neck pulling tight. Ducking his head between his outstretched arms, he closed his eyes tightly and shook his head.

"Oh, God," he gasped. "I just . . . I can't stop."

I arched to get closer, wanting to pull him deeper, more completely into me. I wanted to consume his body, to own all of him, to become one with every part of him that I wanted to feel. And he pushed into me, again and again, and with that thought in my mind, the delicious, ratcheting tension along my skin and in my belly thickened into an ache so heavy that I slipped my legs off his shoulders and pulled all of his weight on top of me as I pleaded.

"Please, please, please, Tyler." I was so close. So close. My hips rotated, and his hips answered rough and wild movements that matched mine underneath him. "So fucking close. I want you so much, please."

LOVE AT PEAK BLISS (MR. STARK)

"You own all me, baby," he growled in reply, before bending to bite my lip and growl. "Take every fucking thing."

I screamed as the orgasm hit, my nails digging into his back and the taste of his sweat on my lips. He swore, his voice deep and hoarse, and with one last powerful thrust, he tensed above me. Exhausted and shaking, he collapsed with his face against my neck.

We slowly returned from orbit, and with our limbs tangled in the sheets, I ran a finger down his chest. He stilled it with his hand, bringing it to his lips and saying, "You blew my mind."

I laughed, pushing his hair off his forehead. "You say that every day."

"Because you do it every day." With his fingertips, he drew spirals over my bare stomach, distracting me. My heart clenched and I wished I could stretch the moment, right there, into eternity.

"So tell me something."

He raised his eyes to my face, smiling a little nervously. "What do you want to know?"

"Do you think what we have is special? I mean have you ever felt this way with anyone else?" I twisted a strand of his hair around my finger, hoping I wasn't pushing him too much.

To my surprise, he answered without hesitation. "I thought I had it once. Her name was Felicia. She was an attorney at a small firm that managed my mother's will. We were together for six months and broke up a few months before I moved here.

"Was that why you moved here?"

A smile tugged at one corner of his mouth. "No."

"Did she break your heart?"

The smile turned into a full-on smirk directed at me. "No, Jen."

"Did you break hers?"

225

Why was I even asking this? Did I want him to say— yes? I knew he was capable of breaking hearts. Sometimes, I was actually fairly certain he would break mine.

He bent to kiss me then, sucking on my lower lip for a few moments before whispering, "No. We realized our chemistry had much burned out. She ended it and I was glad. My romantic life since then was entirely drab. Until you."

I laughed. "Happy to change up the pattern."

I could feel his laugh in the vibrations along my skin as he kissed up my neck. "And oh, you do." Long fingers made their way down my stomach, to my hips, and finally, between my legs. "Your turn."

"To have an orgasm? I already did."

He circled a lazy finger around my clit before sliding it inside me. He knew my body better than I did. When did that happen?

"No," he murmured. "Your turn to spill your history."

"No way can I think about anything when you're doing that."

He kissed my shoulder and moved his hand back to my stomach, drawing circles there once again. I pouted but he missed it, watching his fingers on me instead. "God, there have been so many men, where will I ever begin?"

"Jen," he warned.

"A couple in high school, and Mark of course."

"You've only had sex with three men?"

I pulled back to look at him. "Hello, Einstein. I've had sex with four men."

A cocky grin spread across his face. "Right. And am I the best by a completely wide margin?"

"Am I?"

His grin disappeared, and he blinked, surprised. "Yes."

His answer was sincere. It made something inside me melt into a tiny, warm buzz. I reached to kiss his chin, trying to hide what those words did to me.

"Good," I whined happily, kissing his shoulder. I loved his taste, loved to inhale that musky smell of his. Digging my fingers into his hair, I tugged him down so I could nibble at his lips, but he held himself very still, very clearly not kissing me back. The hell?

I dragged my mouth away and frowned. "What?"

"I want to hear you to say it."

I stared at him, and he stared back, irises growing a familiar shade of angry brown-green. Mentally sorting through the last few minutes, I tried to understand what he was talking about.

Oh! My eyes widened as I remembered "Oh. Yes."

His brows pulled together. "Yes, what, Jen?" Heat pulsed through me. His voice was different when he said that. Sharp and hot as hell.

"Yes, you're the best by a very wide margin."

"That's better."

I winked. "At least so far."

He rolled on top of me, grabbing my wrists and pinning them above my head. "Don't tease."

I laughed and wrapped my legs around him and whispered into his ears. "I love you, Tyler."

He grinned. "I love you too."

The exhaustion of the wild sex we had was finally catching up with me, and the comfort of being wrapped in the warmth of his arms was slowly lulling me to sleep. "Only you."

He'd been holding still before, his shoulders trembled and his breath came out in shallow pants as if his entire body wanted to explode into a wild tangle in the sheets.

"Jenna?"

"Mmm?"

"I want more than just this." His voice was so thick and heavy, I wasn't actually sure he was awake. I froze, my thoughts exploding into a chaotic mess.

"What did you just say?"

He opened his eyes, with apparent effort, and looked at me. "I want to be with you."

Lifting myself on an elbow, I stared down at him, completely unable to pull a single word out of my brain.

"Is that sleep talking, Ty?"

"Hmmm," his eyes rolled closed, and he threw a heavy arm around me, pulling me down onto him and pressing his face into my neck. He mumbled something incoherent as he went to sleep. My own drowsiness had disappeared, and I was wide awake, staring at the dark wall as I tried to make sense of his words.

I was terrified that he had no idea what he was saying, and this would change nothing, and I was even more excited that this changed everything.

"I love you," I whispered into the dark, hearing his breathing slow into a steady, sleeping rhythm.

LOVE AT PEAK BLISS (MR. STARK)

CHAPTER 21

- TYLER -

The sun rose behind the mountains in the distance, its warm golden rays spread across the grass field and reaching the patio. Clear air, bright daylight, and festive atmosphere... It felt like a damn good day. Whistling a random tune, I flipped the turkey over, silently congratulating myself as they turned successfully without breaking the skin. The scent of grilled meat filled the air as heavy footsteps pounded down the stairs. I looked back, expecting it to be Jenna, but it was my brother's tall frame that appeared in the room.

"Morning," I grinned at him as the flames sizzled. I heard the scrape of a chair, then Mark muttered a greeting.

"Need help with that?"

I shook my head as I stuffed the turkey with some onions and lemons and herbs. "No, thanks. I've got this."

"Alright, man," he chuckled as he watched me arrange the dried turkey pieces on the oiled grill and close the cover.

Perfect. I whistled.

"You're in a good mood," he said.

I opened the cupboard and grabbed a bottle of bourbon that I placed in front of him. Hell yes, I was in a good mood. How could I not be? An hour ago, I awakened in Jenna's arms after spending another passionate night with her. I'd wanted to stay longer in bed, but the feeling of excitement had kept me up and I decided to get up to start the day. It was Thanksgiving, and I could already hear music bubbling in the main lounge. So, I'd left Jenna in bed as I came down to make myself a cup of coffee, and then I'd felt like starting the family turkey, while Isabella and her assistants handle the food for the main guests.

"Yeah. I guess I have a lot to be thankful for."

"It's kind of early."

He stared out at the wide expanse of land through the huge window. The day was windy and relaxed, with a bright blue sky overlooking the whitecaps on the stretch of green.

I went back to the toaster and dropped in two more slices of bread. "I was awake, so I figured I'd get up and get an early start."

He scrubbed his hands over his face, then picked up his drink. "Me too. Where's Jenna?"

I glanced toward the top of the stairs. "Still snuggled fast asleep in bed, I hope. Did you go to bed late last night?"

"Yeah. After you, Jenna, and Emma called it a night, Edwin, I and a bunch of tourists stayed back in the public lounge. I knew they'd have beer, so we stayed with them to make sure no one did anything stupid."

"Thanks, man." I felt kind of bad about leaving Mark to watch the guests. Usually, I was the one making sure our guests got back to bed in one piece. But by the time Jenna and I went in to tuck Emma into her bed, we'd been in no mood to come back outside.

I checked on the turkey again. I really wanted it to be perfect, and satisfied with the tender juicy meat with crispy skin, I picked up our drink and led the way to the table. We settled at the table and I refilled Mark's cup.

He had almost finished his drink, and he stared at me with his brows furrowed. "I can cut you some slack for taking early nights now that love and fatherhood has made you largely responsible."

231

"What?" I grunted, narrowing my eyes at him. "I've always been taking my duties seriously, man. You're the one who ran off with your friends for a smoke while I had to cover for your lazy ass with and that Langmore girl you used to stalk."

"I didn't stalk anyone."

"Sure you didn't! That's why her dad kicked your ass when he found you lot behind his house."

Mark's face reddened with embarrassment from the memory. "No one kicked my ass."

I raised my eyebrow. "My memory recalls a certain horrible black eye you sported for a week after the incidents."

He seethed his teeth and ran a hand across his face. "Maybe your memory needs me to kick your ass to get it working proper."

I grinned at him. "I'll take a rain check on that. There's a party here tonight. Don't want to mess this up." I gestured to my face. "Although if I remember correctly, you said a black eye is a great way to meet girls. Maybe I should take you up on it."

"Shut your face, asshole!"

"Boys! Language." Isabella's voice carried across the lawn. "We've got kids around."

Mark and I furrowed our brows. Isabella's words were law around here and she'd scold us like we were still kids if she had to. "Sorry," I called across, "I'll be more responsible since I've always been the most responsible one here."

"You're an idiot." Mark grinned, as he waved his apology to Isabella. She shook her head and stepped away from us.

Mark and I dissolved into laughter as we watched her wander over to the lounge. "I'm glad to be home, brother." he murmured as he clapped my shoulder.

"Yeah, I am too."

I'd been grateful to have my brother by my side for the last two weeks. Mark and Emma had bonded to become very close, and the awkwardness between him, Jenna, and me had evaporated.

A few days after the court ruled in my favor, and Mark and I had started to reconcile, we decided it was time to confront Ellie. She'd refused to see me, but Mark had gone in and convinced her to come to see me and apologize for trying to take away Emma. We'd fixed a couple of meetings since then, but when the time came, she offered up a lot of shallow excuses for why she couldn't make it. I wasn't buying any of it but Emma kept asking about her mother and so we decided to send her another invite to the party and try to give her a final chance to do the mature thing by talking with us as adults. It was Thanksgiving, after all, and this wasn't about us. It was about Emma. We were hoping Ellie would show up to the resort's Thanksgiving party, but she hadn't confirmed anything yet.

Mark blew out a long sigh and I leaned toward him. I knew what was bothering him but most times he tended to keep to himself about this matter since Ellie refused to show up at the last meeting.

"You okay?"

He shrugged. "Yeah, just worried."

"Ellie? You're worried that it seems like there's something else going on?" I brought the cup to my lips and took a long sip. He looked away, but instead of his usual grumbling about her stubbornness and how people that were close to him never ceased to drive him nuts, his mouth flattened into a line.

"What if she doesn't show up at the party?"

"No shit?" I paused, half-expecting the answer to pop into my head, but it remained blank. *I don't know what to do if she doesn't come. What will I tell Emma?*

"She will, brother." I stood and patted his shoulder as I stepped back toward the turkey on the grill. "For all our differences, one thing that always remained clear was how much

Ellie and I love Emma, and how much we were willing to give to be in our daughter's life."

He nodded. "I think so too."

"Yeah." I smiled as I popped the lid of the grill open. "Now we've got a party to attend, and Emma wouldn't forgive me if she believed I had a hand in her uncle turning up late."

Mark grinned and hurried toward the steps before turning around. "You call me if you help with need anything, right?

"I'll be fine," I said, wanting to ease his worries. "Just get your ass in the lounge on time."

"See you at the party."

After Mark left, I finished the turkey, wrapped it up in foil, and headed over to the main lounge. Bella and Jenna had made all the arrangements and decorations for the lounge, with steak and seafood on the menu. Chairs were arranged around tables with a tag carrying each family name placed on it. I walked toward the table in the center that carried *Stark* and looked around at the beautiful hall with bright chandelier lights, and decorated tables completed with champagne flutes.

By the time I was dressed and ready after a long morning of cooking, the party was in full flow. Thanksgiving at the resort has always been a fun event for me, and a chance to get dressed up and take advantage of the open bar and fancy catering as well as talk up some high-profile clients and contacts from the city. This year seemed bigger somehow. The party had spilled out into the yard and the extensive resort grounds. I walked in, grabbing a cut-glass tumbler as I surveyed the scene while sipping on the glass of smoky-sweet Bourbon.

"Hey Stranger," Jenna said, elbowing me playfully.

I turned toward her, and my mouth dropped open. "Now that is one hell of a dress."

"Yeah?" She flashed a little teasing smile.

"Hell, yeah," I muttered with a chuckle. The gold dress hugged her curvy, full breasts and nipped in at the waist before widening over her hips.

"Thanks," she beamed. "Unfortunately, with that look in your eyes I don't think I'll be spending long in it."

We giggled together and she linked her arm to mine as we stared across the room. Mark was happily chatting with a group of tourists by the podium with Emma at his side. Her little dress shimmering as she whirled, swinging her ponytail around. At least someone was being a good host. He'd been quite good with the guests since he came to the resort — he looked like the perfect person for management.

Mark approached and Emma bounded excitedly along his side waving at us. I put my hands on my hips and sighed dramatically. "If it's not my baby girl, looking the best at the annual party."

"You see, even your dad thinks you're the prettiest lady in the room." Mark said with a wide grin.

"Dad..." Emma rolled her eyes, blushing.

"You look beautiful, kiddo." I smiled warmly and leaned to give her a hug, feeling my radiate with warmth and affection.

"Thanks, Dad. I love the dress so much."

I smiled at her mini brocade dress. "It looks wonderful on you. Very grown-up." I nodded, then scanned the room. "Hey, have any of you seen Edwin?"

"No, I thought he'd be with you," Mark answered.

Edwin was our Master of Ceremony for the program and he should have been on stage by now. "Okay," I nodded. "Y'all head to the table and settle down. I'll haul him here."

"Okay." Jenna linked her fingers with Emma's, smiling. "You and me, pretty."

Emma giggled, acquiescing. I watched the two best women in my life head toward the tables along with my brother and I felt peace spread through me. This is how it should be. I hurried toward the kitchen, suspecting Edwin was stuffing his face with food of some kind. The door was unlocked, as usual, so I let myself in and heard the water running.

"Hey, Edwin," I called as I walked in. "You'd better get your ass out there—"

I stopped in my tracks. A person stood at the sink. Short dark hair, wearing a skimpy red dress and a floppy straw hat. She was sipping on a large margarita... and surprise-surprise, it was Ellie.

When she looked up to see me, her breath caught in her throat and for a second, I couldn't speak either. She was here. I finally had the chance to make this family what it should be — unconventional and with baggage, but still a family all the same. A place with love and nurture where Emma would grow without worries or hostility.

My eyes swept up and down, taking her in. She looked like she was tired, staring at me through weary eyes, a deep groove between her eyebrows, her eyes flashing with wariness. Her mouth opened like she was about to say something, but she closed it again.

"Ellie," I muttered. "You came."

"Yeah, and now I'm wondering what I am doing here." Her voice was gravelly, almost monotone.

"You know what you're doing here, Ellie."

"Do I?" She raised an eyebrow, her voice faltering for a second before she could get it to work. "You sent me an invitation? For what? Just to show me what I was missing? What I would be missing for the rest of my life? To gloat?"

I blew out a breath. I didn't answer. Just stared at her because I couldn't believe what I was seeing. This was not the way I'd always envisioned this moment. Maybe I have allowed myself to get too carried away with a fairy tale solution that I had forgotten what Ellie was really like.

She shook her head. "Oh my god, what am I doing? I'm leaving your stupid party."

I stared across the room at her, for some reason I didn't want to give up hope. I wanted to make this work badly. She made for the door, but I stepped forward, ready to block her exit. "Don't."

She flinched backward. "Don't what?"

I swallowed. "You can't leave."

"Of course I can. My choices are the only thing left in my life that you cannot control, so I intend to make good use of them."

I took a deep breath, hoping to stay strong and brave in the face of this confrontation. I needed to get things off my chest if for no other reason than to let it go for my own sake.

"Ellie," I said, summoning all my calm, "I'm angry with you for trying to take away our daughter. I'd like an apology from you in order to move on."

She scoffed. "I knew this invitation was all about your pride, Tyler," she said in a condescending tone. "I don't intend to bow to your wishes."

I didn't correct her. It wasn't worth it. She wanted to skirt the issue, but I didn't care. I shouldn't have expected this to be easy anyway, but I needed to speak my mind, we both need to.

"I have a lot to look forward to in life," I continued on, remaining steady and calm. "And I want to go through that journey with friends and family as close as possible, and of course you know the most important person to me is Emma. I want you close, no I need you close but I cannot do that because I don't believe I can trust you. Not unless you take actionable steps to change your ways."

"This is preposterous!" She shook her head and grabbed her drink again to take a long sip. "Why are you attacking me? You have no idea what it has been like to be under your thumb and control for all these years. You determine when I see her, when I touch her, when I fucking spend time with my own daughter…It's been absolutely miserable. She is a part of me too you know? And I deserve her love and presence, just like you!"

I sighed deeply before I spoke. "Ellie, you were allowed to be with her. No one stopped you from enjoying time with your daughter until you attempted to steal her away without even having a clear plan to care for her. I know Emma loves you because you're her mother and she wants to see you. But what you did isn't something we can just ignore." Her face froze in an exaggerated expression of indignance, and I continued. "You broke our family, Ellie. If you wanted more time with her, you should have asked for that instead of betraying the trust I had in you."

I felt a warmth creep up my neck from nerves, but there was another feeling there, too, and it was strong. Righteousness.

"Oh, that's easy for you to say now," she said, then took a big gulp of her margarita, agitating the ice with a thick straw. "You were going to replace me in her life with that Jenna. I became desperate."

"I was never going to do that. You should have trusted me—"

"Never," she shook her head. "Not after finding out you didn't truly love me. All you did after you found out I was with child was from your sense of duty, not affection. You could easily replace me if you thought I was not good enough for Emma. I could never trust you."

She was right. I had a lot to apologize for and I wasn't going to argue with her. "I'm sorry, Ellie. But I need to make it clear that my intention was never to replace you. Emma loves you."

"She does?"

"Yeah, and you do need to go out there to see her — to see everyone. Emma is who matters most, not us, and if you can't forgive or trust me, trust in her."

Ellie grunted, shaking her head. Great. She probably would say no and retract again.

"Tyler, I can't."

"Can't see your daughter or tell Bella and Edwin you're sorry for running off with her? Of course you can."

"No, I can't see anyone yet." She paused, looking away from me. "I betrayed their trust...I betrayed your trust."

I stepped toward her and placed a reassuring hand on her arm. "It won't be as bad as you think."

"I don't know." Judging by the way she sighed, I could sense I was getting through to her.

"Well, I do. You can take your time, and no one's going to blame you if it takes a while for you to get the courage. But you should know Emma's been asking for you."

"She has?"

"Yes. You'll forever be important to her — to us all. And we need you back in the family."

She stared at me for a couple of seconds without speaking. "Thanks for saying that. But your woman, Jenna—"

"Like I said, you're not being displaced. And Jenna was the one who pushed me to convince you to come home."

"Well," Ellie swallowed, "Maybe I should go out there with you then. It's Thanksgiving after all. And it's all about family."

A wide grin spread on my face. "Great. Come on out, and then there's a little surprise I have planned too that I want you to see."

"Oh. I think I'd really enjoy the night here then..." she used a playful tone and waggled her eyebrows, in a cheery way.

I pushed open the door to lead her out. As the both of us headed back to lounge, I felt a sense of peace spread over me. Our family might not be perfect, but it was ours, and I intended to celebrate that – today, tomorrow, and every day I had the chance, especially after the little plan I had to complete the family this evening.

CHAPTER 22

- JENNA -

I stood just on the edge of the lounge, watching the party which was still in full swing. The sun had already disappeared behind the mountain peaks, easing the heat of the day, but the music from the stereo still filled the air. Laughter and chatter scattered across the room, with people balancing plates of food and drinks in their hands. A bunch had even started dancing.

Mark and Tyler were playing hosts, Ellie was standing with them across the room with Emma. The little girl had been excited to see her mother.

They looked like the perfect family. This was what Tyler wanted, and I was glad I'd been able to help him achieve it. He'd said this was the best thing for Emma, for the family — and he was right. It was clear enough now looking at them, I stamped out the little jealousy that Ellie would always have a part of the man and little girl I loved more than anything.

Tyler was ready to do just about anything for his daughter, but he had shown me enough for me to know that he truly loved me and no one could take that away from me. Tyler was my man and I trusted and believed in him. I also knew that this bit of insecurity I had about this would fade in time. There was enough love to go round, and I was grateful I had the love of both Tyler and Emma — I couldn't ask for more.

Tyler's eyes flicked to me and his lips twitched with a hint of a smile. He'd been giving me that look all day. I'd come over early to help set up, and no matter what we'd been doing— stringing lights around the porch, bringing out chairs, helping

Bella in the kitchen—he'd been looking at me like that. It was making me excited.

If I hadn't known better, I'd have thought Tyler looked hesitant because he was nervous to speak about something important. But this was Tyler. He didn't give in to anxiety. Unless...*Fuck! Unless he had something to say, but he was waiting for the perfect opportunity to say it.*

Did he have some big news about the resort? He acted this way sometimes when he had a big news to drop. I wondered what this could be about. The resort had been going very well for the past months and according to him, we were making almost double the profits we used to make before I came in.

I flashed a smile at him and turned around to walk up the porch steps and settle on one of the chairs. I was still mulling over the look when Ellie appeared and scooted a chair closer. She smiled softly as she sat next to me.

"Hi there, Jenna. Thank you for inviting me. It's a great party."

I nodded and sipped my drink. "Of course. You're family, you should be here."

She sighed and settled in the chair to stare up at the sky. "I want to apologize to you for my words the first time we met. I was scared that you were going to take my place in Emma's life, but now I know better. I also want to say thank you. Emma couldn't stop chattering about you, and Tyler told me just how huge of a help you were in all of this."

I shrugged. "They are happy. That's all I could ask for."

"Yeah," she nodded. "He loves you, you know?"

"What?"

"At first I couldn't believe it was real. He's never been emotionally open to anyone or showed his affection except for with Emma, but that's different, she is his daughter. But the way he is with you..."

I narrowed my eyes. "How is he?"

She took a deep breath, rocking the chair gently. "Like he cannot do without you. Like you complete him or something." She glanced at me. "It's there in his words, in the way he acts. I think your presence in his life is what makes this forgiveness and bonding possible. Hence, I'm grateful."

I gazed at her for a long moment. "You don't think this is what he'd always wanted, and now I've expended my use?"

She chuckled. "You're the glue that holds this together, Jen. I can see that now." Her eyes widened. "I can call you that right?"

I nodded. The little niggle of worry that I had earlier dissipated with her words. Her tone had sounded sincere enough that I knew she meant her words. This would work. The realization filled me with joy and excitement. "Yes, you can."

"Then call me Ellie?"

I nodded again. "Oh sure. I'm glad you're here, Ellie."

"Not as glad as I am, Jen."

She glanced at me, and her mouth turned up into a grin. There was gratitude in her eyes that sent a tingle down my spine. An unexpected spark of joy flared to life in my mind as the fresh night air brushed against my face. *Maybe I don't need to worry after all. I was right to insist that she was invited too.*

Ellie stopped rocking and leaned forward. She took a deep breath through her nose. "He's looking for you. There." She pointed across to the doorway of the lounge where Tyler was standing, holding Emma's little hand in his. The little girl waved excitedly at us, her hair bobbing as she bounced around. "Got to go, Jen. Thank you again."

I remained in my seat, watching her hurry off toward Emma and Tyler. Tyler said something into the little girl's ear and she jogged toward her mother — then held out her arms for Ellie. Ellie hugged her daughter close. Tyler walked across the porch after Emma. I could see his smile as the summer breeze stirred his hair, and warmth stirred inside me. He was so naturally handsome no matter what he did.

"Would you mind taking her?" His voice carried over the distance and then he whispered something else that my ears couldn't catch. Ellie nodded and led Emma toward the house. The girl waved at me again and I waved back.

Once they were gone, Tyler walked up to me. "Hey, you." He leaned over and kissed my cheek.

A tingle of excitement made my heart flutter. "Hey."

"Tired of the party already? You disappeared after the toast."

I shrugged and smiled at him. "Just wanted the fresh night air. I could sense you needed time with the family and the satisfaction on your face tells me I did the right thing."

His smile widened. "My heart's full, Jen. It's good to have all the family in one place."

I nodded, saying nothing as I stared into his eyes and smiled at him.

"Wanna take a walk?"

"Sure."

He held out a strong hand to help me up, and the feel of his skin brushing mine sent a buzz of electricity through me. Instead of moving back so I could step forward, he stayed where he was, just inches from me, his eyes intent on my face. The comforting heat he radiated was both imposing and captivating. He gave me that brooding look again, and for the space of a heartbeat, I thought he might kiss me. But he just flashed a slow, sexy grin that made my legs feel weak.

"Let's go."

He took my hand in his, clasping our fingers together. He held it like it mattered to him to have me close. Like this was important. Like I was important — and that sent a comforting thrill to me. I love him — he was important to me. I knew he loved me too, but I wanted the reassuring feeling that I was very important to him as well. That I wouldn't be cast aside now that he had his family complete.

We walked down the porch steps and cut across the lawn, heading towards the north end of the property. The farther we got from the noise of the party, the harder my heart beat. Being alone with Tyler never got old; on a romantic night like this, I was content to lean close and appreciate his warmth, waiting to see where he would take me.

The moon was nearly full, and the stars twinkled in their full glory away from the fire. We didn't need light to find our way. Tyler didn't say anything, just held my hand while we walked, and it was so peaceful and quiet. He didn't seem to be in any hurry, and I wondered if he had a destination in mind. Eventually we came to the path that led to the private pool at the edge of the property. He turned up it and we kept going, following the route that would take us up to the pool. The path led across to the park and I could see some houses in the distance. Some were dark save for porch lights, their residents probably at not at home for Thanksgiving. Others had lights in the windows or the flicker of a TV peeking through the curtains. Despite the way my heart raced with anticipation, being with Tyler like this felt surprisingly natural. Our fingers fit together comfortably, like we'd done this a thousand times. Like we'd started dating years ago and this was what we'd do forever.

Something deep inside me ached for that version of reality. For a world where Tyler and I were destined to be together forever. Because anything else felt so inadequate.

"What's on your mind?" he asked softly.

"Nothing," I shook my head. "Just thinking how perfect this is."

That was an overwhelming thought to have while I walked hand in hand with him in the moonlight. To acknowledge how much my heart grieved for something I had right now. I'd never felt like this, and I wondered how a few months with him was making me question everything I'd ever been before? It was him – Tyler. He was making me question everything. There was no way I was ever going to replace the feelings he gave me with someone or something else.

He stopped walking just as we reached the edge of the pool's barricade and Tyler grabbed my hand. I looked around in surprise. I hadn't been paying attention full attention to where we were.

"Uh-oh, I don't think I can get into the water in this dress?"

"No." He shook his head, a little smile spreading across his lips. "We're not here to swim."

"What?"

"I came to show you that." He pointed toward something rustling in the wind and I realized there was something strung up on the side of the long rail at the side of the pool. A banner. I walked toward it, blinking.

It read... Oh my god. I gasped, my mouth falling open.

The banner on the railing read: Jenna, will you marry me? in bright gold letters.

"Tyler—" I turned around and started to speak, but stopped short. He was down on one knee. Taking my hand, he smiled up at me, and my heart nearly exploded.

"Jenna, I have carried a pain in my heart since I was a teenager, and you're the only one who's been able to heal it. You're my best friend and the love of my life. I might achieve it all, but it's all nothing if you're not there to share it with me. I want to spend the rest of our lives making you happy. Will you marry me?"

Trembling and nodding, with tears running down my cheeks, I gave him the only answer I ever could. "Yes."

It took me a second to realize he was holding a box and I reached my fingers forward as he pulled out the ring and then slipped it on my finger. Everything was a blur of tears and giggles and kisses and I love yous. I threw my arms around his neck, and he hugged me hard, my feet lifting off the ground. When he put me down, I took a deep breath, trying to collect myself. I looked down at my shaking hand, at the ring shining on my finger.

"Do you like it?" He tucked my hair behind my ear.

"I love it so much. I love you so much. Oh my god, we're getting married."

He smiled again, his eyes flickering. "We sure are. I love you, Jen."

It was about then that I realized applause was coming from the garage bay. Edwin and a bunch of the resort crew walked out, clapping, whooping, and hollering. He cupped his hands around his mouth to shout his congratulations and Bella smiled at us as she clapped. Mark and Ellie were there, and so was Emma who was waving at me excitedly. A crowd of our friends and tourists emerged, clapping and smiling.

"Oh my god. You did all this?"

"Yeah. Originally it was just going to be the banner, but you know how people are around here. It turned into a surprise engagement party pretty quickly."

"I guess it's a good thing I said yes." I nudged him.

He slid his arms around me. "I never had any doubt."

Neither did I. I think a part of me had always known I'd marry Tyler Stark since the first moment we met in my house downtown. Everyone walked towards us and the next thing I knew, I was being hugged by a seemingly endless stream of people. A tearful Bella, then Edwin. Mark squeezed me so tight I had to beg him to stop when he lifted me up and twirled me around. Ellie hugged me almost as hard as Mark had, which was surprising, but I hugged her back just as hard. Dunrad held back at first, but still hugged us both, offering his typical sincere and gruff congratulations.

Ten minutes later, we were back at the party. Someone had balloons and people started setting up tables on the grass near the lounge. A couple of the tourists hung a big Congratulations Tyler and Jenna banner on the side of the railings that guarded the pool.

Tyler stood next to me. "So when do you want to get married? Soon as possible?"

"Yeah," I nodded. "I can't wait Tyler."

Chuckling softly, he drew me in front of him and put his arms around me. "Me neither. I keep thinking about how amazing

246

our future could be together. Even better when I put a baby or two in you."

"Oh my god, did you just say you want to put a baby in me?"

He put his mouth next to my ear. "Yeah. Why? Too caveman for you?"

A tingle ran down my spine. An image of him, me, Emma and a little baby flashed across my mind and I almost gasped with how beautiful it looked. I wanted that — a big happy family. "Actually, no." I giggled.

"Beautiful, we can get married anytime. If you want a nice wedding, we'll have a nice wedding. If you want to get married next weekend at Town Hall, we'll do it. I'll give you anything you want."

"Including a baby?

He kissed my earlobe. "Absolutely."

"Any wedding with you would be a nice wedding." I stared across at where Emma sat on Ellie's lap, sucking on a piece of fruit. "Do you think a baby would be a good idea right now with Emma?"

He shrugged, following my eyes. "Knowing her, I think she'd absolutely love a brother or sister."

I smiled. "We don't have to have a baby right this second, but I'm not going to lie, you murmuring in my ear about getting me pregnant is really hot."

"Yeah? Maybe we should go inside and practice."

I giggled and he squeezed me tighter, trailing light kisses down my neck. "We should probably stay for our own engagement party. At least for a little while."

He groaned. "Okay. For a little while, and then they can go back to pretending this is still the Thanksgiving party."

I watched the people laugh and joke happily, all while wrapped in Tyler's strong embrace. Loved. Happy. At peace. Our souls were inextricably intertwined that I felt confident that there was nothing that could tear us apart.

Every nerve ending tingled with anticipation and I tilted my chin up to give him a kiss. He smiled and leaned toward me. Our lips came together, his pressing against mine in a gentle caress. My eyes drifted closed, and we hesitated there for the space of a heartbeat. With a subtle shift, he slanted his mouth over mine more fully, and we sank into the kiss.

I wound my arms around his neck and parted my lips, inviting him in deeper. His tongue slid against mine, warm and velvety soft. The world around me fell away to nothing as he kissed me deep and slow. I melted into him, surrendering. Secure in his embrace. He what I needed — all I needed.

He was everything and he was mine.

THE END

248

LOVE AT PEAK BLISS (MR. STARK)

WHAT'S NEXT?

Out of interest, who would you like me to write about next?

Fill out this survey: https://bit.ly/3j8tJ8V

It doesn't contain invasive questions at all, I promise. Let me know what other stories you'd like to see.

In the meantime, be sure to check other series that I have going on.

WEDDING NIGHT STRANGER

MR. BUCHANNAN, FULL NOVEL

Small towns filled with billionaire love. Why do they have such an effect on me? ♥ Yearn for their steamy romance heat. ⚱ "Small Town Billionaires" is my ever-growing collection filled with second chances, best friends' older brothers, enemies-to-lovers, holiday romances, and more. Begin with "Wedding Night Stranger" to fall in a love worth fighting for with these hot and sexy "Small Town Billionaires" that satisfy your HEA!

READ "WEDDING NIGHT STRANGER" HERE NOW:

https://getbook.at/WeddingNightStranger

I didn't cheat. Found out at the altar my ex did though!
What are the chances that I end up with a stranger on my wedding night who happens to be my new boss?
Every part of me yearns for him.
I want to forget the man I was meant to marry.
I found out at the altar that my ex had cheated on me, over and over, and with many different women.
So, I got wasted and fell into bed with this stranger out of desperation and loneliness.
I'd spent the entire time trying to get my heartache out of my system.
Now, with mounting debts, I need this new job.
I hear my new boss is a hard stickler for the rules, so I really want to make a good impression.
Wait, is that stranger my new boss?

251

ALICIA'S AUTHOR NOTES

**Did you enjoy this steamy read from my bestselling
Millionaire Doctors' Club series?
Great news, you can check out a FREE sneak peek to
the next story in the series on the next page!**

Much love xoxo

Alicia Nichols

DESTINED LOVE (PREVIEW) (MR. HUNTER - INSTALOVE SPARK)

I believed in our love. Yet he lied to me about his ex, who happens to be my love tarot reader.

Was all this his attempt to win her back?
Sharing a taxi with a handsome and interesting stranger is not how I expected my morning to go.

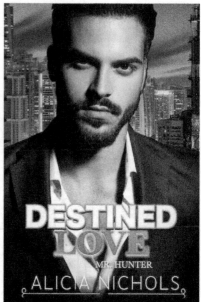

I'm beginning to wonder if he's the man my tarot reader saw in my cards. Wait. No. He can't be.

James Hunter is my new boss.

Yet the longer I spend around him, the harder it is to remind myself why I need to stay away.

Everything else disappears when he enters the room.
No man has ever had such a primal and visceral effect on me.

Who am I kidding? I know I've got a thing for my boss. Why can't I just admit it?

CHAPTER 1

- SAMANTHA -

"You are about to enter into a new relationship, and it is going to be very fulfilling and rewarding."

I held my breath and peered at the card the tarot reader flipped onto the table. The illustration showed a young knight on a horse, holding out a golden cup. Over his armor, the knight wore a clock covered with images of fish. The background was mostly barren, with a few trees and a river flowing between them. I traced the tip of my finger on the worn-out card, the smell of incense wafting up my nostrils.

Was the knight of cups a good thing?

Was my luck finally about to change?

Madame Mystic leaned back in her chair. A thin plume of smoke surrounded her, twirling through the bright beads in her dark hair and the bangles that swished with every movement. We sat at a small circular table in a dimly lit room with blue colored walls, and I wondered if this was the moment my life was going to change forever. I'd followed the way of the cards my whole life and I believed in them with my whole heart. Sooner or later, that dedication had to pay off.

"What does the card mean?" I asked.

Madame Mystic laid her hands down on the table, face up. "You see how the knight is holding his hand out?"

"Yes."

"It's as if he bears a message from the heart. As for the fish on his cloak, they symbolize water, consciousness and creativity."

"In my personal life?"

Madame Mystic's lips lifted into a half smile. "Yes. You see how the knight is not charging forward but moving slowly, gracefully, giving him an aura of peace and calm. The horse represents power, energy and drive. The knight is meant to represent a chivalrous person on the quest for love."

"What about the color? White symbolizes purity and spirituality, but I'm not looking for a spiritual journey. I want love, romance, a man who will knock my socks off and keep me up all night, if you know what I mean. How is this knight going to help me with that?"

She kept her patient smile, but her eyebrow twitched. I guessed that meant she wouldn't want to hear about my nonexistent sex life and my extraordinarily bad luck when it came to dating. I was a hopeless romantic, but I was beginning to wonder if I was ever going to meet the man of my dreams. That was the main reason I was here.

"You are correct, white symbolizes purity, spirituality and light, but you have to consider the components of the card as a whole. The river that flows through the trees represents the power of emotion and imagination, and their ability to create a new life force, even when it seems all hope is lost."

"What about my love life? You mentioned something earlier about a new relationship."

My phone buzzed in my pocket. I glanced at the screen to see a notification from the built-in assistant: *Leave your current location in five minutes if you want to reach your appointment in time.*

The job interview for the biggest media company in town. I highly doubted that my interviewer would see me consulting the cards as a valid excuse for being late or missing my appointment, yet I couldn't bring myself to leave.

Madame Mystic had a reputation that preceded her, and a waiting list that was months long. Having booked her months ago during a late-night, desperate search for a way to improve my love life in the bottom of a wine glass. Since it had been two months and I still hadn't had any luck with finding a good man, I wasn't about to let anything get in in my way.

Even if it meant being a few minutes late to my job interview.

Everyone had and was entitled to their own rituals. Tarot reading was mine and had been since I was a little girl. It was one of the few things my no-good mother brought into my life, even if she hadn't done so intentionally. As a Gemini, I always thought it was my duty to forgive, but never forget. I've forgiven her for the shit she's done, but it's the never forgetting that made my mom split without a word from her in the past five years.

Madame Mystic leaned forward, her face lit up by the glow of the candle. "You have the card of lovers. It represents love, attraction and a deep connection. You will encounter a love that will be unexpected and shake your life up in a big way."

Knots unfurled in the center of my stomach. "Really?"

Madame Mystic nodded. "Yes, but you must be open to it and learn to recognize it when it comes."

"What is he like? What's his name?"

Madame Mystic lowered her head and shuffled the cards again. I sat up straighter and resisted the urge to glance at my watch again. Time was ticking down in the back of my head, seconds drained from a sand hourglass, but I didn't yet know what it would mean for me if I was late. I needed answers, and Madame Mystic was the best one to give them to me.

She handed me a bottle of oil. "Rub three drops of this between your palms. Thoroughly incorporate it into your skin, and then leave your hands facing up on the table."

I followed her instructions, feeling a tingle on my palms as the oil sunk in. Madame Mystic turned over the cards one by one, and with each card, carefully assessing each one.

ALICIA NICHOLS

She nodded and hummed appreciatively at the spread before her. "Now close your eyes, and I will show you exactly what to expect."

"Show me...?" I asked even as I closed my eyes.

Her gentle fingers brushed against my palms, awakening a rush of unexpected sensation throughout my body. I shivered, but it was a delightful feeling, like the cells in my being were awakening for the first time.

"You have so many mental barriers, built brick by brick because of so many years of heartbreak," Madame Mystic murmured. "If you are to truly welcome the love of your life inside, you must smash those barriers one by one. Are you ready?"

I nodded enthusiastically. "I've never been more ready in my life. Please, help me."

Madame Mystic exhaled, and her fingers fully touched down on mine. The tingling sensation pushed through my hands, spreading through my arms and toward my heart. My heart began to race, and I felt a flush of heat rise to my cheeks. Madame Mystic's touch was electric, and as she continued to stroke my hands, I felt more and more in tune with my inner desires. I had always been hesitant when it came to exploring my sensual side, but with Madame Mystic's guidance, I felt like I was tapping into an entirely new part of myself.

"Imagine your perfect man. What does he look like?" she asked. "Don't tell me what you see. Let your mind do the work. I am only your guide."

Images began to flood my mind, vivid and intense. I saw a man, tall and broad-shouldered, with piercing hazel eyes and a chiseled jaw. He stood before me, his expression intent as he gazed into my eyes. He didn't speak at all, and we were in a dimly lit room with a single candle, the rest of the world invisible to me. But his penetrating gaze was enough to send pleasurable shivers racing up and down my spine. Warmth collected between my legs, and I rubbed my thighs together, trying to resist the growing want in my core. That was the look of a man who wanted to do the filthiest things to me, and all I wanted was to fall into his embrace and let him whisk me away into his bed.

258

"Now that you're with him, what does he do? How does he make you feel?" Madame Mystic's voice was distant, an echo from a different world.

"He makes me..." I swallowed. "He makes me feel wanted. Desired. Loved."

In my mental imagery, the man drew me closer. His hot breath tickled my neck, and his gentle lips kissed the taut column. I sighed as he traced the curves of my body, sucking on the sensitive flesh and making me burn all over with the intense need for more.

The heat between us grew, winding inside me like a coiled spring about to burst. His kisses became more frantic, his touch more demanding, and I found myself swept up in a whirlwind of sensation. Sweat trickled down my back and I was panting as the images took over. It didn't matter that I knew it was all a dream, my imagination, but I felt him touch me and god if he just moved his hands a little lower, his fingers vibrating—

Wait, shit, his fingers weren't supposed to be vibrating. A low buzzing sound drew my attention out of the vision, and I fished out my phone again.

WHERE ARE YOU? Lauren's text read. The dramatic capital letters weren't her usual MO but right now, they made sense.

I was officially late for my job interview.

"I'm sorry, Madame Mystic, but I have to go." The chair beneath me screeched as I stood and pushed it back in a hurry. "Can I come back later today, or tomorrow, to finish my reading? It's an emergency."

Madame Mystic smiled. "You will not need to come back, not for a while. I see great things in your future, Samantha Williams."

I beamed and reached into my purse. "Thank you so much."

After setting down a wad of bills, plus a generous tip for the unusual but exciting experience, I raced out of her apartment, pushing my way past a curtain of brightly colored beads. God, what was that oil? Even if I didn't find the man of my dreams soon like she believed, it would be worth going back just to figure out where to buy my own. It would be a lot easier to put up with the lack of eligible, sane men in the city if I could conjure my ideal man to whisk me away for a few hours every night. In the hallway, I adjusted my purse and raced down the stairs, throwing myself blindly into the street. I skidded to a halt before hitting another pedestrian, then found a gap in the foot traffic and bolted off again.

I wove in and out of the stream of people jostling past. The last thing I wanted was to be late for my job interview but considering how well the tarot reading went, I knew staying a few minutes later had been worth it.

When I spotted a yellow taxi in the distance, I waved my hand and took off at a brusque pace. Inches away from the cab, a tall and broad-shouldered man collided into me, sending me stumbling backwards. A spray of coffee flew from the mug in his hand, splattering on my cream blouse. I shrieked from the surprise and the hot liquid drenching my breasts, but before I made a complete ass of myself and fell onto the street, his hand darted out and wrapped around my waist.

"I'm so sorry about this. Are you okay?"

I stepped away from him, pulling the shirt away from my skin so it didn't burn my skin. The thin fabric was turning a translucent shade of dark brown, and it even stained my white bra underneath.

"Great. This is just what I needed," I sighed. "Oh my God, I'm so screwed."

The stranger reached into his pocket and pulled out a pack of tissues. "Here, maybe this will help."

When I tilted my head up to look up at him, I paused to take in his angular face. Dark stubble peppered across a sharp jaw. He shifted, blocking out my view of the sun, and my vision sharpened, revealing expressive hazel eyes framed by long lashes.

My heart sputtered and stopped inside my chest.

Holy shit.

He was the most gorgeous man I had ever seen, and almost an exact replica of the man I'd seen in my vision at Madame Mystic's. Was I going crazy? Had she given me drugs?

Or were the cards finally giving me my lucky break?

END OF PREVIEW

Read Mr. Hunter's Complete Story Now Here:
https://mybook.to/DestinedLove

ACKNOWLEDGEMENTS

ALICIA NICHOLS

Writing a book is the result of many minds and interactions coming together. Inspiration, experience, and insight is gathered from everywhere, and this shows in how this all finally comes together.

I want to begin by thanking you, the readers, who become a part of these stories by reading, reviewing, recommending, and buying the books. It is thanks to you that people like me get a chance to keep tapping into our imagination and sharing new stories. Thank you for your ongoing support.

Thank you also to the team at Light Age Media. Without Erynn, Jordi, and several others, this would not have been possible. You have breathed life into these stories and made it so that they could engage with a wider audience.

I also wish to thank Ty, Marty, Ja, and Josh who have guided my way to publishing and have opened up my world of what was possible from my laptop and with determination. I now feel much more empowered to keep sharing these stories as a way of life.

A special thank you to my Advanced Reader Group who have offered valuable insights early on to improve the story. If you're willing to write your honest reviews and read the books, prior to them being released, here's how you can become a part of it.

Join my ARC team here: https://bit.ly/3NPTOba

A note of gratitude also goes to my early teachers at writing school. I had always wanted to write novels and here's me putting my words where my mouth was. A huge thanks also to the incredible doctors, nurses, and medical staff that I've come to know through my family, from direct experience, and in your continued dedication to your craft. You are truly special.

And thank you to my friends and family who want to see me continue to do what I love. I appreciate your support on this journey and for this craft.

OTHER BOOKS BY ALICIA

COVETED

DR. STONE, BOOK 1

Begin a steamy new series with Dr. Stone. "Coveted" will set you on a course to a satisfying romantic HEA.

And it's FREE. It's an e-book I give to you just for signing up to my newsletter. You won't find it anywhere else.

Also, be sure to check out more dreamy doctors in my "Millionaire Doctors Club Series".

READ "COVETED" HERE NOW:

https://dl.bookfunnel.com/46pg16ndzd

I can no longer deny how my doctor makes me feel.

And he might just feel the same way.

His smooth, tanned face peering intently at me makes me go weak in the knees.

Dr. Stone moves from around his desk and comes to stand in front of me.

My heart skips a beat at his proximity.

I shudder and melt into his embrace, realizing that it had been too long since I'd been held.

The only problem is, he's also my doctor.

SHIVER OF DESIRE

MR. WEST, BOOK 1 – 5

If you've enjoyed Savannah & Asher's story, know that there's an ever-growing collection of Small Town Billionaires! Begin with "Mr. West's" steamy and sweet romance in "Shiver of Desire"!

READ "SHIVER OF DESIRE" HERE NOW:

https://mybook.to/ShiverOfDesire

He'd taken me for granted, and I'd let him, thinking I could change a man like Cooper West

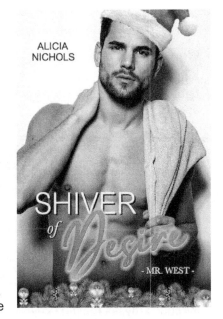

We used to date years ago.

Now he's back in town for his father's funeral.

Despite the heartache, he's still the only one who can make my heart race and my mind go blank.

He looks good.

Like he hasn't spent the past two years tossing and turning, wishing he'd gotten on a plane to come back for me.

I always did have a habit of getting too attached.

I just didn't think Cooper would be the one to leave me hanging.

Why does he still have such an effect on me?

DR. WALKER

COMPLETE SERIES, BOOKS 1 – 5

Begin a steamy new series with Dr. Walker. "Daddy Neighbor" will set you on a course to a satisfying romantic HEA. Be sure to check out more dreamy doctors in my "Millionaire Doctors Club Series".

START READING "DR. WALKER" HERE NOW:

https://getbook.at/DrWalkerBoxset

Who is my new neighbor?

All I know is he is a caring father who drives fast cars and…

…he's breathtakingly gorgeous.

Chills run over my skin from hearing his voice and I don't see signs of a wife.

One night he accidentally catches me staring into his bedroom from mine.

I don't want to seem like a stalker, so I decide to introduce myself the next day.

Something is mysterious and exciting about him. A mystery I can't wait to unravel.

And I'm not sure how I feel about that.

DR. PIERCE

COMPLETE SERIES, BOOKS 1 – 5

Maybe a new start is all your heart yearns for. Even if your life is in shambles and you're forced to return home, back to square one. Will you take a chance at love, even if it requires everything you have left to preserve it? Swoon your way to a satisfying HEA. Start reading Dr. Pierce's series today!

Doesn't he realize that he's the most important thing to me?

But I'm not sure he feels the same way and my love dream is slipping away.

This is my crazy night out before I return home to face my life.

I'm broke and soon might also lose my fashion shop.

Not looking forward to returning to the small town I once left to live my dream.

I eagerly dive into this Mystery Man's arms and his deep blue stare.

Consumed in his kiss, I feel aflame for him.

His are the eyes I saw in my dream.

But before we get too far, he dashes out to save a life, and I don't even have his number.

He's only in town for tonight.

I won't see him ever again, will I?

DR. CARTER

COMPLETE SERIES, BOOKS 1 – 5

If you don't believe in that everlasting love nonsense of romance novels, think again. Dreamy Dr. Carter will leave you satisfied and wanting more. Start reading his series today!

READING "DR. CARTER" HERE NOW:

https://getbook.at/DrCarterBoxset

I wasn't expecting to meet my future husband at the doctor's office.

Well, he doesn't know it yet.

But I can't introduce myself if I'm hiding behind a couch after breaking in.

All for a good cause, I think. I'm helping my friend hide a secret from her fiancé.

How can I meet this gorgeous Viking god in a more fitting scene?

Until by chance we meet.

DR. MACLEAN

COMPLETE SERIES, BOOKS 1 – 5

You've been introduced to Makayla, Dr. Cole Stone's BFF. Now you get a chance to read her own journey to find love. With a Dreamy Scottish Doctor of all things! Read Dr. MacLean. Begin with "Lady of Scots" and dance your way to a satisfying HEA. Start reading his series today!

READ "DR. MACLEAN" HERE NOW:

https://mybook.to/DrMacleanBoxset

At first, the six-year age difference between Ryan and I had been a cause for concern.

Now I love every minute of it.

Ladies' man. Billionaire. He's some kind of Scottish Lord.

My doctor friends want him as a donor for their research.

So, I'm the one who has to lure him in at this important fundraiser event.

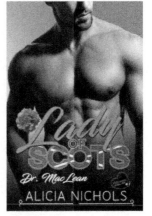

Across the room, Ryan makes his way toward me.

His lean and muscled body is outlined by the dark suit he's wearing.

Each step towards me feels determined and filled with purpose.

He stops directly in front of me, his lips curve into a smile.

And the entire world melts into the background.

I've got to get a grip. I'm not here to make goo goo eyes at a Scottish lord, right?

DR. BLACKMORE

COMPLETE SERIES, BOOKS 1 – 5

Swoon over this new dreamy doctor and ride the wave of Hollywood love in this new steamy rom-com. Squirm and laugh your way to a satisfying HEA. Start reading Dr. Blackmore's series today!

READ "DR. BLACKMORE" HERE NOW:

https://mybook.to/DrBlackmoreBoxset

If word gets out that we're no longer together, millions of fans would be disappointed.

But the man that really sends shivers racing up and down my spine is forbidden to me.

Fans believe I'm still dating my obnoxious co-star.

That's only to save my acting career and the show.

The problem is that I can't avoid the man I fantasize about: Dr. Blackmore.

He oozes sex appeal without even trying.

I rehearse scenes with him to make my character in this TV medical drama more believable.

Do I really want to derail my career for his love when he has nothing on the line? Or does he?

DR. WRIGHT

COMPLETE SERIES, VOLUME 1

If you've enjoyed Jenny & John's story, there's more!

This collection features all my dreamy doctors. Dreamy Dr. Wright will leave you satisfied and wanting more.

Start reading his series today! His Complete Series, Volume 1, with books 1-5 is available.

READ IT NOW HERE

https://getbook.at/DrWrightBoxset

DR. PARK

COMPLETE SERIES

Begin a steamy new series with Dr. Park. He'll set you on a course to a satisfying romantic HEA.

START READING "DR. PARK" HERE NOW:

https://getbook.at/DrParkBoxset

He's moved on, is happily married, and has a family.

I came here partly for him. Was I a fool in denial?

I'm still getting over Cole, the doctor I've had it bad for the last 10 years.

I hate knowing that I'm still hung up on him.

But I have to restart my life. No longer do I want the jet-set lifestyle.

Meeting the right guy and starting a family together feels like such a long shot right now.

I deserve someone who is willing to fight for me and has my back.

I'm nowhere closer to my dream and can't wait to have a stable life.

No sooner said, I meet Dr. Max Park by chance at a convention.

He's seeking investors for his clinics.

But I can't avoid noticing a strong, charming, confident man, perhaps a bit rough around the edges.

What a delicious Lumberjack Hottie.

I don't want to get ahead of myself.

What is it with me and all these doctors? Is my heart aching that bad?

DR. GRANT

COMPLETE SERIES

Love reveals second chances. Even if it seems to have eluded you for years, love is right around the corner. This is Jenny and John's story. Read Dr. Grant and leave your door open for love to a satisfying HEA. Start reading his series today!

START READING "DR. GRANT" HERE NOW:

https://mybook.to/DrGrantBoxset

After two years, I'm ready to put my husband's death behind me.

He and I never really loved each other.
Most days he rarely gave me a second thought.

So, when my friend suggests that we go out next week, I hesitate.

There'll be a silver fox doctor I know from way back in school.

He's handsome and successful.

I once had a thing for him, but never acted on that feeling.

I've been a hermit for two years, and I'm ready to make a change in my life.

Is there still room for me in the outside world? Do I even know how to flirt again?

DR. HAYES

COMPLETE SERIES

Secret relationships in the fashion world. What could go wrong? When love is real, fake blows out the window. But not all is what it seems in this steamy romcom. With Dr. Hayes' new series, find out how love shines through to a satisfying romantic HEA.

START READING "DR. HAYES" HERE NOW:

https://mybook.to/DrHayesBoxset

Liar. Cheater. Dirtbag.

I rehash all the ways Baston duped me with his devil smiles and lies of omission.

He played me so easily for such a fool.

As a fashion photographer, I'm no stranger to looking at perfection.

Yet this guy has something about him that sets him apart entirely.

I can't avoid keeping my eyes off him.

How can I get to know him without this chick who is my archnemesis standing in the way?

DR. CAMPBELL

COMPLETE SERIES

Saddle up for the cowboy! A second chance gets steamy in this small town full of secrets. Maybe that's why these two need a fake marriage. But can she resist the heat from the fireman turned cowboy? And can she trust him? Find out with Dr. Campbell's new series and trot away to a satisfying romantic HEA.

START READING "DR. CAMPBELL" HERE NOW:

https://mybook.to/DrCampbellBoxset

Should I fake-marry the cowboy so I don't lose my ranch... and my new life?
I've never cared much for cowboys or their hats.
Until now.
Enter dreamy cowboy to the rescue when my car breaks down.
He's tall, tanned, and flashes one of his abundant sexy smiles.
After my divorce, my
grandmother's inheritance helped me start over in a small Montana town.
Out of habit, my right hand slips to the ring.
I promised myself I'd pull the ring off before I got there.
Soon I find out this small town harbors a few secrets.
Secrets that will get me into a fake marriage with this cowboy.
Can I even trust him? How did I get myself into this mess?

DARWIN BROTHERS

COMPLETE SERIES, BOOKS 1 – 5

If you've enjoyed Ivy & Blake's story, know that the Darwin family has a backstory! Read their steamy and sweet romance in "Darwin Brothers"!

READ "DARWIN BROTHERS" HERE NOW:

https://mybook.to/DarwinBrothersBoxset

How can I confess my exciting affair with my best friend's older brother?

I might be better off fleeing from the Darwin brothers all together.

The last thing I need is a whirlwind romance that makes me second-guess my sanity.

I've made plenty of mistakes in the past.

We almost lost our family ranch because of them.

And I almost lost my sister.

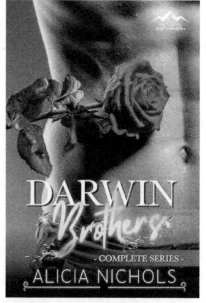

It was partly thanks to firefighters like Jake that all that is behind us.

He has a special aura and is so effortlessly sexy.

He's been nothing but gentle and caring.

Should I give this firefighter a chance? And will his love redeem my heart?

DADDY'S OFF LIMITS

MR. DALTON, COMPLETE SERIES

Love finds you in the small town of West Yellowstone. Sensual bachelors and single daddies fill the steam of whirlwind romances. 🖤 **The Bachelors of West Yellowstone is an ever-growing collection.** 🖤 **Begin "Daddy's Off Limits" to ride your small-town love with a guaranteed and satisfying HEA!**

READ "DADDY'S OFF LIMITS" HERE NOW:

https://mybook.to/DaddysOffLimits

I knew from the look on his face that he was praying I wasn't carrying his baby, and it broke my heart. Was I crazy for wishing the opposite?
It doesn't matter if he's my dad's best friend or that he's single.
Blake Dalton is off-limits. Nothing can happen between us.
Much less now that I'm his daughter's nanny.
I remember years ago going to bed battling fantasies about him.
Carved by the god of beauty himself, he's always the most handsome man in the room.

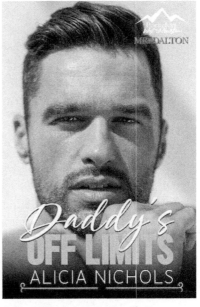

Back then it didn't matter if he barely paid me any attention.
I'm an adult woman now and have more control.
But the moment my eyes catch those smoky gray lights of his, I'm again sparked with desire.
I'm so screwed with this new job.
How am I supposed to stay in the same house with him all day if just being around him makes my brain a mess?

CONNECT WITH THE AUTHOR

Read Alicia's book catalog

https://viewauthor.at/AliciaNichols
https://amazon.com/author/alicianichols

Connect with Alicia and sign up to her email list here:

https://dl.bookfunnel.com/46pg16ndzd

Follow Alicia Nichols' Facebook Fan Page:

https://www.facebook.com/alicianicholsauthor

LOVE AT PEAK BLISS (MR. STARK)

REVIEW THE BOOK

P.S. Readers:

It means the world to me that you bought my book. Your feedback is very important to me.

I'd like to ask you a small favor. Would you be so kind to leave an **HONEST** review on the site where you purchased it?

Thank you so much!

Review My Book Here:

https://mybook.to/LoveAtPeakBliss

Much Love!

Alicia

Printed in Great Britain
by Amazon